The God Machine

The Evolved Book 7

Richard Quarry

ALSO BY RICHARD QUARRY

THE EVOLVED SERIES:
The Big Empty
Point of No Return
The Outcasts
The Evolved
Holobrain
Grinder
The God Machine

The Further Tales of Odysseus:
Man of Many Turnings
Odysseus and the Eye of Odin

The Dance of Light and Dark
Dance of Sword and Heron
Dance of Deer and Shadow
Dance of Cat and Amber
Dance of Wolf and Moon
Dance of Ring and Dragon

Stand-alones

Absent From Felicity
Geneslide
Blue Dread
Trade All My Tomorrows
What Rough Beast
Midnight Choir

Collections:

Soldier of Discontent and other stories
Lord Under London and other cases of Nat Frayne
The Dread Men and other cases of Nat Frayne
Questing Song and other stories
Devolution Day and other f&sf stories

Chapter 1

The holobrain was an awkward damn thing.

Arvada stood by while the Marines used cutting torches to free the mechanism from the shattered hull of the freighter. Around her floated dozens of dead Grinders. Sheets of ice formed from blood and ruptured body organs projected from rents in their silver suits. Within their helmets their heads were no more than pulp, because the Evolved had rigged them with explosives to burst when the suits detected vital signs falling below a certain threshold.

The Marines and Riggers she'd led into the battle to take the freighter had suffered their own casualties, but the last of the dead were even now being loaded aboard the landing craft to be taken back to the *Dysis*. The Peregrines had made fairly short work of the Grinders. But seventeen of them died during the free-wheeling battle in space.

Seventeen men and women who would still be alive if Arvada hadn't insisted on capturing the holobrain.

She didn't think much about it, now. She'd made a judgment. In war judgment involved casualties. Whether or not this particular judgment was justified could only be evaluated at some later date, when its overall effects could better be assessed. But whether or not, perfect wasn't an option. You did your best, fought hard, and kept your eyes pointed toward the future. As she was pointing hers now.

Later, in the night, it might be different. If so, she would face it then. As always.

The actual mass of brain tissue forming the holobrain followed a rough kidney shape, a little over a meter on the long side and two-thirds that in height. It rested within a fluid bath inside a transparent shell two meters in diameter.

Arvada's previous experience with the holobrains, along with that of the *Geniah* expedition three decades before, revealed that while the shell could be pierced by laser or super-speed drill, enabling nanoprobes to be inserted into the tissue, it was opaque to any electromagnetic transmission.

Yet it could somehow transmit a form of thought.

Not human thought, not at least in any manner that anyone other than Hypatia Wren and perhaps Sahan Kotori had ever been able to comprehend. And both their reputations would require significant upgrades just to reach controversial.

But the holobrains hosted, to greater or lesser degree depending on their internal complexity, an embodiment of the Group Mind. And this could communicate with the Living Evolved who oversaw the war against the Peregrine Alliance, and exert total control over the Grinders, who actually fought it.

Though the brain itself could survive indefinitely without external life support by entering some form of sporified state, in active operation it was fed by tubes from a whole array of fluids and filters, pumps and converters, cooling and heating mechanisms, and a variety of nutrients whose composition had been analyzed, but not their function.

Together these occupied about the same space and slightly more mass than a land-based personnel carrier. Either fire from the *Dysis* or the Grinders' efforts to sabotage the mechanism had fused parts of it into the ruptured hull. The support structure itself did not appear badly damaged, but Arvada wanted it whole and intact as possible. Should the holobrain be detached from its support mechanism, it would go on living, but form a core around its outer layers, deactivating itself.

So Arvada couldn't just order the Marines rip it loose. She needed it functioning. Or rather Beck, her Evolved prisoner, did.

Finally they cut it free and pushed it into space. One of the landing craft approached, gull-winged roof opening. The Marines guided it into the craft with small booster rockets.

Unfortunately, having lost her ship, Arvada had no place to put it. So she prevailed upon Solange O'Grady to store the holobrain on board the line of battle ship *Dysis* until Arvada could get another command of her own.

"You do go through them, don't you," was Solange's rather snide remark.

That could be a problem. As soon as the fleet left the Rione system, the site of the battle in which Arvada had led her force to victory over the traitor Raisa Catalan's Collaborationists, her official authority ended. The name Arvada Sattar carried a lot of *cachet* these days, hence her command of the task force. But that command, broadly agreed upon by the fleet, ended with the battle, leaving her in actual fact a Lieutenant Commander addressing senior Captains. The most senior of whom was Solange O'Grady.

The holobrain would then in practice be under Solange O'Grady's control. She might assert her authority and declare the holobrain property of the fleet, to be examined by a broad-based team.

Arvada did not want the holobrain stored aboard the *Dysis*. That would do Beck absolutely no good at all. Unless he remained aboard the heavy, Solange's prisoner instead of Arvada's.

That was no good.

Arvada harbored not the slightest doubt about Solange's will to fight. But the fiery redhead's great passion was ship-to-ship, broadside-to-broadside combat. Admiral Nelson would have loved her. But that was not how Arvada had fought the war to this point. Not how she had scored her victories. Not how she believed the war would be won.

Not against the Evolved.

So she asked Solange — "ask" being all she could do now that the fleet had made their Jump from Rione — if they might have a little chat. Informally. Over coffee. Just girls together.

Chapter 2

He woke lying on his bunk. Frequently it took him a moment to remember where he was, in part because of the swirl of impressions, and partly because the narrow, over-firm bed and the gray steel bunk and walls marked so many of his domiciles. Not just in Navy life, but the Dainichi before. Only for them it had served as the "time-out" quarters — detention, really — where he whiled away so many happy hours.

He quickly oriented himself.

The pain reminded him.

He'd been a bad boy. Again.

He wasn't sure just how. Something to do with the Grinders? Something he'd been trying to tell them? Something they'd been trying to tell him?

We are one.

Had he said that? What had he meant? It was all very vague. Everything was vague. Except the bruises from beating himself against hard objects. Of course they weren't really there. This Grinder body, or rather the simulacrum of one the Evolved had given him, possessed neither the skin nor the flow of blood to leave bruises. The Evolved just liked to tweak his circuits from time to time, remind him that though his mind might live here, the house still belonged to them. And they could make him feel anything they damn well pleased.

Not that it was a whole lot of pain anyway. Just a stiff, bruised feeling in his ribs, arms, and legs. He could move them, but it took effort.

Which he found curious. Because some of this body was actual muscle, though artificially cultured, and some a high-tech pseudo-quantum mishmash on some matrix between steel, plastic, and organic tissue.

But not one molecule of it was his own. No more than any of the nerves or whatever served for them.

All that really remained to him was his brain. And Sahan had his suspicions about that. He knew that by stimulating pain in his brain the Evolved could cause excruciating agony that seemed to come from his own long-lost limbs. That much he'd tested empirically, more than even his generally skeptical nature required.

Of course a brain should not have pain receptors.

Just another little improvement the Evolved had thrown in.

But why leave behind this *bruised* sensation?

Not as a reminder to stay within established boundaries. The Evolved could remind him of anything they wanted anytime they pleased, and make it a lot harder to forget.

Not as punishment, either, for the same reason. It took a lot more than bruises and hunger to get Sahan's attention, as the Dainichi learned early.

Startled, Sahan rolled into a sitting position. He'd forgotten all about the Dainichi. Hadn't thought a thing about them for ... a very long time. Couldn't, because there'd been nothing but a hole where they used to be.

So what were such memories doing in his head now?

The Evolved must want them there. Why else inflict this bruising sensation, no more than a minor irritant?

That had been his life with the Dainichi. Six, eight, eleven, fourteen years old. All through those years the pain stayed with him. Of course the Dainichi never beat him. They were against violence. But they did have something approaching reverence for Tai Chi, and Sahan loved knocking people into floors and walls in Push Hands. A little demented that way, he was.

So since it wasn't safe to put anyone his own age against him, they matched him against older, larger, more experienced opponents. Who in self-defense handled him roughly. Until about fourteen, when they couldn't handle him at all. Not even the instructors.

And so they launched him into outside bouts. Normally the Dainichi kept their own from Alliance matches, because they smacked of the abhorred "competition." But they hoped to humble the boy.

Didn't work. But it did keep up the pain.

Not that he minded. In fact he gloried in it. Wore it like a badge. His reward for pissing off the whole world, which while he couldn't at present remember the details, he was pretty sure he'd been really good at.

As for the pain, you could never make it disappear, but you could learn to set it to one side. Even use the pressure of it to intensify whatever else you set your mind to. He'd learned early to split his awareness into two parts, using the one to stimulate increased power in the other.

Why were these recollections coming to him now?

He ran his hands over his Grinder arms, his Grinder legs, his Grinder face. He still wasn't used to the way the fingers swung out over his mouth and jaws.

Funny thing, fate. In the end, this — *this* — really was his proper place, wasn't it? Enemy to all. Stripped of all the humanity many doubted he possessed in the first place. Even the Dainichi, who venerated humor the way people who seldom get the joke often do, would be falling all over themselves.

Well, he'd amassed a lot of pain and a lot of petty satisfaction. Then he met Arvada.

Smartest thing he ever did — that is, if it really was pain that made him feel the most satisfied.

Sahan held his hands up before him. Long, slender fingers striated as an anatomy book. Skeletal palms with an oily green-gold sheen.

Always going where none had gone before, that was Sahan Kotori.

So where do you go from here, little man?

Finish out the game.

Crash himself against the last, most irresistible pain life had offered him.

Arvada Sattar.

He called out to the Evolved.

"Did you really doubt? Was that why these memories? No need. I'll destroy Arvada for you. You people are into patterns, right? Well me and Arvada, this pattern is *ours*."

He settled back on the bunk.

All his life he'd been splitting himself down the middle. The search for love, and the search for pain.

Time to bring the two halves together.

Chapter 3

"You certainly drive your ships hard," Solange opened, after all of twelve seconds of greetings and small talk. "First the *Viveca*, now the *Geirovar*."

They sat sipping coffee in the Captain's quarters aboard the *Dysis*. Which were slightly larger than the whole officers' wardrobe/council room aboard a fast cruiser. The Captain's table was likewise the size of the council table in a lesser ship.

"I lost the *Viveca* to an Evolved heavy," Arvada reminded her. Oh Sahan, you saved us there. "The *Geirovar* also destroyed the Collaborationist heavy *Filia*."

"Your ships do punch above their weight," Solange acknowledged. "Brilliant victories. And remarkably original. All your victories have been remarkable and original. But my, your crews do lead an exciting life."

Captain O'Grady sat with her back to what appeared to be an imposing vista of space, complete with star fields and swirling gas clouds and the brilliant flares of suns going nova far, far beyond what even a telescope could see. All this courtesy of computer graphics; the scene could as well have included flying saucers with scaled and ridge-headed aliens peering out of bubble canopies. The real thing would have featured considerably more blank expanses and considerably fewer picturesque nebulas, gas clouds, and such.

Captain O'Grady's quarters also featured a separate bedroom, instead of the fold-out bunk of fast cruiser Captains. The wall opposite the bedroom mirrored consoles from the bridge and Engineering.

Did Solange really spend her off hours amid such décor, or had this impression of a constant finger on the battle ship's pulse been laid on for Arvada's benefit? She herself never did. If there was any reason to monitor the ship so closely, the Captain belonged on the bridge. Otherwise she needed some respite from the bright-lit screens with their diagrams and gauges and flashing lights that inevitably revealed *something* of concern.

"Of course the fleet will give you another ship as soon as we return," said Solange, caressing her thin lips with the rim of her mug. It showed the *Dysis* in a 3D kaleidoscope of color, presumably reflecting the light of some cataclysmic space event, since in real life her hull was silver, and scarred by repeated impacts of missiles.

"Will they?" Arvada inhaled the steam from a similar cup.

Solange looked up. "After such a victory? How could they not?"

"By kicking me upstairs. Making me full Captain, then putting me in command of a Strategy Committee or some such. Getting rid of me so they can have the war all to themselves."

"They?"

"The Senior Captains."

They looked at each other levelly. Since the battle at Rione a sort of friendly, almost sisterly rivalry had sprung up between them, born of mutual respect and mutual competition.

"Naval Command is an irrelevancy," stated Solange. "Not even Everson Brooks can sit in his fastness aboard the *Kepler* and decree, 'make it so.' Especially not after this." She lowered the mug. "Nor can I."

"Maybe not," said Arvada. "But after this victory you're certainly in a better position than anyone else."

"You were in overall command," Solange pointed out.

"But you led the heavies to a total rout of the enemy."

"I did, didn't I? So saying, just for grins, final clarification of, ah, the command structure becomes the order of the day. And saying it comes to a vote of all the Captains. Which now it can hardly fail to do, nor will Naval Command or the Citizens' Council dare say boo about it. The fast cruiser Captains will all vote for you. Hypothetically, of course, because we are only talking hypotheticals."

"Of course."

"A number of the heavy Captains would vote for you, too. If, that is, you made it clear you wanted it."

"On the other hand," Arvada returned, "more of the heavy Captains would vote for you. If the choice — just for hypothetical grins, as you say — came down to the two of us, a, ah, an unhealthy tension might arise in the fleet."

"We wouldn't want that. Even a hypothetical tension."

"And I don't want command of the fleet."

Solange raised her eyebrows. "No?"

"Technically I'm still a Lieutenant Commander. Make me a full Captain, and I'm still the most junior Captain in the fleet. To put me in command would put too much strain on the existing structure. On the other hand, a full Captain with a proven record in battle, and more experience than anyone in combat among line of battle ships, who could object to that? Even if she was not the most senior Captain available?"

"We are talking about me, I take it."

"The hypothetical you," Arvada replied. "No one's better suited, and there's no one I could work with so well. So if the matter did come to a vote among the fleet, I think I *might* be able to sway a number of fast cruiser Captains to choose you for overall command. Overall effective hypothetical command. And my endorsement might not be without some effect even among your peers. Which means that for the first time in this war, the Navy could present a united front."

"Except perhaps for Naval Command itself."

"Which as you pointed out, is an irrelevancy."

Solange scrutinized her like a poker player daring their opponent to call. "That would be most ... patriotic, of you. And yet it seems to me that some independent command should still be granted to the Alliance's most dynamic battle leader. A cruiser wing, definitely. And of course her own ship."

"The *Natessa* will do, since Captain Wiritana so considerately avoided putting any dents in her."

"*Captain* Wiritana." Solange mimicked spitting to the side. "My neutered dog has more balls than that clothes rack. But as to yourself, I'm thinking you could best exercise your highly original initiative at the head of a task force comprising ... half the fast cruiser force?"

"Two-thirds would give me more scope. Along with four heavies acting in support."

Solange's conspiratorial nudge-nudge manner hardened. "*Four* heavies?"

"Four hypothetical heavies. That will still give the main fleet—"

"Meaning the two rowboats and an armed freighter you're leaving it."

"— ten Peregrine heavies—"

"You're clearly more optimistic about the *Rajni* than I am. And for all they failed to signalize themselves, the *Druga* and the *Megara* could use some time in drydock as well."

"—plus the two older models from Earth. And if they are ever actually forthcoming, the two new super-heavies they've promised."

"Talk about hypothetical."

Arvada crossed her hands over her heart. "Solange, I'm just putty in your hands. I'll settle for three heavies."

"I was actually thinking more—"

"And you can assign the fourth when the second of the three damaged ships are repaired or the Earth heavies arrive. And I keep the holobrain."

"Take the holobrain with my blessings. No one else is likely to get anything out of it. These three heavies, though...."

"It's not like our commands will never operate jointly. And when they do, you will be Commodore, and if at all possible I will attach them to your command."

"Well in that case." Solange held her coffee mug across the table. They clinked mugs together and drank the toast.

"More?"

"Please."

"What we need to start planning for," said Solange, "though I acknowledge it may be premature, is an attack on Harrar's Reach."

Arvada raised a skeptical eyebrow. "Against the three Evolved heavies remaining in the system? We'd have to overcome the planetary defenses just to get at them. And by the time repairs are completed to the damaged heavies, the Evolved may have sent reinforcements, along with a new Master Holobrain."

"That's why I was toying with the idea of trying it now. The Evolved aren't invulnerable. At Demeter we didn't understand their capabilities. We used tactics developed for use against Earth and let them concentrate too much firepower on our closed formations. Then instead of adapting on the spot, the people in command ran away. That's the truth of it. We know more now."

"That doesn't mean the Evolved heavies have gotten any weaker. What kind of odds would you need?"

"Two of our heavies against one of theirs...." Solange grimaced. "In truth I like their chances better than ours. Three to one, and now the Evolved are starting to have some serious nails to bite. I'm presuming the Collaborationists won't fight any better than they did here. If to that we could throw in those two new Earth heavies with their greater firepower, I'd say the fight is ours to lose. Even without them, though, I would consider odds of four to one. It would be a shambles, but in the end the Evolved would be gone."

She stared moodily down at her coffee cup. "You're right, though. Even if we had fifteen heavies to throw at them, we'd be lucky to get half through the planetary defenses."

"Give me a chance to work on some things," said Arvada, thinking of the holobrain.

Now it was Solange's turn to look dubious. "Something dark and mystical?"

"Honestly, I don't know yet. But we both now we can't invade Harrar's Reach unless we can find some way to neutralize the planetary defenses. *Or,* make them come to us."

Solange started to speak, then checked herself. "I'm not sure I even want to know." Laughing, she shook her head. "I remember hearing about Arvada Sattar while you were still a cadet at the Academy. You and that pet Dainichi of yours. The pacifist who kept breaking people's bones. Many thought you a privileged adolescent who would soon grow bored with service life and follow your mother into politics."

"And you?"

"I withheld judgment. Not least because despite all the doubts about Sahan Kotori, and the jokes at his expense and yours, I noticed no one ever beat him. Clearly there was something dangerous there. As I recall, you were pretty good in the Decahedron yourself."

"I don't think 'pretty good' quite expresses it."

Again Solange laughed. "No. And just look at you now. There was never a chance you'd work your way up the ranks. Well, it looks like we're stuck with each other. But I have to ask. All this trouble to get a holobrain ... does that have anything to do with Sahan?"

Arvada wanted so badly to tell her the truth. She so badly wanted a friend, and somehow Solange O'Grady, whom she'd always found so forbidding, had turned into the leading candidate.

But as Sahan once told her, truth was like the Uncertainty Principle. You didn't want to present it in such an unshielded way that if you put forth one interpretation, all other possibilities instantly collapse.

"The holobrain," she said, "is actually for Beck. He's got me about half convinced he'll go mad, maybe even die without it."

Solange raised an eyebrow. "You didn't build your reputation on solicitude."

"Solicitude is not exactly what I have in mind. I think I can turn him."

"Through the holobrain? Strikes me that could very easily become a two-edged sword."

"Indeed. I did, however, learn a thing or two from Sahan. We have gotten accurate intelligence from the holobrains before."

"Well, I'll leave that to you. Since there's nothing I can do about it anyway. Can I take it we have an agreement, then?"

"You may." Arvada extended her hand, and they shook.

She didn't know what fingers Solange kept crossed with her other hand. The ones of her own offhand that remained crossed through their manly handshake were because ever since Beck told her Sahan might still be alive, in a highly altered form, Arvada had begun to frame the whole thrust of the war as a battle between him and her.

And she had no idea whether love or hate would win.

Chapter 4

The terror came to him during what Sahan defined as sleep.

Not sleep as he once knew it. Not unless his sleep had been nothing but nightmares.

Maybe it had. Because the scenes that came to him were all familiar; Arvada betraying him, Arvada mocking him, Arvada laughing as she took a succession of lovers to her bed.

He could tell this was "sleep" however, because of the rapidity with which the visions rotated.

Sahan did not find this restful. He yearned for some cessation from Arvada's endless taunting presence. For a moment, just a moment, of pure sweet peace.

Then as if in answer to his plea the parade of torments thinned and died, leaving him staring at blackness where a moment before he'd seen Arvada's mocking grin.

He tried to relax into the momentary peace—

But at once fear crashed through him. An overwhelming terror he could not define, though he heard a distant whimper he knew to be his own, and felt sensors in his brain inform him that his imitation Grinder body was trying to fold into a ball.

The universe, *his* universe, turned vast and empty. He felt himself falling. He reached out for anything, anyone. Even

Arvada and her mocking laughter would have provided one still point.

Nothing.

Nothing nothing nothing.

Nothing but this void into which he fell. Sahan tried to claw deep inside himself in search of a place to hide, and found only more emptiness.

Then another, separate fear descended on him from out of the nothingness. An external force, chaotic and flailing. Sahan cowered away as its tendrils touched him.

As this new terror, this Other, enfolded him, what was left of Sahan's mind dissolved in what he could only conceptualize as its soul.

Need. Raw, gaping, need. An inner emptiness so profound as to echo the external void into which Sahan fell.

An urge to weep seized him, right through his terror.

Need, yes. He understood that.

Such pain, scratching against the walls of perception!

The Other reached deeper into him in panicked hope.

Sahan's fear peaked.

Suddenly he realized that a Presence so familiar he'd come to confuse it with his own thoughts was winging away from him.

The Evolved. They didn't like it here.

Here in the Terror Barrier.

Take me with you! Sahan tried to shout, but his mind was as mute as his voice.

A voice called to him. Or did it? He strained to hear, but couldn't be sure.

Help, or one more Siren luring him to his doom?

The familiarity he'd first sensed in this Other finally came clear.

The ghosts. The Christian ghosts reaching out for the faith that had been scorched from their heads.

How had they found him here? What unknown echoes did he carry that led them to him?

Like attracted like. His life too was ruled by an insatiable hunger. Then and now. First frustrated love for Arvada, now the need to wipe her from the universe, and finally scrape her mocking laughter out of his head.

He had to escape. Whoever inhabited this realm, whether ghosts of the Christians, or those of the Evolved who'd fallen into this realm while failing to make the transition to the Group Mind, they were too many, too strong.

He still held one weapon. One which never left him.

Arvada.

For even through his terror her image stood firm, and her laughter never left his ears.

Pain. Let it give you strength.

Rage. Let it hurl that strength against all that besets you.

The scenes of her betrayal crescendoed, while her laugh beat against whatever substitute for eardrums the Evolved had given him. He used them to flail himself, to cauterize himself against all but hatred.

The whole universe might dissolve around him, but he was still Sahan Kotori. Still holding to his purpose.

Arvada.

Not even the Terror Barrier could dissolve that out of him.

***

SAHAN WAS BEGINNING ANOTHER training bout with the Grinders when he realized their attitude toward him since the mock-up of his battle aboard the *Enodia*, where he'd slain several, was changing.

You'd think they'd hate and fear him all the more. Only it didn't work out like that.

Sahan did feel something like a surly tone emanating from the Evolved, who'd arranged that episode to increase his authority over the Grinders through fear. When you think yourself All-Knowing, miscalculations are more jarring than for mere mortals.

But for now they let events take their course. They did not cause the Grinders to hurl themselves in a frenzy at him. They'd refashioned Sahan into a leader they hoped would get more out of the Grinders than they'd been able to. At some point they had to let him lead. Not manipulate him and the Grinders into more and more scenarios which however much they fit some idealized model, might not stand up to reality.

So the Grinders moved in against him in measured fashion, and not wholly without an improvement in the skills he sought to teach them.

The outcome remained the same, of course. Sahan was bigger, and even though they wore powered suits and he didn't, at least as strong. Though he could tell from previous battle experience with the Grinders that the top power range of their suits had been disabled.

He was also Sahan Kotori. And even though his current body felt almost fuzzy in comparison with the old, he still, aside from years of accumulated knowledge, possessed a level of perception and anticipation that could not be trained into Grinder brains.

Or could it?

When Sahan sometimes took as much as ten minutes to work with an individual, moving slow enough that they could actually see what he was doing, some of the Grinders rewarded his patience with surprising progress. Not simply mastering a set series of maneuvers in a set sequence, but beginning to understand the logic behind them, and altering the moves to meet altered circumstances. On occasion he even saw them trying to help others.

Something else surprised him.

They showed ... gratitude?

Or maybe they did. Not easy to tell, with Grinders. Their vocabulary was so pared down it was generally easier for them to communicate their simple needs through grunts and gestures and the occasional blow or bite.

But the way their eyes followed him, no longer with the murderous, fear-checked intensity they once displayed, the way they gathered around him in the training hall like a pack of dogs, they way they made muddled half-bows, a gesture perhaps less of respect than submission, it all reminded him....

It reminded him of the way people used to fawn on Arvada back at the Academy, where she began her career as queen of creation.

Sahan suppressed the memory. With effort. He did not want to answer any softening, even loyalty toward him among the Grinders, with rage and broken bones.

The Grinders' changed demeanor toward him eventually brought with it a new level of communication. Again, hard to be sure. But he thought they wanted something from him. Not just training. It went beyond that.

At first it remained elusive. Then another memory added dimension to his speculations.

The Grinders bore a deep-seated need. Unvoiced and undefined, but gnawing at them constantly, giving them the air of cats crowded too close together, and ready to lash out at whatever came near.

Sahan had previously dismissed their reflective belligerence as a dull-spirited response to a life of overwhelming monotony and lack of choice.

Now he perceived their underlying hunger more clearly. And linked it with another.

The Christian ghosts of the Terror Barrier, moaning for a Redeemer to make them whole.

Of course among the Grinders that sense of despair remained faint and flickering in comparison. The Evolved had not bred them for deep emotions other than rage, and none among them had the slightest memory of any religious concept sparking about their neural circuitry. But as one who'd felt the ghosts reaching for him, Sahan recognized the similarity clearly enough.

Did the Evolved know?

How could they not? Didn't the holobrains read and control everything that took place within the Grinder brains? And Sahan's?

On the other hand....

If that need originated in the Terror Barrier, the Evolved might see the results, but misjudge the cause. The Barrier kept its secrets, even from them.

Did these two hungers spring from the same source?

It would make for a long and tortured inheritance.

But tenuous as that legacy might be, it might help explain why the Grinders seemed to draw closer to Sahan every day.

The ghosts had sought refuge in him, but found he could not provide it.

The Grinders' need, at least superficially, was more here and now. They needed someone to make them....

To make them feel human again.

At first he rejected the task. He wasn't one of them. Despite all that had been done to him, despite this wholly artificial body, he still existed in the same realm as Arvada.

Only you don't, do you?

Whatever realm you do inhabit, you and the Grinders appear to be sharing it.

And when you're feeling sorry for yourself, like now, and every now and then the sentiment overflows, where can it go?

The Evolved? Yeah sure.

Arvada? If this was a real body I'd be laughing.

He lined up to meet the next Grinder, aware of the others watching in fascination and whatever else their truncated little hearts and minds could watch in.

Just you and me, guys.

A poor thing, but mine own.

Chapter 5

A CRAMPED CARGO HOLD aboard the *Natessa* was not the sort of place Arvada would normally choose to while away the hours. Yet in a fast cruiser crammed full of Marines and combat Riggers over and above her normal crew complement, free space was hard to come by. And so she came to visit her precious, hard-won holobrain within these gray steel walls.

As always, she was struck by the holobrain's resemblance to an old-fashioned gimble-mounted globe of the sort that once graced Victorian studies. Within its translucent shell it displayed only a featureless golden brown expanse instead of marking nations and oceans. But to Arvada it was still redolent of the same mystery many regions of Earth must once have held before steamships, railroads, and machine guns standardized the planet into the customary arrangement of those who prospered and those who starved, those who issued commands and those forced to follow them.

As the Evolved desired to issue commands now.

The dull-silver profusion of pumps, filters, heaters, coolers, pipes, and gauges that serviced the holobrain even brought to mind fanciful depictions of Earth-era laboratories, making the comparison to *Frankenstein* inevitable. For all the Evolved's sophistication in things of the brain — creating a Group Mind that provided life after death was no mean trick, after all — it had often been remarked that their material development was not significantly advanced over that of the Peregrines.

As had become his custom, Beck sat facing the Evolved machine. Less than a meter separated him from the faintly sparkling globe, since supply containers filled the steel racks from floor to ceiling on three sides, leaving but a compact cave for the device itself.

"Does it help to stay so close?" Arvada asked, leaning against one of the shelf arrays. "I'd think your quarters would be more comfortable."

"So they would. But since the holobrain is the closest thing to a companion I have aboard this ship, I appreciate the proximity."

"More of a companion than me?" Arvada affected a wounded look.

"Perhaps instead of 'companion' I should have said 'friend.' The holobrain does not make light of my pain or threaten to kill me at regular intervals. In fact it is innocent of all those sadistic impulses that figure so largely in your own barbaric though admittedly scintillating personality."

Arvada laughed, oddly flattered. "Sadistic or not, I did get you your holobrain. Do you imagine that was such an easy thing?"

"I was there, if you recall. At your insistence. I have never questioned your competence."

"Just my benevolence."

"Does anyone actually believe in your benevolence?"

Shocked and not a little offended, Arvada searched through her roster of friends, smaller than she'd assumed once she took a closer look, then professional acquaintances.

"Well no," she concluded reluctantly. And here she'd been going around thinking she was basically a good person at heart, too.

"Did you have questions for me, Captain Sattar?" He looked up from the hard metal chair that reminded her with a pang of Sahan sitting much the same way.

Beck was a tall, spare man with a long, spare face. It surprised her every time she saw him how much like any Peregrine he looked. Though it shouldn't; any progress toward a super-race the Evolved may have achieved lay purely in the mental realm, and even that, as far as she knew, centered almost entirely around the Group Mind, which only came into play after what most humans would call death, though you could get an argument from Beck about it.

"First," she said, "would you like a more comfortable chair?"

"I am quite content, thank you."

Again his quiet, stubborn asceticism reminded her of Sahan, who she often thought deliberately hoarded discomfort. He would look distant and long-suffering if she suggested anything to soften his existence, like the slightest relaxation might weaken his will. With Sahan, maybe there was something to that. And maybe he undertook some of it just for practice.

He'd been like that when they met at the Academy. At first she thought him just another poseur, trying to look wounded and sensitive. Only most people, their pose crumpled at some specific quantum of challenge. It might be adversity, surprisingly often it was sympathy. But they all had it somewhere, and to maneuver them you simply had to feel out that point.

Not Sahan. That point simply didn't exist. The world and Arvada had together inflicted enough pain on him to prove that.

She cleared her throat to hide a spasm of guilt.

"Has the feeling of isolation you complained of lessened?" she asked Beck.

"It has indeed, Captain. For which I thank you. Though perhaps if you had simply turned me over to you governing authority as part of some sort of exchange, as you may remember I several times suggested, fewer people would have died to address my discomfort. Not that I flatter myself that my comfort was uppermost in your thoughts."

"And as you may remember *I* suggested, we are at war. People are supposed to die. Even on your side, shocking as you may find it."

He raised one eyebrow in a supercilious gesture and started to turn away. Then checked himself. He stared up at her with a challenging air.

"Despite the plethora of religions and sub-religions and cults and superstitions that throughout human existence have produced thousands of interpretations of death, the actual experience remained absolute and universal. Now we have entered into a new era, where death can take several forms."

He waited like an instructor expecting you to muff the question.

"There is plain old death," Arvada stated in reply. "Which everyone but the Evolved expect to come to, however they picture it. There is a form of death, or I would call it so, where" — thinking of Sahan she clamped down to avoid affording Beck the satisfaction of her grief — "part of a person's mind survives, but part of it, perhaps the greater part, has been taken from them. Perhaps even used to force them to a course wholly opposed to what they would choose on their own."

Beck shrugged his head sideways. "I was not including that in my own count, but yes, I will acknowledge that the suborning of an individual's inborn will through invasive manipulations of the brain can possibly be considered a form of death."

Oh you'll acknowledge it, will you?

Arvada pressed on past her anger. "Then there is the Group Mind. Which to hear you talk of it, is not death at all, but rather a form of collective immortality."

"Yes. Though 'immortality' forms but a shallow accounting of the possibilities. Leaving that aside for now, can you think of another?"

"Just one. The Terror Barrier. Though maybe I'm being too parochial here? Just as the Christians thought you had to die to go to hell, I'm thinking you have to die to go to the Terror Barrier. Of course some awareness functions there; it would hardly be the Terror Barrier otherwise. But would you call it life?"

"I would call it death. The most horrid imaginable. In fact beyond imagining."

"It wasn't beyond imagining for Sahan," Arvada pointed out. "He went there and came back."

"A most remarkable man, your Sahan Kotori," Beck admitted. "And one of unique experience. I doubt such circumstances shall ever be repeated again. But what I'm asking you to understand, the old conceptions of death have finally been made real. Not the fairy-tale aspects, the lakes of fire and forked tales, or working in the vineyards singing praises to the Lord. What sort of dreary, dead-end destiny would that be? What kind of God would create us in the first place, if the whole exercise was simply to weed out the ones with any spirit or initiative, and keep the dullards around just to sing his praises? But the comparison I meant to emphasize was that the old ideas of heaven and hell have finally come true. In a real and incomparably more vital form than all the dreams of the afterlife ever set forth."

"You mean the Group Mind and the Terror Barrier."

"Of course. The Group Mind is the proper fate of humanity. Not the Terror Barrier. That was an accident. Someday, when we are free to establish a true Homeworld of our own, we will learn how to dispel it and at last free those trapped there."

"Ticklish work, when you're so frightened of the place."

"Ticklish indeed. But to be conducted by a more knowledgeable entity, as the Group Mind itself continually evolves. But first we need peace."

"You have an odd way of getting it."

"This should not be happening!" Beck cried in sudden passion. "You should have ceded to our terms following the collapse of your fleet at Demeter. Many of you did. Even now, surely some settlement cannot be so far away."

"If only the Alliance would be reasonable, right?" She sighed theatrically. "Funny things, wars."

He frowned at her sarcasm. "Don't you see? If we win, there should *be* no more wars. Not after this one. We will establish the conditions to make further war, at least further interstellar war, untenable. Whether Earth likes it or not, peace will reign in human and post-human space."

Arvada exploded in laughter. Leaning against an upright, she rolled from side to side clutching her ribs. She couldn't help herself.

"No more war!" she gasped at last. "So *that's* your fantasy! Same as they told us we were working for back at the Academy. All this firepower, all these pretty, *pretty* ships bristling with weapons coursing through the star systems with all these painstakingly trained killers aboard, all that money devoted to devastation ... and for why? To end war! You know something? I almost swallowed it. For a while. Sahan opened my eyes."

"You appear cynical enough on your own," Beck observed acidly.

"War's been a great learning experience. Especially war with you lot. The vaunted Group Mind, whose knowledge spans realms far beyond mere human whatever. Now you tell me your whole rationale is to put an end to war. *After* you invade us. Oh, that's just too funny. Didn't your great pacifistic Group Mind ever think of talking to us *before* killing three thousand Peregrines at Demeter?"

Beck shot to his feet, so fast Arvada remembered his physical capabilities. "You were too damn proud, and we knew it! Just look at you! You would never accept any limitations on your precious technology unless we proved it useless to fight against us!"

"I advise you," she said levelly, "to sit down."

***

BECK'S EXPRESSION HELD IMMOBILE. Arvada saw no tightening or trembling of his body. But she could all but feel the heat pouring off him.

They stared at each other. The room was of course being monitored, and Security stood right outside the door. Nor was she exactly helpless. But a lot of damage could be done by a dedicated practitioner in a second or so, and he'd surprised her before with his speed of movement.

He sat down.

"Only as it turns out," she said quietly, "that technology you meant to disparage wasn't so useless, was it? In fact I'd say we've utilized it rather well. As your status as honored guest should demonstrate."

"But at such a price." A stiff calm once more prevailed. "A dreadful, needless waste."

"Waste? I have lost a damn sight more in this war than you have!" Calm yourself. Who's running this conversation, you, or him? "And I don't call it a waste at all. Sacrifice, yes. A most noble sacrifice. But never a waste. So if this waste you talk of so troubles you, go back to where you came from."

"And have Earth follow us? They will never forget what they claim happened to the Christian colony aboard the *Hawking*."

"A claim by now pretty well substantiated, I think."

"You and Earth, you push and push and push a people already on the thin edge of survival. You did it at L5, you did it aboard the *Stephen Hawking*, you're doing it now. Having deliberately planted a subversive colony in our midst, you cry genocide when we defended ourselves."

"We? You mean the Peregrines?"

"Understand this. My people are not going to spend our entire existence running away. We have tried to accomplish something beyond all previous human achievement, but your pursuit—"

"Expansion?"

"— makes it impossible to further our goals. Which will in the end bring the ultimate blessing to all humanity. Once we contain your vengefulness and militarism."

"You still might at least have considered asking. Maybe even saying 'please.' Because you're saying it now, aren't you? When you ask us to take up arms against Earth, it's no longer followed by a big 'or else.' Or do I misread the situation?"

He tried to wave her objection away. "Let us cease this quibbling. Try to understand what is really at stake here. The ideal my people have striven to create, that all humanity has always sought in vain, is now in sight."

"The Group Mind?"

"Life after death. And beside that, the *certainty* of knowing what the afterlife holds, so humanity no longer fight needless stupid doctrinal wars over something it knows nothing about. But try, just try, Captain, to realize the wonder of it. Because the Group Mind far transcends mere immortality. Immortality as portrayed by every religion in history never surmounted the individual being, with all its pain and limitations. *This* is different. I cannot come close to comprehending its full scale. How could I, since I still live in the same realm of individual existence as you? But the wonder, the joy, the vastness of the experience! I can't begin to convey it."

"How do you know, if you're in my same realm of existence?"

"All of us who serve and nurture the Group Mind—"

"The Living Evolved, you mean?"

"I find that offensive, and misleading as well."

"That's what Sahan called you, and you're just going to have to put up with it."

"Can't you be bothered to even try and understand? Are you really so imprisoned in your own bitter fantasies?"

"Elucidate me."

"All of the Evolved still functioning in this realm share glimpses of the wonder," he said. "We could never comprehend the full scale, that would shatter our minds. But just a glimpse ... I tell you, Captain Sattar, I *do* know the meaning of sacred. For all his experience, your Sahan never knew that."

"I do not hold you as equipped to make presumptions about Sahan. Many of your kind did, and died for it. Or worse."

"Try to step back from your chauvinism and aggression for just a moment. The Group Mind could be yours. I mean, the Peregrine people. Maybe not your generation. I doubt there's time left to accumulate sufficient transcripts to carry your essence over into the Group Mind. But the next generation, paradise could be theirs. If only you'll allow it."

Paradise. Arvada tried to comprehend. Immortality, yes of course that had to tempt anyone. As for the Group Mind....

What did it really represent? Transcendence had always been at least an ideological goal of the *Hawking* voyagers ever since Maeda Rao first preached at L5. The meditation, the internal arts, these were practiced for greater sensitivity in the suits, and for skill in the Decahedron, but ultimately the goal of *satori* was always held to be the ultimate achievement. And there was no lack of those in the Peregrine world who claimed to have achieved it. Sahan was always fascinated by the possibility. But Sahan was born for combat, not sainthood.

The Group Mind, however, must represent some form of transcendence. After all, weren't the limitations and illusions of the individual ego just what *satori* was held to overcome?

"Tell me," she said. "Within the Group Mind, is there still any ... perception, or recognition, or identification with, the individual personality at all?"

"Of course. But that is unimportant. What matters is the experience of pure *life* beyond anything remotely possible to individual existence. A pure creation that possibly may transcend the life of the universe itself."

"Possibly?"

"The Group Mind is still in its relative beginnings."

Peregrine meant wanderer. That was a core value of her people and their experience: to wander the stars, in search of whatever wonders might be found. But the Group Mind would far transcend any physical wonder space might have to offer.

What would it be like, never to be lonely again?

What would it be like, to join once more with Sahan, and together explore the wonders of the human spirit? For she and Sahan were cast by fate to adventure together.

The vision pulled strongly at her.

And yet....

"Your Group Mind," Arvada told Beck. "For all the razzle-dazzle, I can't help thinking it sounds like the triumph of the dead over the living."

Beck slapped a hand to his forehead in by far the most human gesture she'd ever seen him make. "Are you truly so wedded to your petty little existence? To say something like you just did ... that's nothing but xenophobia. Throughout human history, throughout human awareness, our species has always sought to construct gods. Then live in terror of the laws they believe these self-created gods will impose. *That* is the triumph of death over life.

"But with the creation of the Group Mind we have for the first time the means to see beyond death. More, to *exist* beyond death. And exist as something far grander than anything we might ever have experienced within our individual awareness. If we carried all our same individual loneliness, biases, irrationalities, and fears into the afterlife, what would be the point? We would merely construct anew the muddle we left. The *fulfillment* of humanity, free of fear and selfishness and greed. *This* is what we offer you."

Arvada felt dwarfed by the prospects.

But right here and now, she *was* locked in her own individual fear and selfishness and greed and all the rest of it. And locked into a war, besides.

"Only you didn't exactly *offer*, did you?" she told Beck. "You came booming in with a fleet of warships and a host of demands. If you were promising eternal life, you can see how we might get a little confused, the way you started out spreading death. And trying to deny us the same technology that eventually led you to that point."

Beck tried to brush that aside. "We couldn't expose ourselves to you until the most dangerous of your interstellar capabilities were neutralized. But you Peregrines, you're descendants of the *Hawking*, same as us. The conclusion of this whole affair was always intended to be a homecoming. For both of us."

For the first time since she'd known him he gave way to a look of despair. "It all went so horribly wrong."

Arvada shook her head, the spell broken. She was too small for such grand visions. Too dependent on the here and now.

"It's looking to get wronger," she said. "Your people are still maintaining three line of battle ships at Harrar's Reach.

They're not trying to negotiate anything and neither are we. The conclusion I'm drawing is that the Evolved are sending reinforcements. Including a Master Holobrain. To smash us into submission. That's the real homecoming you offer us."

"We need to establish certain conditions," Beck said, almost pleadingly. "Our vulnerability is extreme. We need to protect ourselves."

"Yeah, we need to protect ourselves too. Funny how that happens in war. Maybe I do understand something of your Group Mind after all. Because like it, war too is the domination of the living by the dead."

Chapter 6

"Douse the stimulants!" Sahan shouted into his suit mike as the Grinders came streaming back from the domes of the mining colony, yellow spears of rocket fire prodding them like the Devil's pitchfork. Those, that is, who didn't lie huddled or sprawled in bloody silver bundles amid the hummocks of Aulaire.

The Grinders' movements turned spasmodic as the collision of terror and artificially induced rage left them too clumsy to control their suits. They fled hopping, leaping, tumbling in arcs, bouncing up and down. At times one would halt, teeter, then spin around and march back toward the hostile guns in a stiff-legged puppet's march.

Most often a rocket would blow their suit open within a few meters. There was just enough gravity to hold the viscera of the fallen bodies inside their suits, but veils of blood drifted like red a mist through the perpetual green-tinged twilight of the planet.

"Kill the fucking stimulants!" Sahan roared again.

"Negative," came back the voice of the AI, rendered deliberately mechanical. "Plans specify an all-out attack against the complex entrance. A second wave will be landing shortly. Send them into the attack immediately. The survivors of the first wave will serve to draw fire. We are currently experiencing difficulty turning them. But increasing stimulant dosage should at least hold them in place."

"You're killing them to no purpose! I need these troops!"

"Orders are—"

"First wave!" he screamed into the command channel. "Retreat! I repeat, first wave fall back!"

An echoing emptiness came back; the AI had muted the channel.

"The plan of attack—"

"Don't tell me the friggin' plan of attack! *I'm* leading the Grinders, not you!"

"But we retain overall command. Our analysis—"

"Is what? Feed the Peregrines so many bodies they'll run out of ammunition? Your analysis is too high on Artificial and too low on Intelligence! Now turn field command over to me before you slaughter the second wave too."

"The decision tree specifies—"

BREAK he thought, directing it toward the frequency foremost in his mind. No use arguing with the rivet-heads. Evolved ships carried a living commander to override the AI if necessary, but in this operation Sahan had no authority over them at all. And they weren't any better than any other senior officer with too much time polishing chairs and not enough getting shot at.

Only one authority in range could override them. The holobrain. And though it could play alchemist in his mind, he was barred from communicating back. He'd tried, and been rewarded with nothing but vacancy. Or PAIN.

Turning away from the screens that gave him multiple perspectives of the battlefield, Sahan stood and peered over the ragged edge of the trench hurriedly dug with shaped charges.

The hillocks spread across the bare, dusty ground looked like a succession of waves. Over which what was left of the first attack force struggled back with a herky-jerky motion as the AI pumped still more rage-inducing stimulants into their brains in an effort to make them turn around and get slaughtered.

Sixty percent gone, at least. He was going to lose them all if the rivet-heads didn't back off their obsession with human sacrifice.

Grinder. Not human sacrifice, Grinder. Like him.

Sahan flinched and ducked back into the trench as an explosion twenty meters to the rear sprayed dust over him. Ragged black pieces of metal flew like witches through the air.

His landing craft. Knew the Peregrines would find it eventually. The thin atmosphere, non-breathable, muffled most of the sound, but the flare lit the green night into a luminescent seascape all around.

Sahan jumped out of the trench and ran forward in great hopping low-g bounds. He made almost a hundred yards toward the complex of domes and bunkers before the lancing yellow trails of rocket fire began to seek him out. He dived behind a meter-high hummock. As it exploded, showering him with dirt, he slithered forward behind the intermittent shelter of others.

When he leapt up and ran forward again, the rockets had moved back to the easier targets of Grinders wallowing like five-legged spiders as fear and stimulants warred within them. A few isolated flechettes glanced off his armor with that nerve-grating scraping whine that wedged your throat tight as you listened for the alarm that signaled "suit breach." None penetrated; the distance was too great.

He began to pass Grinders fleeing in the opposite direction. As rocket fire once more turned his way he dived flat and crawled forward, coming to the fringe of dead and wounded scattered among the sandhills.

The dead, instantly recognizable by the paste that was once their brains scattered across their helmets, by far predominated. The Grinders' suits might seal off a breach to the lower leg or arm, but anything beyond that triggered the explosive charges surgically implanted in their heads. Such instantaneous oblivion bypassed the last-millisecond primordial terror that came with the soul's final unshielded sight of death.

This represented no tender mercy on the part of the Evolved. Instead, since the Grinders' minds were in direct contact with the holobrain, these micro-bursts of fear would accrete to the Terror Barrier, deepening and widening that trap that surrounded the Group Mind like a moat. So the Evolved sought to obviate it.

The first of the wounded Grinders Sahan reached was a woman with her lower leg mangled. In minutes, he guessed, her blood pressure would fall below critical threshold and the suit monitors would pulp her head. Now, though, she kept dragging herself along, hopping forward on one leg, invariably twisting sideways and landing in a heap. Then flail around as she tried to rise again.

Gently Sahan pressed her down. The stimulants in her brain remained at such a level that she tried to bite his arm.

He had no way to speak to her. Words for "quiet" and "easy" existed among the Grinders, but only as commands, with an edge of threat.

Sahan brought his helmet close to hers so that she could make out his face. Gradually she ceased to struggle against him, though still quivering from the hormones. He felt her reaching toward him as dying focused her emotions and sent them through the holobrain.

She called on him for something rare among the Grinders; recognition of a common existence, with common fears, and a common sharing to ease the loneliness that made those fears so much worse. As Sahan knelt in the shelter of a hillock and held the wounded Grinder close to him, her hands scrabbled against his suit, trying to grip him close. Trying to reach the shared pain she sensed in him.

Sahan held her helmet to helmet, rocking her gently. The woman's pain peeled back the layers of defense he maintained reflexively. That surrender was all he had to give, but he gave it wholly, so that in that moment they were neither of them alone.

His head rocked sideways at the explosion that ended her life.

Still Sahan held her. He saw flares and rocket fire and dismembered bodies all around him. These things were real, emerging from the eternal green twilight of Aulaire.

But he saw them, and felt them, as if from some other place.

Inside himself he heard a cry.

WHY?

A cacophony of calls from the panicked Grinders filled his ear phones.

The cry couldn't be coming from them. But Sahan heard it so.

WHY?

Floating distorted before his vision he saw that same question, same accusation, shouted from the dead faces of the Marines and Riggers who'd followed him into massacre.

In some mental feedback loop it spread back and forth through the green night between the shrill wails of his dead from the *Enodia* to the growls and snarls and terrified howls of the Grinders. It echoed from the red mist floating around him. It exploded in the spurting dust storms of hillocks exploded by rocket fire.

Softly he lay the dead Grinder down. He stood, heedless of the rockets.

WHY?

Why had he brought so much harm to others, and they to him? Why the whole bitter, blood-stained trajectory of his life?

WHY?

Still filing back, the Grinders quieted their struggles with themselves. They stared at Sahan. Listened to him. Not through their ears, but the holobrain that linked their consciousness. And to which they were now exposed more than ever before.

Two landscapes churned before Sahan. One was Aulaire; the other his nightmares from the *Enodia*. Flares lit both, flaring out of one green background and one black. Dismembered bodies in battle suits lay or tumbled past. Grinders hopped out of one into the other.

As he sank further away from the green night, distant purple sheets rippled in and out of view.

Sahan floated back to the surface. In the green light of Aulaire the retreating Grinders either made it back into the shelter holes blown out for them or lay dead or dying amid the hummocks.

Still seeing the purple landscape of the holobrain through the green sheet of reality, Sahan started back toward the trenches. Three hundred meters beyond them the landing sleds of the second wave were sliding down to the surface in great clouds of dust.

The AI screamed in his ear. Sahan called up the codes to control his inputs, physically repeated the numbers, and manually shut off their channel. A few moments ago he would have failed, but now his immersion in the holobrain gave him the power.

The Grinders were his … people. Not the Evolved's. Not the rivet-heads'. His. His people because no one but Sahan felt one damn thing when they died.

And he'd lived through one massacre too many.

Chapter 7

Sahan stood at the edge of the trenches with the Grinder refugees of the first broken attack huddled at his feet. Seen through infrared, the line of figures still twitching as they tried to fight off the stimulants the AI pumped into them brought to mind a scarlet worm writhing in sudden exposure to the sun. A memento of his youth tilling the soil. The memory darted up out of his past and even as he tried to fix it darted away again, leaving the impression of not another life; but another dimension.

In the emerald-tinged distance the second wave of Grinders, over three hundred of them, scurried out of the dust cloud kicked up by the landing sleds. They loped forward in ungainly low-gravity skips. As rocket fire once more lanced from the domes many Grinders flattened out and dove forward close to horizontal, belly-whomping down in clouds of dust, sometimes flattening whole hillocks.

Sahan ignored the rockets. At this range they were more an expression of optimism than a serious deterrent.

He saw and understood these things.

But this reality was superimposed in a shallow film across the still more immediate reality of the holobrain. The instrument through which the Evolved ruled Sahan and the Grinders.

Only maybe not so much as they believed. Because the Grinders who'd made it back from the initial attack were not going anywhere without Sahan, no matter how much the holobrain juiced up their blood.

And he was being recalcitrant.

Rejected, the AI tried to bring him back into line. Sahan's body possessed no organic heart, but whatever conglomerate they'd stuck in his chest wasn't so much pumping as slamming fluids into his brain, along with their attendant cargo of stimulants. The artificial nerves that controlled his limbs burned like wires too thin to contain the electric charge forced into them.

And now a third layer of reality, intermediate between Aulaire and the holobrain, forced itself upon him. He saw Arvada standing before him, taunting him, daring him, just as she had when she beat him down and dumped him into the cockpit of the hunter-killer for his last doomed episode as a human being.

The fresh wave of Grinders vaulting toward him, their spirits still undimmed by casualties, added their mad urgency to his own. And to the surviving Grinders of the first wave, a number of whom scrambled back out of the trenches, hopping and waving their weapons in their eagerness for another chance to have their brains blown to jelly.

Still Arvada egged him on: *are you frightened, little man? Because even if you win here, you will still have to meet me. And that terrifies you, doesn't it?*

In a moment they'd all rush headlong against the bunkers. Some would even make it. Probably just enough to overcome the surviving colonists. The rivet-heads were good with numbers. And with brute-force solutions, suitable when your working tools lacked all pretense of humanity.

The situation teetered on the edge of another massacre.

WHY? WHY?

Because I was too weak! he screamed back at them. Because I was determined Arvada would not fail, and she meant more to me than your lives!

WHY?

He opened himself up to the voices, and the shame and guilt they brought. They'd guided him into the holobrain before; let them take him deeper now.

Then he he was right there, amid the flares and darkness and screams. Watching the dismembered bodies of his dead tumble past, still calling out:

WHY?

Sahan bellowed out his pain, pleading for forgiveness.

The force of his cry, the despair and shame contained within, drew the Grinders deeper into the holobrain after him. Until Sahan saw their own images of guilt and shame and fear and rage spinning within minds too agitated by stimulants for any thought beyond myth.

The myth of their own massacre.

He saw humans in machines with great black tires riding the wind through storms of flame and choking black cloud. Falling upon the Grinders in their still-human form. Beating them down, crushing them, then peeling away their skins, revealing the shameful insectoid structure beneath. Driving them from idyllic green pastures into a world of unbroken gray metal and slavery and shame. Shame at their form, shame at their own minds which they knew to be dull and subhuman; shame at their sterility, which left their very creation to the whim of the masters, and shame at their own uncontrolled barren sexuality.

That shame they tried to bury beneath rage, screeching and howling and wailing in their frenzy to avenge themselves. To take back the humanity they'd lost from those who'd taken it from them.

But as to the exact nature of that humanity, of that they had no idea beyond the superficial appearance. How could they? It defined everything they were not. All such memories had been taken from them, leaving in its place only an aching void.

Like him.

Cracks broke through the pain that had so long possessed him. And through those those cracks his battered soul tried to issue muffled screams of love.

Love for what, he didn't know. For everything his life or his pride had always cut him off from, only he could not now remember. For the dead of the *Enodia*. For the Grinders. For the living Evolved he'd cast down into the Terror Barrier. For Arvada — or if not her, then for that part of himself that had managed to love her despite all, when never in life had it allowed him to love anything else.

From deep in the holobrain, that disembodied love filtered its way to the Grinders. Who could make little of it, such feelings having been lost to them along with their God and their human form.

Yet though they could not fit his love into their own emotional range, one idea did get through to them.

Here was someone, a being more powerful than themselves, who actually cared for them.

Sahan became aware of them crowding about him. Every now and then one cried out as a rocket sent pieces of them gushing bloodily through the green night.

Sahan went on wide transmission.

"Back to the landing sleds," he ordered. "Everyone back to the sleds."

Hopping the trench, he strode off in that direction. The Grinders followed.

The AI screamed at him. Ran flame along his nerve-endings. Gave him terrible shooting pains in the stomach he didn't have. Sahan bent, but kept walking.

"This operation is now under my control," he told the AI. "Either accept that, or kill me if you can. And take your chances with the Grinders."

"Any demonstration of mutiny—" the AI began.

"When I mutiny, you'll know about it. Until then, screw yourselves. Better yet, unscrew yourselves. Sahan out."

Behind him the Grinders shambled across the plane, exhibiting a mood he'd never before felt in them.

The eagerness for bloodshed, that was familiar. But always before it had been artificially induced.

Now they were entering into combat for something else.

Themselves.

And maybe for him.

And maybe for all of them together.

Chapter 8

Four unmanned sleds with horseshoe bows streaked low across the pockmarked landscape of Aulaire. Rocket fire from the surviving bunkers surrounding the domes shot yellow spears at them through the green atmosphere. Two of the craft took hits, but kept going forward with large but intermittent blobs of flame flickering back along their sides. Aulaire's atmosphere did not contain enough oxygen to support showy conflagrations.

Partially shielded by the empty sleds, two waves of six more followed, crammed past capacity with Grinders. Some were strapped into their chairs, the rest relied on the strength of their suits' grip to keep them anchored in the event of a sudden swerve or deacceleration.

Sahan guided the whole formation from the cockpit of a sled in the second rank. Though outfitted for a pilot, the cockpit was all but vestigial since control of the craft was invariably left to the AI. Though some Grinders were trained to fly, they'd rarely been trusted.

Five hundred meters from the colony perimeter one of the decoy craft exploded, followed almost immediately by another. An occupied sled in the first wing took a hit. Sahan could hear the screams of the Grinders as fire ravaged the interior. He ordered the atmosphere evacuated to kill the flames. Hopefully some would survive.

With a mental command he kicked the surviving craft as close to straight up as the jets could push them. A collective groan sounded from the Grinders as their insides were squeezed by the inertial pressure. Several bumps against the fuselage behind him indicated someone's hold had broken loose. Sahan's artificial eyeballs ached, but since he was watching everything from within the optical centers of his brain, vision remained.

Though he kept his main attention on the formation, a semi-autonomous part of his brain focused on a screenshot of the landscape below. The colony of Aulaire lay mostly underground. A ring of large silver domes surrounded three landing bays circled by gauntlets. The metal doors of the bays had been blown open by an earlier barrage from robot gunships from the Evolved mother ship. Several of the domes had also collapsed, and the area all around the perimeter looked thoroughly chewed up. Only not enough to take out the rocket fire that had killed so many Grinders in the first attack.

Up and up flew the sleds, unimpeded by the weak gravity. Rocket fire blew the engine off one. As it veered toward a tumble, Sahan released control to the autopilot, which he hoped would milk enough thrust out of the remaining engine to land the craft a safe distance from the bunkers.

In the lead, the burning decoy slowed, wobbled, then fell into a spiral dive.

A thousand meters above the surface Sahan triggered the warning for abrupt maneuvers. Then swung the whole flight around in the tightest arc the sleds could hold. There came more groans and thumps. Then down they dived toward the three ragged cavities of the landing bays.

"AI," he called mentally. "Time to get back in the fight."

The ground was coming up too fast. He called for reverse thrust on all sleds. They slowed, but not enough to escape going *splat!* if they hit at any angle short of horizontal. He lowered the landing gear.

"AI! Quick, dammit." Smug bastards must be gloating.

"Acknowledged."

One of the sleds disintegrated in a short-lived flash. A lucky hit; the sleds were coming in too fast for the surviving missile stations to lock onto.

"Take over guidance of the other craft," he told the AI. "We're going through the holes. The unmanned sleds first. Then—"

"At your current rate of deacceleration impact will be—"

"Shut up, dammit! As we go through you'll level out the sleds. We'll take the impact on our bellies."

It *should* work. Maybe.

The bays rushed up, their jagged teeth agape like dragons poised to swallow the whole flight.

"The impact will still—"

"We'll talk about it later." The sleds had too much momentum on them to pull out now.

Yellow flashes filled two of the cavities below as the lead unmanned sleds dived nose-first into the service bays. That should give any reception committees something to think about. Nonetheless Sahan experienced a moment of doubt. The ground was sweeping up awfully fast.

Then they were in. A metal claw of the bay cover took the sled's wing off and sent them spinning even as the craft began to level out. The distance from cavity to floor was sixty meters; with the spin, they'd still hit nose down and kill everyone aboard.

Though dizzied by the rotation, Sahan managed to swing the craft into a gantry. Gantry and bow both disintegrated, but the collision slowed the craft and helped level them out as the tail swept level with the bow. They thumped down belly first. The landing gear barely slowed the impact. With a sickeningly loud crash the fuselage folded into ripples. Even in his suit the impact jarred Sahan's neck and spine.

And exploded the engines, shrouding the sled in flame. But as the gull-wing roof blew open the Grinders scrambled through the flames or jetted on max thrust up out of the craft. Grabbing the battle-saw from its magnetic clamp, Sahan dived straight through the fire gushing along the port side of the crumpled cockpit. He hit the ground folded into a ball, rolled, and ran clear of the flames, which still flickered in places along his suit.

Ten meters away another sled came down hard, crumpling and opening cracks in the fuselage, but not catching fire. More Grinders poured out.

Another blunt-bowed craft flew through the shattered bay doors. Only this time the AI didn't get them leveled out quite quick enough. The craft smashed at a nose-down angle into the service bay floor. As the bow disintegrated the tail swayed for a moment, flames running up on all sides, then teetered over sideways. Amazingly, some survivors fought clear.

Sahan almost gave the order to get the wounded clear, but what was the point? Anyone left behind would have had their head pulped by now.

Sahan turned away. Vishnu send that the survival rate for sleds in the other bays was better than here.

(*Vishnu?* That plucked at a memory, but....)

The Grinders ran toward whatever cover they could find as hand-held rocket and flechette fire peppered them from behind an improvised bulkhead of heavy machinery, tractors, and storage containers. Others huddled in the burning shelter of the sleds, invisible to their enemies, but equally helpless to affect the fight.

He had to get them moving. The fire from the defenders was hardly overwhelming; ten, maybe a dozen guns. Most likely the entrance to the corridors was not where the defenders chose to stage their final defense.

A direct attack would certainly carry the barricade, but Sahan had a visceral dislike of throwing bodies across open ground. Delay was not an option. The attack via sleds had taken the defenders by surprise, but surprise had a short half-life.

Sahan bounded toward the open cockpit of the most intact sled, dented but not burning. Several flechettes tore through his leg. He ignored the pain, and the hiss of the suit as it melted and reformed the fabric over the tiny holes. He took the impact against the sled on his left shoulder. He hopped into the cockpit as a hand-held rocket launcher scarred the fuselage where he'd stood a moment before.

Had the engines survive the crash? Sahan called for power. The sled swung to the left as the engine below the stubby right wing came into a rather gurgling sort of life while the left scraped against the floor. Sahan maxed out opposite rudder but of course there wasn't enough air resistance to do any good.

The fingernail screech of the pancaked fuselage against the metal floor cut right through his suit's effort to filter it out. But as Sahan held full power, forcing the sled into a circle, some twisted configuration of the undercarriage dragged it slightly forward. The Grinders using the sled as shelter scrambled back from the exhaust. Rocket fire tattooed the hull. Sooner or later it would break through.

Folded up between the chair and the console, Sahan held full power. Trying to keep his eye on the barricade, he switched his view from screen to screen as the sled rotated.

Closer, closer, but oh! so slow. How long before the accumulated rocket fire punched its way through?

Five meters from the barricade, the console erupted in sparks and broken glass, then caught fire.

Sahan windmilled over the chair. Having switched to his own sensors, he saw the defenders running for an exit on a side screen.

The right engine slammed into a heavy tractor. A ball of fire swallowed him as he tumbled over the edge of the cockpit. Flames crisscrossed along his faceplate.

Sahan rolled across the floor, putting out as many of the flames as he could. The suit would insulate him against the heat — until the fire burned through. And if it burned through his air hose, he'd die gasping for oxygen in Aulaire's parsimonious atmosphere. Ten minutes, maybe fifteen. Even this body could not long keep his brain supplied with oxygen without some external source.

Then the Grinders were on top of him. Smothering the flames with their own bodies.

That came as a surprise.

Chapter 9

The fighting in the tunnels was close and bitter.

The defenders doused the lights stationwide, knowing their superior sensors and keener mental implants gave them an edge.

Sahan expected them to blow some of the corridors to try to trap the attackers. It didn't happen. After repelling the first attack, the Peregrines never took the trouble to arrange a defense in depth.

Deeper and deeper into the colony he led his troops. Fighting by the red shapes of infrared, the yellow of echo-location, the green of radar, the gray-green of night vision. The attackers' strategy was to force hand-to-hand combat, canceling the Riggers' superior aiming technology with shoulder-fired weapons. The defenders fought from behind a succession of hastily improvised barricades, trying to loose a few volleys then fall back to the next shelter before the Grinders could close.

But Sahan had developed a counter-measure, consisting of blunt mortar-like launchers whose projectiles created clouds of electromagnetic interference. This not only blinded the aiming apparatus on both sides' weapons; it played havoc with the suit sensors as well.

The foggers, as he called them, came into their own at a broad plaza, the major crossroads of the entire underground complex. Here all manner of shops, darkened in the blackout, served the community. Here too the defenders had time to set up head-high barricade from one side to the other, complete with loopholes from which they could fire their rocket launchers and flechette rifles while sheltered from return fire.

This would be their final stand. Below the concourse were only the emergency and storage tunnels. Retreat down there, and the Grinders could seal them off and wait them out.

Sahan, the Grinder horde at his back, stopped as he came to the concourse. Trying to cross that twenty-five meters to the barricade would create a shooting gallery. The rivet-heads might try it, figuring to win on sheer attrition.

That wasn't his way.

He ordered the mortars to keep up a continuous dampening barrage for two minutes, then sent in drones mounting additional interference devices. The drones swirled and swooped above the barricade. In the darkness the electronic distortion rendered them hard to shoot down, and they didn't need to last all that long.

When his own sensors were thoroughly distorted, Sahan led the attack. He held his battle-saw across his chest. The standard Grinder close-quarters weapon was the vibra-sword, but he preferred the weapon that had brought him through so many close-quarters shambles.

Blind fire came from the barricade. Most of the Grinders advanced in looping hops, while others slithered across the floor, avoiding any one plane where the fusillade could create havoc.

To Sahan, the barricade itself was no more than a series of quivery green balls and yellow dashes twisting in his radar, along which sparkled the red flashes of rockets and flechettes. He took several hops forward, the rocket trails passing below his feet or passing over his head, very narrowly, as he landed in a deep crouch.

Finally, at five meters from the barricade, he gave a great leap and landed on the other side. More Grinders splashed down like rain on either side of him.

Into a dreamscape. Or rather a nightmare that could turn literal in a flash.

Blobs of red dashed across his vision, giving off tendrils, changing shape so radically he could not be sure whether he was looking at one person or two. Both sides carried transponders that gave off different signals, but they fluttered like butterflies amid the jamming. Echo-location yielded a field of short yellow dashes churning this way then that, incoherent as a swarm of bees. He doused radar because it took too long to decipher.

But if he couldn't see, neither could anyone else. And with the Riggers' greater skill nullified, numbers invariably began to tell.

Stepping forward into chaos, Sahan saw a twisting dull red blob parting into three. One advanced on him amid a disturbance of yellow lines, inciting a rising pitch in his aural centers. A flurry of yellow dashes told him a saw was sweeping up toward his left thigh from the lower quadrant. Sahan side-slipped to the right. In low grav it paid to keep your feet tight to the ground.

With infrared nothing but a dizzying pattern of bouncing scarlet balls, he gave a short quick chop to the center of a yellow swarm he hoped signaled his foe's arm. A sharp pain in his thigh told him his timing might no longer be what it once was.

No matter; he felt the familiar tug of his own spinning blade meeting a suit, then cutting through.

Through all the confusion, through even the Grinders' rage and fear, he felt an emotion spread among them. At first he could not interpret it. Then it came to him.

WE ARE ONE.

***

The battle was over.

The fighting around the barricade had been most bloody and confused, but in the jumbled cut and thrust of blades and colors, the Riggers' will broke first. They were rational men and women, and such combat was inherently irrational. At last they streamed down into the survival shelters deep down in the rock of Aulaire. There they sealed off the hatches and battened down for a last-ditch defense.

Which never came. An agreement was reached with the Evolved (with the AI, actually, though the colonists didn't know that) that the Grinders would be temporarily withdrawn, leaving the way open for the surviving colonists to come to the surface, unarmed, and be transported to the Evolved mother ship. From there they would be taken back to Harrar's Reach, to be either interned or allowed to live whatever life they found open to them, according to the decision of the government of Admiral Raisa Catalan.

The Evolved's goal was still a negotiated settlement, not a succession of massacres. Sahan's suicide mission against the Master Holobrain had made them leery of total war.

Considering the alternative was death by Grinder or slow suffocation, the Riggers spent a surprising amount of time talking it over. They had their pride. But at last the surviving colonists of Aulaire came to the surface and were duly transported in two large landing craft to the Evolved ship.

Before this, however, the Grinders were pulled out of the tunnels, because emotions from the fighting still reverberated too strongly in their skulls to guarantee the safety of the prisoners.

In leading the Grinders to victory, Sahan had gotten himself well knocked about. One leg was gone — he found that funny, before he passed out, like the curse followed him from body to body — and his left hand to balance it. He had numerous deep cuts that would have killed and/or paralyzed any real body. Most dangerous of all, a rocket had eviscerated a substantial part of his internal workings. Though this body didn't truly bleed, it did leak, and his brain needed nutrients like anyone else's.

It was a problem for the Evolved. The Grinders had no medics. Robotic facilities aboard ship could affect certain repairs, but now that the Living Evolved had been withdrawn from Peregrine space there existed no trained personnel to rush down to the planet and plug in a new filtration pump in place of the "heart" seeping perilously close to the end of its reservoir.

So Sahan was brought up to the ship, where the robots would do their best.

Since all the landing sleds had been destroyed in breaching the surface defenses, a small auxiliary freighter set down as close to the entrance as possible.

Various mechanical trundles were available on-station to transport him through the corridors to the surface. The Grinders rejected them. He was theirs; they would carry him themselves.

And so six Grinders emerged into the eternal green night of Aulaire bearing an unconscious Sahan Kotori on their shoulders. His head hung down; his arms were splayed out.

Around this procession the other Grinders clustered in a tight-packed mass. The atmosphere was just thick enough that had an outside observer been stationed close by, he would have heard a low, continuous moan sounding through their helmets.

Chapter 10

"It's come," Beck told her one day. "The Master Holobrain."

He'd asked her to meet him in the cargo bay harboring the server holobrain she'd taken at the battle of Rione. Beck spent nearly all his time in this cold, cramped place, with its hard gray walls surrounding a mad-scientist array of tubes and pumps, cooling units beaded with sweat, smooth-faced metal boxes containing computers interested in no business but their own, and of course, the gimble-mounted, golden-brown sphere of the holobrain in its impregnable shell.

Arvada did not ask how he knew.

Beck had put on a little weight since getting this holobrain to share whatever he shared with it. Still slender, but no longer gaunt and hollow-eyed from corrosive loneliness and lack of sleep. Dressed in navy-standard magenta fatigues, no Peregrine would give him a second glance.

Most marked of all, the inherent twitchiness that had possessed him since his capture and separation from the holobrain had ceased, and with it the desperate and querulous tone in his speech.

He retreated into absolute stillness, as though in a trance. "I do not think there are any living Evolved in Peregrine space.

They have all been evacuated back to the homeworld." He turned to her. "I am the only one left."

"But how can that be? The Living Evolved captain their ships, as you did. They serve as advisors, or rather puppet-masters, to the Catalan government. They—"

"Have all been withdrawn," he insisted.

"But why, if there is once more a Master Holobrain in-system?"

"The certainty of knowing we will be absorbed into the Group Mind seems far less certain in time of war. Death comes too suddenly. The destruction of the *Elipida* proved that. Hostilities will now be conducted by the Master Holobrain and the server holobrains, through the AI."

"I see," said Arvada.

Thinking: hostilities will now be conducted by Sahan Kotori.

∗∗∗

Shortly later, when news came of the capture of the colony at Aulaire, Arvada's last doubts died.

"Experience has made me reluctant to question your assertions," said Solange O'Grady, from the privacy of her quarters aboard the *Dysis*. "But Sahan Kotori? Are you sure? I thought he was dead."

"Only in part."

Arvada answered from her own more austere cabin close by the bridge of the fast cruiser *Natessa*. Both her task force and Solange's fleet of heavies were still in orbit around *Kepler*. Since Rione, the war had entered a lull while the Alliance ships damaged in that battle and those they'd captured were refitted.

"You can see him in the footage from Aulaire," she told Solange. "That Grinder bigger than the others, cutting through our Riggers? That was Sahan. He doesn't have quite the timing he used to, but I still recognize that style. And the battle itself. Diving those sleds through the bays and belly-landing at the last second? No Evolved or AI thought of that. That's pure Sahan."

Arvada struggled to keep her voice under control. Her emotions were a churn. Horror at what had been done to the man she once — she still — loved. Wonder, that even the Evolved could bring him back in such a form. Disbelief that they could turn Sahan against her. Speculation about whether there might be any chance to win him back.

And a faint sliver of something almost like pride, that Sahan, her Sahan, was still such a terror. It took a Master Holobrain to control him, and Arvada would not be at all surprised if the Group Mind itself got its experience broadened far beyond its expectations.

But below everything, she felt dread. Because she knew his true purpose, the reason he'd been revived by the Evolved, was to hunt her down.

Sahan. The one always at her side. Her final resource when all else failed.

Now she was thrown onto her own resources. And though she did not slight them, this was the last enemy she would have chosen.

"Very well," said Solange. "I accept your assessment. It's a shock, though. Sahan Kotori? A Grinder?"

"That's the form they gave him. Beck said his body was beyond all saving." And much of his mind, though that she kept to herself.

"Arvada, look." In the viewscreen Captain (now Admiral, by authority of the Captains of an Alliance fleet that possessed no formal authority to make her so) O'Grady wrinkled her freckled face in a rare moment of doubt. "I have to ask. Before, ah, before his attack on the *Elipida*...."

Another sore point, that had won Arvada the official designation of "War Criminal" from both Naval Command and the Citizens' Council

"Yes?

"Well, the rumor mill had it that you and Sahan were lovers. Was it true?"

"Yes." You know damn well it was true. Everyone knew. We hardly tried to hide it. "But only in our last days together."

After I spent ten years breaking his heart. And mine.

"And do you think he will fight you now?"

"I think that's what the Evolved sent him to do."

And if it works, they could not have made a better choice.

Chapter 11

Standing before Beck, who was seated in the cargo bay as per custom, Arvada slammed her fist against the holobrain. Or rather its shell. The golden fluid beneath did not even ripple. Her hand ached, but she refused to show it.

"I put myself at risk to get you this trinket! I put my *people* at risk."

"That 'trinket', as you call it, was but an incidental part of your battle plan," Beck retorted. "You meant to engage the Collaborationist fleet. *That's* what put your people at risk. The holobrain was no more than an afterthought, following the enemy defeat."

Arvada noted his use of "Collaborationist" and "enemy" for those who had once been his allies.

"If you truly possessed such clear-eyed insight into my thoughts as you seem to think," she declared, "you would be trembling now. Allow me to give you the big picture. When I took the risk of capturing this holobrain, I did it with, perhaps not the expectation exactly, but a reasonably calculated hope, that you and it together would be of use to me."

"You mean that I would ignore all other loyalties, including to my own kind and my eventual afterlife, to serve as your spy."

Arvada clapped her hands. "You *can* read my mind! But results have so far proved sparse. Dangerously so. For you."

"What would you have of me?" he complained. "Total penetration of the Master Holobrain? Even if I could do such a thing, which if *you* knew as much as you seem to think you do, you would realize is quite impossible, do you really believe they wouldn't notice?"

"Or perhaps the truth is, your efforts to date have been half-assed. Which I'm fairly sure I did not list as an option. Meanwhile, who knows what information the holobrain is learning from you?"

"It can't learn anything unless—" He stopped abruptly.

"Unless you deliberately open yourself up to it. Yes, I know. Which *ergo sum* means that whether through design or inaction, you are in fact spying not for me, but *on* me." She clicked her tongue in disappointment, as one might to a child. A child about to receive a reckoning.

"That's absurd! Do you call that logic?" But he was beginning to get nervous.

"I call it results-based. Now, once upon a time you were a prisoner of war. Entitled to certain considerations."

"Which you totally ignored."

"Oh dear. If you think that was total, you *have* led a sheltered life. But perhaps we can broaden your parameters. Because if you are a spy, my freedom of action widens. Even legally."

"But I am *not* a spy."

"Not my spy, certainly."

Beck's face started to bulge in indignation. He composed himself. "No more threats, Captain Sattar. Please. You are not going to kill me. And even if you do, a Master Holobrain once again reigns in the system, so I will not be trapped in the Terror Barrier."

"You're right. I am not going to kill you. So just out of curiosity, what is the, ah, effective range, I guess you'd call it, of this holobrain?"

"This one? To send information? At least as far as all occupied Peregrine space. For the Master, of course, much greater."

"We're talking basic, ones and zeroes information here?"

"You know that technically I am not obliged to give you that information."

"For politeness' sake, then. Oblige me."

Their eyes locked.

Beck issued a deflated sigh. "It is not simple binary transmission. Otherwise you would have been able to intercept and decode it. It is something like thought waves, but partially analogous to coherent light. All wavelengths in phase. The transmissions from the holobrain are a form of thought, from many sources. Collectively the information resembles something like a hologram. It accretes from smaller, discrete impulses into more complex structures that no human brain can read. Due to my implants, I can. But only on the most basic level. The Grinders read it at a lower resolution still. Mainly in them it stimulates pre-planted images, and hormonal centers. Only another holobrain can interpret the full content."

"And the Group Mind?"

"And the Group Mind, of course."

"And yet you say the holobrain allows you to, what? Share the thoughts of others of your kind? Mind-reading?"

"Only in the most general way. It is not some elevated form of conference call. Emotions are much easier to transmit than specific thoughts, such as, oh, open the door."

"And it is the lack of these emotions, or ... what, an emotional net? ... that you say can kill you through sheer loneliness if you are separated from it for a long time."

Beck's face and upper body showed no sign of tension. But his heel began tapping, ever so slightly. "When I am in contact with the holobrain, I can *sense* others. The Living Evolved, as you call them. Beings like myself. And in the background, and this is most important, the Group Mind. I feel hints of the Collective. Even on such a reduced scale, it builds up a form of...."

"Addiction?"

"Communication, extending over vast distances and vast stretches of time. It is almost like you can see the whole future unfolding before you from the smallest segment of the present."

"You'd think the Evolved would be better at strategy, then."

"But the true scale of the fulfillment such communication offers," he said, ignoring her, "can only be measured in contrast with the devastating isolation we experience when cut off from it. Like our one thin consciousness must fill the whole empty universe. Such loneliness can make a mortal die. Of fear, Captain. Such is the fear contained within the Terror Barrier. Nothing in your experience can allow you to imagine it."

"Maybe not. But Sahan knew that fear. Better than you. Sahan ventured into the Terror Barrier. More than once. And when he returned" — she winced, recalling his pain — "he brought some of it back with him."

An incipient defiance began to form on Beck's face, as if he would question Sahan's authenticity. Then he recognized that would be an exceedingly bad idea.

"Then you have at least some conception," he conceded.

Sternly Arvada pushed those memories of Sahan's agony to the back of her mind. "But surely you can get more from the holobrain than you have so far. Sahan did, and he wasn't even Evolved. Several times he discovered the enemy's plans."

Of course Sahan had the help of poor mad Hypatia Wren, reduced to a spirit adrift in the holobrain. But Arvada was not going to provide Beck with excuses.

"I don't know how your Sahan Kotori did it," said Beck. "I'm beginning to suspect he was a madman. With all respect. That might help."

Arvada held herself back. Hitting him would only reinforce Beck's sense of superiority.

"Sahan was a little mad, sometimes," she acknowledged. "Motivated, as well. Motivation is a great thing. I am coming to seriously question yours. But later for that. What is the maximum range at which the holobrain can enfold you in its whatever?"

Instantly he was alert. "What do you mean?"

"I mean, you have indicated that the holobrains can send some sort of information over vast distances. Independent of relativity. But all this cooing and cuddling that can save you from a fate worse than death, after the loss of the *Elipida* there were still holobrains still in Harrar's Reach. They didn't seem to help you so much."

"They lacked the Master Holobrain to amplify them, and more vitally, give them sufficient coherence for clear transmission of thought and emotion."

"Ah. So now if I detail a minesweeper, say, to take you through Jump after Jump, while I keep this holobrain aboard the *Natessa*, I'd have to send you ... where, all the way to Earth, before the Master Holobrain stopped playing mother?"

"Some distance, certainly." He couldn't quite hide his apprehension.

"Ah. And I suppose that serves for the Grinders too."

He hesitated. "That is military information."

"Look, we're just starting to make friends here. Don't spoil it by stamping your pretty little foot and making me do something that later I will have to swear to all kinds of committees I was sorry to do."

"I see," he said. "Yet another threat."

"Understand my position. I have a holobrain aboard ship. I need it. I also have you. Apparently I can't move you beyond range of the holobrains without going to a great deal of trouble. So I have to ascertain whether you're spying for me or against me."

"On what authority do you claim I am doing either?"

Arvada tapped the small golden sunburst medallion on the shoulder of her fatigues, symbol of a ship's Captain. "This authority. Which as far as you're concerned is absolute."

"Of course. You have your qualities, Captain. You are clearly a good strategist, and an able leader. But personally, you are evil."

"Oh? Did I invade *your* homeworld?"

"What do you want of me?" Beck asked wearily.

Yes, what? Arvada about half-believed him when he said he had yielded up all he knew. Likely he could do a little better with some constructive prodding, but the difference was unlikely to prove decisive. And while she really did rather enjoy torturing him a bit here and there, it wasn't an urge she should indulge purely for its own sake. Petty temptations could easily spiral into compulsions.

But she had taken a Living Evolved, and she had taken a holobrain. These *should* be major prizes of war. Arvada was determined to put them to good use. Even if she had to make up that use as she went along.

"You will show me how to enter the holobrain." The statement about half took her by surprise.

He started at her in disbelief. "You jest."

"I wouldn't count on it."

Slumping, he clapped a palm across his face. "Teach you to enter the holobrain. Do you realize the absurdity of your request?"

"Request? I'm not sure we're on the same wavelength here."

"Captain Sattar, I have special implants. And years of training in how to use them. Just as you people do with your power suits. Even so, I can only skim the surface of what the holobrains contain."

"Sahan went deeper. Hypatia Wren went deeper."

He grimaced perceptibly at that name. "Hypatia Wren is a wraith. Likely a myth. The Evolved have searched for her for years, and though some activity has been seen which might be significant, they have never gotten a definite sighting."

"Hypatia Wren was a Peregrine woman who entered the holobrain."

"You're believing in fairy tales, Captain."

"Sahan met her."

That brought him up short. For a moment.

"Whatever the truth of that, it is madness to think I could bring you into the holobrain. And if I could, you'd be madder still to trust me. Either my motives or my abilities. Captain, this is your *mind* we're talking about. Even if you found a way in, nothing awaits you there but the Terror Barrier."

"Maybe."

Maybe indeed. The holobrain had certainly taken its toll on Sahan. And his skills at meditation and martial arts far exceeded her own.

But Sahan had penetrated far deeper into the holobrain than Beck, unless the Living Evolved was a much better liar than she believed him to be.

And Arvada believed, for reasons she could not come anywhere near to explaining, that if she could penetrate just a little way into the holobrain, she would find Sahan there waiting for her.

Which looked at objectively, exceeded every warning Beck made by orders of magnitude.

She still had to try.

Chapter 12

Sahan went through an indistinct period.

After an initial hyper-alertness in which he tried to remember who and where he was, without success, he relaxed into it. No pain, for once. No bad dreams. Or where they memories? Whichever, they left him alone.

He couldn't move. Not that he could tell, anyway.

But for now, that was someone else's problem.

Sometimes a most uncomfortable urgency came over him. Hints, fragments only, of unpleasant memories, pointing to an unpleasant present. Something he'd just as soon not wake up to, but if he did, he better brace himself for.

But mostly he just tried to turn off his mind. He did feel some guilt over his passivity, but what the hell? Just what was he expected to do about it?

Anyway, he had a premonition that whenever he did come back to whatever life he'd left, he'd look back on this inertness as the good times.

***

It was a phase change.

Emerging from a long nothing, all at once he had a past. He still couldn't move, still couldn't see beyond this circumscribed mote of self-awareness. But the memories came flooding back. And with them, the anger.

At Arvada first and foremost. And at all the humans who'd made use of him then cast him out, so that now he shared this form of shame with all the other Grinders.

The Grinders.

He ... he....

Sahan? That sounded vaguely familiar — he stumbled over his own emotions as memories of the Grinders returned. Scenes came to him, of carnage in the green twilight, of fighting blind amid a cacophony of colors in the corridors of ... somewhere.

And of a bonding whose nature he did not understand, but found himself clinging to nonetheless.

Somehow he'd made the Grinders his. And in so doing, he'd become theirs.

Together they—

That's when the Evolved came.

Sahan knew it was them right away. And automatically cringed in the expectation of PAIN.

But this time was different. The Group Mind talked to him.

In a way.

They were talking *to* him, he knew that. But he couldn't understand. The Evolved knew that. Just as Sahan knew, from somewhere, that if the Group Mind truly talked directly to him, they would disintegrate his mind.

So they talked *around* him. Forming an enclosure with their language. Supporting him on all sides, as if to resist the pull of gravity from all around a surrounding sphere. But gently this time. Extraordinarily gently.

Never had Sahan felt so fully supported. So able to relax every muscle in his body. Never so safe. Never so aware of his customary state of perpetual alertness, and the peace it had robbed him of.

But now the tension eased. Leaving him open, but unthreatened. And profoundly grateful to be free of that expectation it now seemed to him he'd carried since his earliest memories, that at any moment he might have to fight.

The softness, the warming ease, spoke to him:

We will enfold you. We will make you one of us.

One of us one of us one of us....

He never questioned it. He could do nothing but BE.

A web of tendrils connected him like an infinitude of umbilical cords to the universe. Feeding back and forth, so that all existence was reflected within him. And he himself was but a subset of the ultimate Knowing encompassed within the Group Mind.

Softly, softly, his awareness began to expand outward along along these tendrils to those other BEINGS. Who were after all but a reflection of himself.

Come. We will show you.

He came.

***

GAS CLOUDS SURROUNDED HIM. A sun being born. Its pinwheel arms slowly circled, all degrees of the spectrum sparkling in the glow of the gravitational furnace only recently ignited at its center.

He swam through the clouds. Swam alongside others of his kind. Cetaceans of a sort, but big as planets. They exchanged joyful noises among themselves, complex melodic peals that travelled freely through the vacuum.

Sahan could not make such noises. Not yet. Nor could he perceive their full multi-tonal quality, that gave voice to the processes he beheld: the musical whistling of the gas cloud as it spun, its component atoms rising and falling from one energy state to another; the crashing rhythms of fusion forming the beating heart of the still-birthing star; the harp-like extrusions of sound as the whales plowed through the clouds with mouths spread wide, leaving behind them a wake of molecules forming in and out of new configurations, each reflecting the linked beauty and logic of the universe.

Yet even the bits and pieces he did hear made him weep for their beauty, and long to join in the song that would unite him in this ecstatic vision.

Because he could weep! Figuratively at least; real tears would not long flourish in space. But the emotion, even the physical sensation, was there.

He could laugh, too. Copious displays of both issued from him as he gamboled with the others through the clouds, feeding as he went.

This was his destiny.

Rather, this was the destiny he must achieve. All the visions of transcendence he'd chased throughout his life turned shabby and remote in comparison. Not that he'd ever achieved them, but all those hours of lonely, often painful discipline — what kind of joy, what kind of union had they ever led him to? Fighting yes; he knew how to fight.

And he now sensed, with infinite regret, that he must soon return to it, and the loneliness it would once more shroud him in. Where was the joy there? His rage might at times have approached a transcendence of its own, but never joy.

Never, he realized swimming here amid the star whales, could anything he'd ever done or ever could do in his human life relieve the loneliness that formed the curse bestowed on him, as it was bestowed on all humans, at birth.

He must face the fighting, and endure, and win.

Only then could he return.

To his true brethren.

Chapter 13

Beck told Arvada he had no idea how to teach her to enter the holobrain. Such a question had never been raised among the Evolved.

But he did at least have a serviceable motivation. Early on he'd assumed that any officer of the Alliance navy would of course abide by the Alliance's own regulations regarding treatment of prisoners.

His disillusionment in regard to Arvada Sattar had been swift and unconditional.

But that still didn't provide the handbook.

"What do you expect?" he expostulated. "Some telepathic linkage? You to me, me to the holobrain, the holobrain to you? Based on what, exactly? The commutative principle? Come, Captain Sattar. This was your idea. Do you have even the most tenuous plan to actualize it? Or do you believe that in this as in all other matters the universe should simply accede to your will?"

More like the latter, in fact.

Arvada had learned from Sahan that his own entrance into the holobrain involved nightmare images and the final death-realization of those he led to their deaths aboard the *Enodia*. Since there had been a holobrain aboard, the dying Marines' and Riggers' last micro-second's death-terror burrowed its way into the Terror Barrier. Their cries, and likely his own crushing guilt, had ushered him into the holobrain.

Not an experiment to be repeated.

In any case, she had no wish to penetrate so deeply into the holobrain as Sahan. She had no conviction at all that she would ever find her way out.

No, all she wanted was to go far enough for him to find *her*.

Then what? He might kill her. That's what she presumed he'd been programmed to do. Within the holobrain, she'd be helpless against him. He might do worse. Shred her mind. Trap her within the Terror Barrier. Arvada could not know his power in that environment. Nor the depth of his hatred.

But there might, just *might*, be a chance that if Arvada could only reach him, some surviving impulse of love might make Sahan reach out to her in turn.

Long odds, given what the transformations the Evolved had likely wrought in his brain.

Yet it was either that, or the next time they met in this world, it would be to kill each other.

Standing by the side of the golden-brown sphere, Beck waited with an infuriatingly insouciant look on his face.

Which raised an idea. Sahan's entry into the holobrain had involved a great deal of agony. What if the open sesame was agony itself? After all, Sahan seemed to have spent a great deal of his time in and around the Terror Barrier.

What if Beck's agony created, oh, perturbations, say, in the holobrain through which she might gain entry?

"Why are you looking at me that way?" Beck asked, smugness narrowing into apprehension.

No. If his agony was that great, he'd be too distracted to help her.

"I cringe when you get that speculative look," Beck said. "It means the sadist never far below your surface is about to emerge. Again."

"You misjudge me. I look upon us as collaborators."

"As lab animals collaborate with the researchers?"

Arvada affected a laugh.

Which definitely inflated his alarm. "Wait. I do have an idea."

"Tell me."

"You do Push Hands, don't you?"

***

ROTATING TO HER LEFT in response to the pressure of Beck's hands, Arvada let the force of his push sink straight down into the ground through her left foot.

But she tightened her knee, to a degree barely perceptible even to her, just before his force was completely discharged.

Immediately sensing her stiffness, Beck committed to the full Push. Arvada crouched and pivoted further left, swinging her arms up as she moved to deflect his force upward. Even before the deflection was complete, she lunged into a shoulder push. It was a favorite move of Sahan's when he was in a bad mood. He usually moderated his force with her; she did not thus favor Beck. She wanted to launch him straight across the room, and with luck break a rib or two, less on the chance that pain might facilitate entrance to the holobrain than a mood of general beastliness.

Instead it was Arvada who got launched, straight into a stumbling run ending with a most ungainly crash-landing against the blue mats of the gym floor, smelling of sweat and old shoes.

She stood, rubbing her nose to see if that peeled feeling meant she'd scraped off the skin. To her relief, her fingers revealed no blood. It still hurt like hell.

Beck awaited her, still and wholly neutral, though she swore she could detect the hint of a sardonic smile lurking behind his lips.

"Are you considered expert at this among your own people?" she asked. They'd spent fifteen minutes doing Push hands in the blue-padded cubicle and he hadn't hit the floor once. He was good.

"Average, I'd say." Cocky as hell. "And you, Captain Sattar?"

"Oh, maybe a little above average, once upon a time. Just a little. I never came close to Sahan's level."

Well close, maybe, but she wasn't going to admit that after being tossed around the gym the way she had been so far.

Dammit, this smug bastard of an Evolved should not be able to shove her around so easily.

He was quick, and stronger than his slender frame might suggest. Like Sahan. But quickness and strength could be self-defeating in Push Hands. Sensitivity came first, followed by balance, then that particular explosiveness, coordinated through every muscle in the body, known as *jing*.

The skill was to deflect the opponent's pressure, most often to either side, sometimes back or down, more rarely up, if you had the skill for it. If your foe was drawn off-balance, you could pull him past and fling him away. Else feel him try to pull back, then hurl him by adding your own force to his withdrawal. If the opponent stiffened you could uproot him, if your jing was sufficiently strong.

Beck had done all these things to her.

She still didn't rate him quite equal to Sahan. Not quite, not unless he was holding back, which he might well be doing. But he was good. Fighting him was an exercise in frustration. And painful. It was like pushing air. Until suddenly it became a tornado, and bounced her off the gym pads.

Arvada was soon widely bruised from hitting the mat. It would have been nice to roll into the falls as she'd been taught, only the mat came up too fast.

As for the holobrain, it might possibly be laughing at her, but Arvada did not feel herself coaxing any other reaction out of it.

"It occurs to me, Captain Sattar," Beck said as they took a break, stepping under an overhead duct to cool away the sweat caused less by physical than mental exertion, "we may be trying too hard. I know Push Hands was my idea, but a competitive element has entered into it which can hardly promote the rhythmic flow I had in mind."

Arvada raised her eyebrows. Competitive? Me?

"An initial period of testing was likely unavoidable," Beck continued, "given the, ah, 'enmity' isn't quite the word I'm looking for, perhaps more, ah...."

"Enmity will do," she said graciously.

"But having expressed that, I believe our endeavors would be better rewarded if we returned to a more collaborative basis, as I believe you referred to earlier."

"You mean having gotten some of your own back by beating me black and blue, you are now ready to get down to the business of helping me enter the holobrain?"

"Perhaps we both had to discharge a certain degree of aggression. Now it is time to concentrate less on each other and sink more into the process. Though your Sahan Kotori, as best I can understand it, more or less bludgeoned his way into the holobrain."

"Sahan was very good at bludgeoning."

"But it is not an approach I can either offer or advocate. Following the ideas of Maeda Rao, we believe the universe contains certain fundamental rhythms, superimposed over one another, and exhibiting a feedback relationship with time and local circumstance."

"So do we."

Not that most people took it all that seriously anymore. Or that Arvada really understood it all that well herself, beyond what Sahan taught her as a byproduct of their Tai Chi training. The mystical teachings of Maeda Rao were one of the few aspects of Dainichi culture Sahan took with him.

"The holobrains," said Beck, "Master and server alike, are extraordinarily sensitive to these fluctuations. Again among my people, Tai Chi and Push Hands are considered direct though physically demanding ways to harmonize with these rhythms. To make ourselves more sensitive to the local moods of the universe, as you might think of it."

"Was it the mood of the universe that told you to invade our homeworld?"

Beck ignored that. "You yourself are not without skill," he said, the 'for a Peregrine' echoing unmistakably. "Perhaps if we can treat the Push Hands more as an exercise than a competition, we may be able to better harmonize with the prevailing rhythm, and effect communication with the holobrain. Though I must state yet again" — he looked around the featureless blue room — "I take it we are being recorded?"

"Of course." And half a dozen armed Security personnel waited outside the entrance. She wanted Beck to be more or less at his ease during this experiment. But that didn't mean she trusted him.

"Then let me state once more, for the record, that I think it is a bad idea for you to try to enter the holobrain. You have neither the physical adaptations nor the cultural familiarity to navigate such an unfamiliar landscape. And should you encounter the Group Mind, it will regard you as an enemy, not a friend."

"Sahan managed it."

"With respect, Captain Sattar, we did learn something about Sahan Kotori. He entered the holobrain already on the border of madness, through a portal leading to the Terror Barrier. And he never wholly escaped it. I know you loved him—"

"Love him."

"But had he lived, the Terror Barrier would inevitably have swallowed him up."

"He *does* live. And I mean to find him."

"And that," said Beck, "is the most dangerous part of all."

Chapter 14

Sahan held a review of the Grinders.

Only they didn't know it, because they were sleeping. They did a lot of sleeping. The holobrains routinely kept them in an agitated state, nursing their grievances against humankind. Such aggression, and the adrenalin rush that propelled it, tired them quickly.

Sleep also helped keep them from getting perhaps dangerously bored and restless. The Evolved did not encourage a variety of pursuits. Though so much had been expunged from their minds, the Grinders' brains were still human. No point in stimulating their imaginations past the basic requirements of battle and vengeance. Who knew what ideas might bubble up from the dim distant past?

Besides, the Grinders were quite highly susceptible to the holobrains when sleeping, in more subtle ways than rage or lust.

And it was thus that Sahan visited them, via the holobrain.

His own mental state had altered since his communion with what he thought of as the Star Whales. His mind swelled with pulsations outlining some universal order which if only his imagination could reach that far, would bring him an ecstatic sense of belonging.

To the universe. To the glory of the Star Whales.

To the Evolved.

The suggestion of some fiery light burned toward the back of his mind. Whenever he tried to fix it in place, though, it slipped away. Sahan thought the light might represent the fusion glow at the center of the swirling gas clouds upon which he and the other Star Whales fed.

Yet it might be more, too. Hints came to him too of some moment in his life he felt to be transcendent, but whose nature he could not decipher, whether blessed or damned.

This new bond with the Evolved distanced him from the Grinders, despite the camaraderie that had grown between them during the battle on Aulaire. Now he saw them as the Evolved saw them.

That they were ugly and distractingly insectoid had not disturbed him before. They hadn't chosen their appearance for themselves, any more than he had.

Now the Grinder form repelled him, even as he shared it. It was a shameful regression from the beauty of mind and body that could be the only fitting end for human evolution. Evolution that must free itself from the chains of nature, the chains of chance, to create a grandeur of form commensurate with the grandeur of the universal knowledge which he himself had ghosted alongside in the musical vibrations of the Star Whales.

The Grinders' minds were distorted and ugly, like their bodies. Vengeance was the height of their dreams. As they were of his. But saying either of them achieved it, what then? Did the Grinders hope to reclaim their original form? Did they dream of reverting to a peaceful, bucolic existence, by now too obscure to clearly imagine, but sensed in neurons and synapses not wholly excised from their brains?

But without the Evolved, they could never be anything but a short-lived menace to all.

A tool need not be pretty. But once its job was done, it was best put away.

The Grinders were his tool, no more. His weapon against Arvada. He must wield them skillfully, then be done with them.

And when he accomplished his one great ambition? He would be as purposeless as the Grinders.

Unless.

Unless the Evolved truly did incorporate him into their vision, and he lived forever in a state of bliss.

Over and over he kept seeing the bond between himself and the Grinders, and rejecting it. Because the Evolved had shown him a vision so far beyond.

How could he actually *feel* for such creatures?

He could only have been driven to such self-abasement by despair. After all, the Grinders might have myths of being stripped of their natural form, but he alone had actually lived it.

The Evolved had given him a Grinder form as part of his own personal evolution. But that was no more than a temporary interval. A larval stage, as humanity itself was but the larval stage for the Group Mind. When he'd completed the task, they would usher him along the next stage of his journey.

Sahan clung to that belief, trying to fight off the despair that saw in his past and future mirror images of anger and pain and futility.

✳✳✳

"YOU HAVE TO SEND two of the heavies out of Peregrine space," Sahan told the AI.

"Negative," they replied, always a fairly safe assumption for their initial reaction. "All five ships are required to assure adequate protection of the Master Holobrain."

They weren't at the command post of the ship that had carried him back to Peregrine space. They weren't even in some official council room. Sahan sat on the same rough dull green blanket rumpled across the same stiff mattress in the same steel-gray quarters he'd always had. Except for the fact that he had the room to himself, they were the shabbiest quarters he'd seen since his Academy days.

No place on the ship went unmonitored by the AI. Sahan saw no screens or speakers, but their voice came from ceiling, walls, floor. Of if they desired, they could send messages through the holobrains directly into his mind, and receive them in like manner.

You might think that after initiating him into the wonders of the Star Whales, the Evolved might show a little more largesse by way of his quarters. Maybe they didn't want to spoil him.

Or maybe for them a Grinder was a Grinder. Even if you did remind him which side he was supposed to be on by offering him scraps from the high mystic table from time to time.

Still, they had shown him a vision. And if it hadn't quite reached true transcendence, in that he'd returned much the same, it had been a vision of joy and peace, and thus unlike most anything else his life would seem to offer.

And there was a promise, an assurance to it that all other avenues lacked. In the end the Evolved would do whatever they pleased with him. But they *could* bring him into that vision. Sahan believed that. Most of the time.

Still a nagging sense of division ate at him. Sahan knew his only possible destiny lay with the Evolved. They'd shown him wonders. The Grinders could show him nothing but a life nasty, brutish, and short.

And yet surveying his own gold-streaked green skin, Sahan could not help feeling the currents of fate pushing him toward the Grinders.

Why? Sharing the same shade of green didn't make them soulmates. They couldn't offer him anything like transcendence, as the Evolved could.

So he'd tried to push all such empathy away. Tried to cultivate contempt for them and their primitive slave existence.

It was a weakness, that was all. One of many that had plagued him throughout his life. Just look at Arvada.

"You can protect the Master Holobrain all you want," he said, speaking aloud because he didn't like the rivet-heads grubbing around in his head, not that they gave a damn. "Up to a point. And that point passes when Earth starts sending its new model heavies here."

"Perhaps. That still assumes Earth will aid the Alliance."

"If Arvada Sattar still lives, it will. She will either inspire or shame them into it."

"Your thinking exhibits a great tendency toward Sattar-centricism."

"Isn't that why you brought me back? To centricize her right to death?"

"And what part in that does reducing our defenses play?" At a certain point, when it didn't think it was getting due respect, the AI's external voice turned mechanical and inflectionless, as if talking down to the slow-witted humans.

Sahan swung up his legs and lay flat out on the bed, setting his long thin Grinder hands on his long thin Grinder stomach and twiddling his long Grinder thumbs, with their distinctive swelling at the top joint, in a manner wholly foreign to the Grinders.

"If we leave Harrar's Reach in search of her, we'll spend a lot of time running around, and never catch her until she wants to be caught. At which time we might find ourselves having second thoughts. And there's Earth producing its super-heavies like a ticking clock. We have to lure her into the attack and eliminate her, thereby causing Earth to keep its firepower for its own defense. We do that by making an assault on Harrar's Reach seem feasible."

"Reducing our defenses to three line of battle ships makes such a possibility much *too* feasible." The AI added overtones for emphasis. "Five is the minimum we feel consistent with security considerations."

"Five Evolved ships is a damn juggernaut. If you could go back to taking colony after colony, you might still force the Alliance to a settlement. But you don't have enough Grinders left. And I notice you didn't exactly send out a vast horde with the Master Holobrain."

"Reinforcements have arrived."

"Four hundred of them? In addition to the three or four hundred already here? That's all I know about. And don't tell me there are things Sahan Kotori was not meant to know, because I'm the one you brought back from the dead to kill

Arvada for you. What am I supposed to do with eight hundred Grinders? We can't take new ground, we can't even hold Harrar's Reach beyond three or four colonies."

"Then why did you insist on attacking the colony at Aulaire?"

"To provoke the Alliance," Sahan replied. "To give them a sense of urgency, so they wouldn't get any ideas about sitting around with their thumb up their butt waiting for us to leave. Just like I advocated spreading hunger through the Reach. We need to build civilian pressure to drive the Evolved out of Peregrine Space. But no matter how much the pressure builds, Arvada won't attack if we insist on maintaining five heavies here. With them and the planetary defenses, no offensive action is possible."

"We agreed to let civilian conditions in Harrar's Reach worsen not with the thought of provoking battle, but to force negotiations upon the Alliance."

"The Alliance isn't *going* to negotiate! If you've accomplished damn all else, you've made a whole lot of Peregrines determined that the only ones who are going to negotiate are you. And it's going to come with a 'please.' You've made them willing to endure loss and hardship just for the chance to grind their heel in your face. If you think stalemate favors you, just keep on the way you're going. Or if you've got another fifteen or twenty heavies to bring in if Earth does start sending its own new-breed heavies, then I suppose there's no hurry. Personally I don't believe it. But you'd know more about that than I would. Just understand this. In the long run, you can't hold the Peregrine system and you can't turn it against Earth. Unless you take Arvada Sattar out of the situation and inflict enough of a defeat on the Peregrines that they will negotiate, sooner or later you'll end up running back to your Homeworld. Having created just exactly you were hoping to forestall — Earth and the Peregrines chasing after you in a blood feud that will last generations."

"We believe your assessment of the situation accords too much leverage to the Peregrines. And Earth."

"Then you're welcome to live or die by that assumption. In case you ever have any doubts, however, you better start thinking about creating a situation where I meet Arvada face to face, and destroy her."

"And why would we assume your victory is the inevitable outcome?"

"Because before," Sahan told them, "she always had a shield. Me." He thumped his chest. "My heart. But you took that away from me. And for that if nothing else, I thank you. Now it's just me and her, and the field has been levelled."

He held up his Grinder hand to cut off any retort from the rivet-heads.

"And this time I am going to stuff that laugh of hers right down her throat."

Chapter 15

ARVADA BANKED THE SLED around the lozenge-shaped stern of the *Megara*, one of the Collaborationist heavies taken at Rione. The line of battle ship lay stationary in drydock, lit up in dazzling silver by the lights mounted on the skeletal frame of the dock. Robots crawled like ants across vast expanses of the ship's hull, and floating repair platforms obscured several sections. The starboard exhaust nacelle was well-shredded, and some of the external gun platforms gaped open.

For a ship "forced" to surrender in the midst of battle, however, she fitted Solange O'Grady's contemptuous assessment: "A few tubes of glue and a new coat of paint will do her up fine."

The Admiral herself sat at Arvada's side. That Solange would let Arvada take the controls was quite the complement. Solange took well-earned pride in her ship-handling, large and small. But Arvada was a legend.

And as the current darling of the Alliance, best placated even if inferior in rank.

Levelling out, Arvada headed the sled toward the *Rajni*, one of the Alliance heavies also damaged in the battle. The *Rajni's* drydock floated some distance away. When the Collaborationist fleet destroyed so many of the ships docked in response to the Citizens' Council demand to stand down for negotiations, they'd destroyed most of the service facilities as well. Riggers from all over the Alliance had since flocked in to repair the facilities, but it was a massive project.

"How would you feel about taking back the Aulaire colony?" Solange asked.

"I don't consider it a viable target," Arvada responded. Technically she should add "Admiral," but the authority between the two of them was still semi-improvisational.

"I feel the same. But pressure's building among the civilians throughout the Alliance. We established such a good record recovering occupied colonies. Now many see this as a set-back. And there's a whole, well, cult, not to put it too strongly, saying Arvada Sattar will soon take it back."

"No she won't."

"Fine. I think it's a waste of resources, myself. But what are your reasons?"

They entered the gulf beneath the massive bulk of the *Kepler*, its twin cylinders slowly spinning in opposite directions. The colony still served as the informal center of the Alliance.

Not an entirely comfortable one. Naval Command and the Citizens' Council had never been formally dissolved, though the fleet under Solange paid them no attention at all. No legal precedent existed for the fleet to so disregard their authority, as the two institutions shrilly proclaimed throughout Resistance space. So a certain tension existed, uncomfortable to all.

Simply sending in Marines to sweep them out of their offices would look uncomfortably like military dictatorship, an anathema to the citizens of the Alliance. So both bodies continued to issue directives which the fleet wholly ignored.

Social media was alive with the controversy. Most of it, rather to Arvada's surprise, in favor of the fleet.

But that could change quickly, if the military appeared to be over-reaching itself.

"First of all," said Arvada, "there's nothing on Aulaire but Grinders. The colonists were all evacuated. It's not a rescue mission if no one gets rescued."

"Agreed."

"Second, Sahan took the colony for a reason. I think it likely he intended to keep war fever at a pitch and increase the pressure on us to invade Harrar's Reach. Like he's worsened the conditions among the citizens of the Reach themselves."

"You really think it's him directing all that? That the Evolved would allow him such authority?"

"It's him."

They came in view of the *Rajni*, tucked tightly into the drydock frame. Its once cigar-shaped nose was smashed into a bulbous mass of twisted metal. A small city of drones, robots and service sleds clustered about the starboard wing, trying to rejoin it to the hull. The engine mounted on the stubby wing had been detached and brought to an auxiliary frame, to be dismantled for parts. Much of the ship's skin looked like the face of the moon.

"Now that," said Solange O'Grady with satisfaction, "is how a warship should look following battle."

"Will she be ready any time soon?"

Solange shrugged. "Depends what you mean by soon. A couple of months, with luck. Like several of the wrecks. I'm thinking we can't wait around that long. If we're seen twiddling our thumbs like the last crew, the people will switch from us back to the Council. They were at least elected. And all that bullshit about a negotiated settlement may start up all over again."

Arvada suppressed the temptation to whip around an external arm of the frame at high-g's. She used to enjoy nothing more than setting Sahan's teeth on edge, the superior bastard. But Solange might not get the joke of being white-knuckled by a junior officer.

Sahan! I saw you! They've made you into a Grinder, but I know, I *know*, you're still Sahan. I cannot imagine what ordeals you've been through, and the distortions they've forced into your mind. But at the root of it I believe you're still Sahan. *My* Sahan. And I will find a way to bring you back.

"Arvada?"

"Sorry. Trying to think up a radical solution."

"Radical's always been easy for you."

"Solutions are harder."

"Has your prisoner yielded any usable intelligence?"

"He told me a new Master Holobrain has arrived in Harrar's Reach. He also believes that all living Evolved have been evacuated. From now on the war will be run exclusively by the holobrains. And Sahan."

"And you're reasonably sure," Solange said, looking away with uncharacteristic deference, "that Beck isn't passing information on to the enemy?"

"I make very certain no information comes to him."

"Of course. But what I'm concerned, that is, ah, wondering...."

"Yes?"

Solange braced herself. She sat up straight in the co-pilot's chair, fixing a stern expression on her face. Authority speaking.

"These adventures in the holobrain you insist on undertaking. They clearly took a toll on Sahan Kotori."

"Of which I am quite familiar." More than anyone. She was willing to accept the Admiral's authority, but only so far.

Not in matters regarding Sahan.

"I trust," said Solange, "that in your eagerness to gather information from the holobrain, you are not exposing yourself to undue risk."

"There is some risk," Arvada acknowledged. "But I believe I can recognize it in time to pull out." Sure.

"Do you trust Beck?"

"Up to a point." She hesitated. "Do you and I have an 'off the record' mode?"

Solange thought about that. "Yes."

"Then off the record, Beck knows that if he misleads me, serious consequences will ensue. Most serious. If I am incapable of enacting them, then members of my crew will."

"Good." Solange had no trouble with that at all. "We can't afford to lose you, Arvada." Which showed just how far things had changed since the early days of the war, when Arvada was universally regarded as an insubordinate, glory-hunting cowboy egged on by a mad mystical XO with a death wish.

Fair enough, actually.

"I think," said Arvada, "this is where I'm supposed to promise 'I'll be careful.' I've never understood the point of that. Like you haven't been careful before? Look. If I can, I'm going to enter the holobrain. Hopefully I'll be smart enough and strong enough to find my way out again. But it's no land for promises."

"I always find it so reassuring, talking with you."

A wholly unrelated idea came to Arvada, the way they sometimes do when you've been thinking so hard about something else as to clear the way.

"When will the damaged ships be ready?"

"It varies. The *Rajni*, quite a while. And she still can't be completely armed because the ordinance she needs is inside Harrar's Reach. The others, Catalan's ships, not so long, since they showed so little enthusiasm for dying for their Supreme Leader. The more immediate problem is installing crews. Most of the captured crews swear they're just dying to serve the Alliance. But will they feel the same when that dying appears right in front of their face? Do we spread them around the fleet and create the possibility of introducing potential saboteurs aboard every ship? Or leave a majority of those we think we can *probably* trust crewing their old vessels, and hope they don't switch sides again in the middle of a battle? I'd love to crew the ships with proven people, but we just don't have the numbers."

"So fix up the propulsion systems and run them from AI. You can leave any weapons systems that still function, but there's no need to add new ones. And you can leave life support and the inertial dampers offline. Now how long will it take to get them ready?"

"Three weeks? If we push the crews really hard. The facilities took a beating."

"There is a war on."

"Maybe two, then. But we've tried employing line of battle ships as drones in exercises. They're poor performers as combat ships."

"How about as shields?"

"Shields?" Solange swallowed down her instinctive rebuttal. Her heavies, the pinnacle of human achievement, dismissed as shields?

On the other hand....

"Shields, huh? Another plan from the devious mind of Arvada Sattar. Okay, hold that thought. We'll talk about it later. Right now I'm due for another meeting with the so-called civilian authorities, surprise, surprise. They keep demanding to know if a formal declaration of martial law has been imposed. If so, what's my legal authority? And if not, under what authority do I deny them their constitutional oversight of the military? I'd dissolve the whole bunch, only it would look like we're running a military dictatorship."

"Aren't we?"

"*Shhh!* Never use the *D* word. Officially we are in a power-sharing arrangement. Since the Council fucked up standing our ships down while leaving the Collaborationists cruising like sharks around the *Kepler*, they have no great support among the general population. On the other hand, Peregrines are extremely touchy about their freedoms. As you being your mother's daughter would know better than most. Right now we're walking a tightrope. What if many of the Riggers signing up for military service stop because they won't fight for military rule? Even worse, what if the ones we already have demand a greater voice in how we use them? We don't have enough Marines left to go it alone."

"God help us. I ran afoul of that one aboard the *Mettalise*. Led by Sahan's mother, of all people. We had to put it down hard."

"Hard how?"

"Sahan had a heart-to-heart with his mother. I don't know if he actually threatened to airlock her, but I do know for a fact he threatened to beat her deputy to death before her eyes."

"Was he bluffing?" Solange asked incredulously. "I mean, his own mother...."

"About the deputy, no. Of course I'd never let him airlock his own mother, and he knew that. So if he ever said it, which I don't know for a fact, then yes, that would have been a bluff. Of course if I wasn't there ... with Sahan it's — it was — often hard to be sure."

"I can see how you'd miss him," said Solange. "But that option is closed to us. Anyway, that's my sob session for today. Take her back to the barn. And thanks for avoiding the acrobatics. I know your reputation. I had to intervene twice to save your pilot's license from being lifted."

"That was you? I never knew. Thank you. I know something of your reputation, too. Want to compare emergency maneuvers?"

"Not with you. Maybe after the war, when we're expendable."

Chapter 16

Back and forth they glided across the blue-padded floor, joined at the forearms in the slow dance of Push Hands. The unseen ventilation wiped the perspiration off Beck's forehead with a cooling hand. The air recirc scrubbed all but the faintest smell of cleanser from the gym, but could not quite whisk away the scent from years of sweat infiltrating the supposedly nonabsorbent surfaces.

Surprised at Arvada's skill, Beck wondered how much she'd practiced with Sahan Kotori. The renegade Dainichi had accomplished feats within the holobrain believed impossible. In fact totally beyond conception, before the war. He'd even deceived the Master Holobrain at Harrar's Reach long enough to destroy it.

A lesson might be learned, thought Beck, not without trepidation because it was not after all his role to advise the Group Mind. War is not simply the continuation of accepted reality by other means.

Yes, Sahan Kotori had put a shock into them. Most especially the Living Evolved who died aboard the *Elipida* in the same flash that destroyed the Master Holobrain.

Had the holobrain survived them by just the few milliseconds needed to absorb their spirits into the Group Mind? Beck forced himself to believe so. Because otherwise they might be screaming their souls out in the Terror Barrier right now. Now and forever.

The Group Mind itself sent out mental shock waves as the Master Holobrain died. Beck's head had still been ringing with them when he surrendered himself to Arvada Sattar.

What was he supposed to do? The Master Holobrain was dead. No one had believed such a thing possible. In one blinding flash all certainties were exploded, all norms suddenly open to question.

Was he supposed to go down with the ship and thus condemn himself to the Terror Barrier over a minor — yes, most definitely minor — point of honor? Clearly it was his duty to carry on the war by any means possible.

Only instead of returning him to his own people, the way any civilized person would do, the way her own civilian government would have done, Arvada Sattar kept him to herself. Just to watch him squirm.

During those terrible early days of captivity Beck had managed to maintain his surface equanimity, but inside he'd been terrified that the Evolved might abandon the war, and him with it. For if the Peregrines could produce one Sahan Kotori, might they not produce another?

It would not be beyond Arvada Sattar, blind to any consideration but vengeance for her genocidal lover, to keep Beck in her own private zoo. Just so she could come by and laugh while his mind disintegrated from loneliness in the absence of the holobrain.

Until when it finally came, the "release" of death would send him straight to the Terror Barrier.

Those had been very bad days. As bad for his faith as for his nerves.

In hindsight Beck could see the Group Mind had no choice but to fight on. To acknowledge the victory of this inferior people would mean fleeing yet again into unknown space, continuing the dangerous and degrading saga begun when the *Stephen Hawking* first fled Earth.

But now he was seeing that Sahan Kotori might not be needed to rid the Evolved of Arvada Sattar after all.

Not if Beck could lead her deep enough into the holobrain that she could never find her way out.

Her crew would kill him, of course. They were cast in the same savage mold as their Captain.

But that didn't matter, because once again a Master Holobrain lived within the Peregrine system, ready to enfold him within the Group Mind.

Not that such a solution did not entail sacrifice. Beck was still young by Evolved standards. His experiences as recorded in the holobrains had not achieved that critical mass that would allow him to function as a fully self-aware entity within the much larger expanse of the Group Mind. But all the transcendent wonder, all the communion, the ecstatic absorption into the miracle of LIFE, the immortality of the collective, all that would still be his.

Dying now would redeem him for his failure to die when he surrendered his ship.

First, though, he needed to lead Captain Sattar deeper into the holobrain.

How? He did not know.

Beck had experienced a most profound satisfaction at bouncing her off the blue mats of the training cubical, bruising her flesh and even more her pride.

Now as they moved more slowly, a deeper rhythm arose between them. The energy flow, which in fast practice exhibited small turbulences and discontinuities each sought to exploit, now seemed to thicken and smooth as it passed from body to body. A soft warmth filled Beck as his flesh relaxed more and more deeply, absorbing that flow. Its strength gathered force.

Now Beck realized that the currents were beginning to carry him, at least, into the holobrain. A roiling, effervescent sensation burgeoned within his mind, bubbles roiling feverishly.

Only these bubbles carried not heat, but sound — the voices of his comrades. Faint and indecipherable, but each clear in their individual tone and spirit, so that despite the overlay, he recognized each one.

The voices of the dead.

For these were the voices of those who'd accompanied him during the initial invasion of the Peregrine Empire. The campaign that would finally put a stop to the flight begun aboard the *Stephen Hawking* back at L5.

And now the others were dead. Almost all of them. Dead at the hands of Sahan Kotori. Dying aboard the *Elipida* in the same blast that destroyed the Master Holobrain.

Suddenly he was staggering back across the blue pads. Caught off-guard. Even in slow practice, concentration was all.

"I didn't employ much *jing*," Captain Sattar intoned with insufferable smugness as he rose to his feet.

"I let my mind drift. My apologies, and I hope you enjoyed yourself. Again, Captain?"

Touching the backs of their forearms together in the basic stance, they reentered the gentle rhythm of push, deflect, root, and push.

He tried to push away as well the nagging fear. So long as the Master Holobrain still functioned, no such ghostly afterlife could claim him. And it was inconceivable that such a disaster could repeat itself.

After all, Sahan Kotori himself had now become the Master Holobrain's tool. Arvada Sattar remained a danger, but....

For how long?

The energy flow between them had turned so strong Beck believed he felt them sinking into the holobrain together.

He would lead her as deep into the holobrain as their combined resources allowed. Just as she'd asked of him.

As for finding her way out again, the good Captain Sattar might find that a most fascinating challenge.

***

THIS TIME, ARVADA BEGAN to sense the holobrain around her.

She did not hear the dead's accusing cries of "*WHY?*" But those had been Sahan's dead, not hers.

Terror did not riven her soul. Ghosts did not flock around, probing her with incorporeal fingers.

That too had been Sahan's path.

Though she was vaguely aware of the gym with its blue pads reflecting light all around her, a purpling twilight gradually filled Arvada's mental landscape. Suggestions of echoes surrounded her, but when she tried to fix on them, they wisped away.

Suddenly aware that her attention had wandered, she tried to fix back on Push-Hands before she found herself coming in for a rough landing.

Nothing happened. Nor did Arvada feel vulnerable. Because she felt herself absorbed even more deeply into the flow of energy created by herself and Beck. In this state she would be as sensitive to any disturbance as a spider guarding its web.

She began to see the ebb and swell in streams of orange, blue, and green. She even saw the upward and downward currents. A vibrant red turned deeper toward dark as her legs lowered, discharging *yin* energy into the ground, while at the same time gathering energy into the relaxed muscles. As her legs extended and the energy turned more *yang*, the color again turned bright.

Easing wholly into the flow of energy, Arvada floated free from her own self-conception. She existed as an event in space-time. Not the point-source Arvada Sattar she'd always known, but a probability cloud of Arvada Sattars whose likelihood of being found in any particular life-line was determined less by her own will than a primal chaos of passions and branching trajectories of chance and effort expressed through eruptions of force swirling her spirit along with them.

Was Sahan then her Strange Attractor? Because she knew that his presence alone, of all her possibilities, would always flow along within the time stream.

Arvada leaned further into the current, submitting her body to its guidance in the hope it would take her to him.

***

HE DRIFTED BEFORE HER. A slight condensation in the dim, purple-shaded atmosphere of the holobrain, echoed in a similarly elusive presence in her mind.

Sahan.

Arvada's heart tightened. She almost veered out of the energy flow.

Soft, soft. Everything soft. In your feelings as in all else.

He did not speak. Gave no sign of noticing her.

But Arvada recognized her own reaction.

She tried to draw him into the Push Hands flow that had brought her here. Creating an emptiness around that part of her mind that perceived him, hoping he would by old habit expand into whatever emptiness she revealed. No matter that so often that resulted in propelling her across the room as she tried to recover her root. To secure any contact at all....

Was that a flash of recognition? It passed too quickly for her to be certain.

But following in its wake came a procession of ... not thoughts, exactly; or at least not clear enough for her to read. More like fragments of emotion gradually building toward some culmination. She reached out to grasp it, and found—

Rage.

A flood of it, tearing away the banks of her mind as they tried to channel it away.

Arvada hit the ground with neck-jarring force, took a slight bounce, and settled, still badly shaken by what she'd seen.

Beck stared down at her in surprise.

"I'm sorry," he said. "I didn't intend to do that. You stiffened so quickly, my reflexes must have taken over before I could divert them."

Arvada got to her feet. Her left hip was sore from the fall. She tried to concentrate on the pain, to hold the greater shock at bay.

"No problem."

"Did anything, ah, unusual, happen?" His attempt at nonchalance fell short.

"Nothing I shouldn't have been prepared for."

"Did you encounter the holobrain, by chance?" Eager. Way too eager.

"I believe I may have. Only I may have reached too hard, and made myself vulnerable to your Push. That's enough for today. My concentration's lagging. Thank you."

"If you'd care to keep going....?"

"Tomorrow."

If I can stop these hateful images from raging around my head.

And if I can figure out some way to keep my supposed collaborator from trapping my mind someplace far, far away.

Then there's Sahan. Arvada did not believe he'd even known she was there.

If such a shallow penetration could do that to her, what risks lay in going deeper? Her confidence that the force of their love would overcome the Evolved's conditioning had just been badly battered.

The thought of meeting Sahan face to face in that strange land....

Terrified her.

Chapter 17

The Grinder's hands, strong enough in the powered suit to snap a human forearm by grip strength alone, dug into Sahan's artificial skin at the right bicep and left wrist. Around them other Grinders in silver-green suits shuffled for a better view. Some clambered up on the equipment racks along the near wall.

Arvada. Why did the thought of her keep piercing him through even the most violent activity?

Sinking her weight, the Grinder pushed Sahan's bicep and pulled on his wrist, no doubt hoping Sahan, who'd been teaching them not to resist an enemy's force when they could instead make use of it, would try to spin into the pressure to hurl her down and around. To which the Grinder no doubt had some diabolically clever counter planned.

Would Arvada never allow him a moment's freedom? Why must thoughts of her still drill through his skull, as when he was helpless before her? Why must they still *hurt* him so?

Without shifting his feet Sahan emitted expanding *jing*. The Grinder flew three meters through the air, suit and all, bounced, then slid three meters more across the slick black floor that alone relieved the uniform gray of the training hall.

The other Grinders shouted and hopped in appreciation. Sahan idly ran his fingers over his bicep where his opponent's amplified grip had the torn loose the fiber. He did not bleed, of course. But the pain was the same as if his real skin had been peeled away. To move this body with full facility, the pain receptors had to be activated head to toe.

The Grinder he'd thrown got slowly to her feet, muttering a guttural expression of thanks. Sahan bowed to show his respect for her ingenuity. A gesture they were coming to appreciate. The next opponent stepped forward.

Slower, now. Not so much *jing*. His students could learn nothing from tactics they could not understand. They appeared to value this interaction between them, this exchange of skill and pain, as if some special communion took place. But that wasn't why he spent most of his time in such exercises. Not even the pain, though it helped divert him from thoughts of *her*.

The Evolved were running low on Grinders. Though clones, they didn't just spring forth as adults ready to grab their weapons and go forth in pursuit of mayhem. They had to be grown. Conditioned. Most of all, their still-human brains had to be altered in infancy. Without driving them wholly insane or reducing them to a vegetative state.

Sahan assumed there must be some failure rate, even for the Evolved. Brains were not simply mechanical devices. Whatever it was, he didn't want to know. As for how those failures were dealt with, he knew damn well, but tried to hold it out of his mind.

And then, the successes, the Grinders, had to be controlled.

Meaning that like all other slaver societies throughout history, the Evolved lived in constant fear of revolt. They'd instilled numerous and deep-seated mechanisms of control, along with fail-safes that in a worst-case scenario could kill the whole population. But they'd created the Grinders for a reason, and to exterminate them in one go would eliminate their entire infantry.

Thus the Evolved had deliberately limited the number of Grinders. They'd built up the population in preparation for war. But that war had far exceeded their projections both in duration and casualties. Because in this as in so many other aspects, the incomparable powers of the Group Mind allowed insufficient respect to their own origins.

Hubris, was the name for it.

Thus, frustrated in their attempts to fit Sahan and Arvada Sattar into their projections, the Evolved pulled him back from the edge of death so that they might pit one against the other.

Now he led the Grinders. In ways neither the august Group Mind nor the AI had foreseen.

They didn't like that. That's why they let him swim with the Star Whales, to lure him into dreams of transcendence.

It worked, too.

For a while.

But the Star Whales, while certainly more elevated company than the Grinders, were a vision whose full realization Sahan had gradually come to understand would be forever denied him. The Evolved were not about to incorporate him into the Group Mind, even should such a thing be possible. They only wanted him panting after it like a dog.

Like he had for Arvada.

Two visions of beauty. Equally out of reach.

Not like here, with the Grinders. Losers like him.

Though he tried, Sahan could not regard them as no more than cannon-fodder. They were his troops. *His* troops. No different than those he led to their death aboard the *Enodia*, just so Arvada could claim her victory.

That memory tortured him. But a sense of her presence spying on him right here tortured him worse. Like her laughter was so corrosive it even penetrated the holobrain.

Laughing not only at him, but at his new soldiers.

That was good, though. Remember that. Good. Because by the time she learned neither he nor the Grinders were any laughing matter, she'd be staring into his over-size Grinder eyes as she watched herself die.

So here he swayed back and forth with his Grinder opponent, trying to impart a basic sense of ebb and flow, of balance, of trying to read the opponent's movements instead of flying at them in a blind frenzy. Which if they kept their head, was sure to cost you yours.

Yet hints of Arvada were never far away. So that Sahan had to remain constantly alert not to inflict gratuitous injuries on his trainees.

He did let them fasten their hands on him more than he probably should have. It wasn't always that easy to grab trained Riggers, and if you didn't *immediately* use that grip to create an opening you were most likely gifting them your arm.

But he needed the pain when he threw them off. It felt like being skinned alive. It soothed him.

And in his mind, though perhaps not theirs, it bound him to the Grinders through a living reenactment of their own creation myth.

See, he tried to tell them, I too have been stripped of my flesh and my humanity. Arvada Sattar took them from me. This marks the bond between you and me.

The bond that will lead us both to vengeance.

***

HE LAY NAKED UPON the table, feeling not at all undiminished by his Grinder form. The desire for humanity no longer troubled him. At first he'd been shamed to think of Arvada seeing him this way. Now it just marked how completely he'd broken from her.

Projecting from wheeled and telescoping mounts, robot arms manipulated his now ragged limbs and body. They ran softly hissing machines like irons over the torn-away patches of his outer wrapping, restoring green in place of frayed gray. The pain receptors to his extremities had been shut down. Lying inert, he no longer needed the pain.

The arms tending him looked remarkably human. They had reason to: they came from Living Evolved who had passed on or been elevated up or swallowed down or whatever brought them into the Group Mind. Now not only the limbs but the brains were superfluous. But a dead brain still possessed the circuitry to evoke pathways long laid down between it and its limbs, with a delicacy beyond the threshold of machines. No mystery, no Frankenstein weirdness; if you can make a dead frog's leg twitch, you can make a surgeon from the dead.

The tricky part, stimulating the right pathways in the brain, was easy money for the holobrains. They'd been accumulating transcripts and schematics throughout the donor's entire life. If they could usher a dying *persona* into rebirth within the collective mind, zapping a few synapses here and there was mere mechanics.

Still, Sahan found something chilling about the arms. As he did about the Evolved in general. Everything seemed pointed to, and directed by, the dead. Or should he say The Dead? In nuts-and-bolts technology the Evolved had advanced scarcely at all beyond the Alliance, and what gaps existed were closing fast.

It was as if The Dead, or rather the Group Mind that revitalized them, retained little interest in the material universe. Which might explain how a people who knew the brain on such a level as to treat death as just a way station on the road to bigger and better things could prove so inept at both diplomacy and military strategy.

Such thoughts must be at least borderline heretical. Why did they not invoke PAIN?

Because the Evolved wanted this Sahan Kotori to make up for their own deficiencies. So long as he fulfilled his role as hunter-killer to Arvada Sattar, they weren't going to chastise him over a few lapses of faith.

Not like the Dainichi.

The last wrappings were — steamed? whatever, it left a smell similar to burning glue — into place on his "skin." The weaving arms, reminiscent of multi-armed Kali in her dance to death, withdrew to the corners of the gray — what else? — room. Another example of the Group Mind's indifference to the mortal world. The universe of the Star Whales seethed with colors generating musical tones and waves of rapture. For everything else, gray was good enough.

Sahan turned his attention back to the mix of scenes from Harrar's Reach. The holobrain could transmit them direct to his visual and audio centers.

Riots were breaking out throughout the Reach. On torus, cylinder, and in underground corridors, people massed in the streets and pedways to shout and wave and hold up signs denouncing Raisa Catalan and the Evolved. In some habitats where Collaborationist troops were thin on the ground, or had in several cases gone over to the protestors, Riggers were sealing locks and docking ports to prevent the Grinders from getting in and whipping the populace back into line.

In the cylinder *Dobrilla* and the double torus *Clarissant*, suited Grinders marched on the demonstrators. Pushing, shoving, occasionally lashing out, which could well be lethal against an unarmored human. In both habitats small groups of suited-up Riggers tried to block them, but were immediately overrun, leaving bodies lying with twisted limbs on the pedways.

Such scenes, transmitted by the participants in defiance of directives and ineffective attempts at jamming by the Collaborationists, naturally fueled further protests throughout the Reach.

Admiral Raisa Catalan still held the cylinder *Gudrun*. Most of the habitat population had worked for her since the first days of the war, and didn't see much promise in now trying to pretend they'd been loyal citizens of the Peregrine Alliance all along.

Besides, the citizens of the *Gudrun* weren't hungry yet.

Unlike much of Harrar's Reach. The war, you know. Breakdown of trade and all that. Blame it on the Resistance. That was Catalan's line. Which damn few looked to be buying.

Of course all the larger habitats featured their own gardens. Actual starvation was unlikely. But as Sahan knew better than most from his upbringing, even if cabbage soup (Sahan's imaginary stomach came close to turning inside-out) was plentiful, it could still inspire extreme depression or extreme rage.

All part of Sahan's strategy.

The demonstrations were making the AI nervous.

"This will stiffen resistance against accepting our latest terms," it told the center of his head. "Even in Harrar's Reach, aside from the Alliance."

The "latest terms" had been whittled down to little more than "kindly let us maintain a presence in Peregrine space, and deny it to Earth warships."

"Your antennae are gummed up," he replied. "Why would the Peregrines accept any terms you offer? Oh, I know, it best serves their own rational self-interest. As calculated by you."

"That is a gross simplification."

"I'm a grossly simple man. Why do you have this quasi-religious reverence for 'rational self interest?' Has rational self-interest played any part in humanity's history of religious wars, ideological wars, nationalist wars, land-grab wars, and wars for the sheer hell of it? What counts is grinding the other guy's face in the dirt. After the defeat at Demeter, when the Peregrines hardly knew what hit them, *then* they might have agreed to your terms. If, that is, you dumb rivet-heads hadn't overreached yourself and demanded war against Earth. Since then you've been redrawing that line in the sand so far back you've now got your ass in the ocean. Get it into whatever passes for your heads. You aren't going to win this war. That probability cloud has collapsed."

"We can still bring the remaining warships from the Homeworld."

"What, all four of them? Five, maybe? So what then? You can't occupy any more colonies; you don't have enough Grinders left to hold them. And even with eight, ten heavies at the outside, your Shock and Awe days are done. Listen to me, and listen with 1's and 0's. If Arvada is left alive, she will inspire the Alliance *and* Earth to fight you to the bitter end. *Then* follow you back to your Homeworld and flame every last holobrain. Your worst nightmare come true. It may take a while, but since you can no longer maintain an offensive, it *will* happen. Imprint that on your circuitry."

If the AI was chastened, it never missed a beat. "And what does your plan entail?"

"Just what you made me for. Kill Arvada Sattar. With your help and mine she has created a legend. Just like she always wanted. Legends take on a life of their own. Uproot it, and if you act fast you can declare victory and get the hell out of Peregrine space. Put off the reckoning for another generation or two, anyway. Let that legend flower, and your — or should I say your Masters' — existence is a roll of the dice. And if Arvada figures in the odds, I know which way I'd bet."

"Your scenario is quite Shakespearean. But your heuristics are based more on your own melodramatic fantasies than probabilities."

Still lying flat on the table, Sahan shrugged his green shoulders.

"Did your probabilities calculate me? Did they calculate Arvada?"

For once, he made them pause.

Chapter 18

Arvada sank more quickly into the energy flow this time. Perhaps she and Beck had crossed some Push Hands threshold, growing more deeply attuned to each other's currents of *chi* generated through the push and deflect, sink and expand, step and counter-step.

Or maybe having penetrated the holobrain once, even if only to the shallows, the entity recognized, even encouraged her.

Was that a good thing?

Certainly Arvada did not trust Beck. Following the destruction of the Master Holobrain, she'd been confident that the threat of death, invoking the much more horrifying prospect of the Terror Barrier, would keep him in line.

Now a new Master Holobrain reigned in Harrar's Reach. Freeing Beck from the prospect of an eternity spent screaming. Arvada did not think Beck wanted to die. But if death led him into the Group Mind, he might seize the chance to remove Arvada Sattar from the time-stream, hoping to redeem himself for his surrender to what the Evolved deemed an inferior race.

To let this man, this enemy, lead her into the holobrain was sheer lunacy.

Check that. It was stupidity. The lunacy still lay in wait.

The voice of responsibility kept telling Arvada she had no right to risk herself in such a foolhardy enterprise. To be guided by an enemy in such a strange land as the holobrain, in search of a man who hated her and wielded vastly more power, yielded no positive outcome reason could find.

But that man was Sahan.

And Arvada simply lacked the will to surrender all hope that the love they once shared would not somehow lift him up out of the world of rage the Evolved had plunged him into.

She just could not imagine Sahan hating her so.

She hit the mat hard.

"Mind somewhere else?" Beck asked smugly.

She rose, disguising the pain in her neck and right hip. Again they touched arms.

Maybe that rage had not been so very difficult to instill. She had hurt him over and over again through the years.

But she'd never been indifferent to his pain! She'd had her duties to perform, her life to lead. Sahan knew that. And clung to her anyway. Because they made such a good team. And maybe because all through those years there lay implicit the promise that....

Yes? Did you ever truly feel any such promise?

But it wasn't like she'd gloried in his pain. Maybe from time to time she allowed herself to be ... thrilled? — no, proud, admit it, proud — of her hold over him. But she never hurt him purposefully. It was just their roles, that was all. She could hardly be expected to live like a nun.

Besides, where would Sahan have been without her?

Wham!

She hit the mat again. And this time sprang to her feet. Again they began the dance.

Don't try to excuse the past. Whatever the truth of it, your efforts to render yourself faultless can't help but invoke some element of hypocrisy.

She felt herself swaying off balance, sensed Beck gathering energy for a really strong push, and just barely rooted and deflected it.

She didn't really know what the truth had been between them. And now, seeking out Sahan's spirit, whatever lies she told herself would only lead her astray and make her more vulnerable. Like tensing up in Push Hands. She must try to eliminate her defenses, and go in with whatever her heart held now. It would either work or it wouldn't.

But remorse struck deep as she thought how easy it must have been for the Evolved to turn Sahan against her. Wonder was he hadn't done it himself years ago.

And yet he hadn't. Through it all, Sahan *did* keep loving her.

Now she must reawaken that love in him, and use it to drown out the hate.

Win or lose, whatever happened between them now would finally complete the story. Finally reveal the meaning of the whole saga.

Only first she must find him, and hope this love she set such store by reached whatever passed for his heart these days before he tore her mind to shreds.

The *chi* flow of Push Hands enveloped her. Soothing, warm, redolent of the underlying rhythms of *yin* and *yang* as they performed their own slow dance to create the ever-changing, ever-constant universe.

She saw the landscape turning purple about her, its boundaries loosely defined by swaying yellow electric fields.

***

ARVADA LOST ALL SENSE of either dimension or direction. She knew her feet must still tread the mats of the gym, because the flow of *chi* still coursed through her, and she could not perform Push Hands ungrounded. But her sense of up and down spun about every time she tried to fix on them.

Though she'd come to find Sahan, the atmosphere of threat pervading the holobrain made her less and less sure she wanted to press deeper into this land.

You must try. That is why you came. That is why you determine your course *before* you enter fear-inducing situations, rather than improvising according to the reactions of your body.

What now? Arvada feared that if she called out too forcibly, she would jolt herself out of the *chi* flow that kept her here.

Perhaps if she could incorporate memories of the love between her and Sahan into the flow, it might counter those the Evolved had planted in his mind.

Arvada tried. At first the process felt dreadfully mechanical. She could visualize past scenes of happiness, but the emotions attached to them remained distant. They were all of another world, and deny it as she might, the man she'd known there was dead.

Besides, no single scene, however poignant, could encompass their relationship. Their love was not defined in bed, nor in the victories they'd won together. It was not defined in rare moments of carefree joy such as playing together in the ocean aboard the *Kepler*. Nor even in their long ritual of collaboration, two naughty children in possession of a starship, with all space for their playground.

A true reckoning of their love could not ignore the pain. The years he'd longed for her while she held him distant. The verbal sparring, part joking, part challenging, and too many times bitter, when one or the other or both of them tried to work themselves up to a final parting.

Love included her own selfish pride that this strange man of unique abilities served only her. A pride on occasion reinforced by sticking pins into him to affirm her faith that he would never leave.

And love included the peculiar intimacy that bound them since their first acquaintance at the Academy. Even when Arvada believed herself sailing wide on the great stream of life with Sahan but one of many sails, it was most often him she checked with to set her course. Always the two of them plotting together. While others spent great energy to be included in Arvada Sattar's circle, Sahan had only to come into view for Arvada to go to him, her fingertips lingering possessively on his arm.

Their love included all those things.

And God, she'd loved him so much more than she ever let herself know.

Movement.

Pressure.

A faint rustling, as of distant wind.

He was here.

Sahan.

Arvada could not stop herself.

"Sahan!"

A blast struck her mind. A spewing inferno of hate. She threw up her hands against it. But in this realm they lacked materiality. Emotion counted for all.

The inferno swallowed her up and spewed her out. Arvada was dimly aware of bouncing across the gym mats. A chiseling pain dug into her shoulder. Beck must have thrown her, hard.

All previous purpose now subordinate to fear, Arvada tried to grab onto the pain and use it to drag herself from the holobrain.

The purple landscape clutched her tight. Sahan was upon her. Not in any physical form, but as a crushing pressure of rage, gushing forth images of her own sneering, laughing face.

Arvada sought some way to flee. But she floated helpless as a space walker whose jetpac had just sputtered out. Her lungs pumped madly, yet the force of Sahan's anger blew out her breath like a candle.

Where was Beck?

More images invaded her mind. Images of her and Sahan in his human form. But twisted into cruel perversions of reality. In all of them Arvada saw herself laughing at him. Scorning and insulting him. Forcing him into hazardous enterprises — like that aboard the *Enodia* that left him shorn of a leg. Then refusing help, or bringing it too late.

She saw him pacing his quarters like a caged animal, groaning inside, his heart on the verge of bursting from his chest, while she cavorted with other lovers.

It was all so wrong!

Or mostly wrong. The lovers, sometimes....

But Sahan knew the reasons! The fleet could turn a blind eye to some surreptitious liaisons. But an affair with a subordinate officer, especially this one, that would have wrecked her career. Salacious rumors already pursued them.

And she always encouraged Sahan's own affairs, half-hearted as they might be.

As for the rest, yes, she'd sent him on dangerous missions. Having Sahan at hand, who else would you send? Nor had she ever delayed bringing help. When his offensive was surrounded by Grinders aboard the *Enodia*, Arvada delayed launching a counter-attack only because the torus was already breaking up, and she had to get the civilians out. That was her sworn duty.

But that done, she risked her life to pilot a sled through a field of hurtling debris in order to rescue him — against Sahan's own urging. And at Philomel she imperiled her entire ship and crew by waiting till the last moment to pull away from the sun, because she feared Sahan might still be trapped in the holobrain aboard the enemy ship.

Arvada tried to reconstruct these scenes from her own memory, hoping to show Sahan the truth, and deflect his anger.

His wrath swiped her attempts aside before they were half formed.

Such hate! Only within the holobrain could a human mind contain such intensity. And then maybe only Sahan's.

Relentlessly he pounded her. Now Arvada saw herself and Duncan Mallory in bed and crawling all over each other.

"Sahan, no!" she tried to shout, even as the force of his anger blew the words straight back into her mouth. "That never happened! Even after I believed you dead, I never—"

His anger swatted down her protests. From far away she smelled burning wires. Claws dug into her brain. Piercing deep, they ripped gaping chasms into her mind. Terror unique to all her experience swirled through the rents.

She was dissolving! Not into nothing; that would be mercy. Into the panicked awareness of dissipating forever, her molecules, her very atoms drifting further and further apart, yet still screaming out to rejoin each other.

Gathering up her last shred of will she cried: "Sahan! No! Don't do this! You condemn us both!"

It seemed impossible that any other emotion could break through such wrath. Yet one did.

Amusement. Just a glimmer, but enough for Arvada to comprehend in the rapidly thinning remnants of her mind that he *wanted* to condemn them both. To send them both spiraling down to the Terror Barrier in mutual, eternal embrace.

His final triumph. He would have her at last. And forever. But to truly possess her, he must feel her. Feel every agonized moment of her torment, reflected in his own.

It was the ultimate realization, and the ultimate perversion, of the union Sahan had sought for so long.

Her last thoughts unraveled in terror, until there remained only:

SAHAN, NO!

Come, his spirit whispered, sharp as a knife. Come, and let us lay together in the Terror Barrier.

In agony beyond your imagining.

You and I.

Forever.

***

From a distance Arvada heard herself whimper. Sahan's wrath streamed into the place where Arvada Sattar used to dwell, bringing with it a rivening terror the remnants of her mind could not resist.

Eternity beckoned.

Then Arvada became once more aware of herself. In paroxysms, choking.

Sahan was backing away from her. He had assumed his own form. His human form.

"Sahan!" she wheezed.

If he heard, he made no reaction. Another figure advanced on him. A woman, fully formed yet insubstantial. She radiated such suffering Arvada wanted to weep for pity despite her own crisis.

Still Sahan retreated, while the woman followed after with unbalanced, almost staggering steps. About her swarmed some form of ... nothing Arvada registered as life, but ... spirits? Arvada thought she heard their despairing cries, but could not be sure because they gave the eerie impression of coming from another dimension.

The woman reached out her hands. She and Sahan both appeared locked in the same trance. Like a form of Push Hands with no contact, but some palpable force linking them all the same.

Contrasting emotions played across Sahan's face. One was fear. In Sahan, who a moment before had been willing to spend eternity in the Terror Barrier just to bring Arvada with him!

And the other? Total fixation, but conveying what? The closest Arvada could come to any palpable emotion was longing.

And pity? Could such an emotion touch the demon who so recently sought to make Arvada his own in an eternity of pain and fear?

What was going on here? Should she take a side? Whose? How?

With a cry so piteous Arvada wilted beneath its poignancy, the woman lunged toward Sahan. Who flurried away, then disappeared. The woman let loose a howl of pain, of terror, of loss, far beyond what any single awareness should be able to contain.

Then she too vanished.

Leaving Arvada alone and lost and terrified.

She struggled to resist panic. Being lost was not a sensation she'd developed reflexes to counter. Even in the most mammoth habitats you could not lose your bearings for long.

In this world she didn't know if there *were* any bearings. Not that she possessed motive power in any case. She knew, probably, that she was no longer doing Push Hands with Beck, because she felt no movement of *chi*.

At any moment Sahan might reappear. Her fear must echo like a siren in this place.

Nothing, she reflected, is quite so scary as helplessness.

Your recklessness borders pathological.

Was that her? Or.... Arvada's heart, already redlining, all but swallowed itself.

"Is someone there?"

Maybe. Or maybe you are talking to yourself. Certainly it was not sanity that led you here.

The voice echoed all around her head, making it impossible to locate the source. A woman's voice? Barely, if so. Yet Arvada knew it did not originate in any machine. She took a leap of faith.

"Hypatia? Hypatia Wren?"

The voice in her head laughed, echoing back and forth inside her skull.

Hypatia as ever was. Though perhaps not quite.

"Please help me. I must get through to Sahan."

You just did.

"The Evolved made him hate me, but—"

You provided fertile ground.

"If I can only get past his anger—"

Past his anger to what? Past his anger there lies only more anger still.

"He loves me! Somewhere inside him, he still loves me."

Talk about clinging to your basic fragile reed. You know, long, long ago I was young as you. I think. It did not end happily. In a universe built on random chance, you'd expect a higher percentage of happy endings, wouldn't you? There must be some sort of Strange Attractor that tilts the probabilities toward tragedy. Someday when I have more time perhaps I'll—

"Hypatia?" Recalling that Hypatia Wren had slaughtered her own crewmates during the *Geniah* expedition, Arvada did not speak without a certain trepidation.

Are you still here? I wouldn't be. Your survival genes are short a few strands of DNA.

"Who was that woman?"

Mirai Allan. Though 'woman' is relative. She resides in the Terror Barrier. Where you may make a closer acquaintance, if Sahan gets another grip on you. Figuratively, I mean. Social interaction is actually quite limited.

"Why is Sahan frightened of her?"

Because if he allows her to touch him, he will take her place. Not through some mystical fol-de-rol. Because he can't help himself. The Terror Barrier itself is not sufficient to move him one way or another. Not anyway what the Evolved have left of him. But to go there without you, without his revenge, that one outcome in all the universe is Sahan's great fear. Such obsession is almost enough to make me jealous.

"It looked to me almost as though he wanted to go to her."

Strange, isn't it? Seems even the Evolved could not quite scrape the last little dregs of compassion out of him. They're still squirming around in there somewhere. Just not for you.

"And Mirai Allan? Why does she seek Sahan?"

Because he has a foot in both worlds.

"Who is — was — she?"

Your dedication to learning is commendable. Your good sense, on the other hand ... oh dear.

"Please."

Very well. Mirai Allan was a teenager when the Christian colony had their heads opened up and their religion scooped out. Transcripts were made for future study. They traced the growing horror as each strand of faith was burned away, taking all the memories, associations, and certainties along with it. Knowing records of this episode would soon be erased from the history of the Riggers, Mirai Allan joined the research staff in order to copy the transcripts. When it came her time to die, she incorporated them into her own brain circuitry. By then the Master Holobrain was still in its initial stages of development. But early failures to enter the Group Mind had already created the Terror Barrier. Mirai Allan killed herself, not quickly. She needed to be sure her final death-terror would carry her and her memories, as it were, into the Terror Barrier, beyond reach of the Evolved. She hoped that someday those memories would reemerge."

Arvada was horrified. "But why? How could anyone condemn themselves to such horror?"

For love. She loved one of the victims. A boy who kept bees. Now begone. I don't want Sahan jaunting off to the Terror Barrier with you while you're still trying to explain how much you really loved him all those years you were doing such a proficient job of demonstrating otherwise.

"That's not fair."

No? Well then, little Miss Selfless, try to grasp this simple concept. You cannot stop Sahan. I cannot stop Sahan. Even the Evolved don't have half the control over him they think they do. Not here. Now I feel him returning. Mirai Allan's spirit has sunk back deeper into the Terror Barrier, and conjuring her up again is a sometimes thing, and most exhausting. I trust you will prove realistic enough not to count on me to rescue you again.

"But—"

"Yes?" said Beck, reaching down a hand to help her up off the mat.

Chapter 19

The aura around Mirai Allan floated, little more than a vaporous cloud, through the purple atmosphere of the holobrain, weaving among the sparking yellow sheets. The suffering contained within pulled Sahan after, even as it sank deeper toward the Terror Barrier.

He did not know why he followed the woman and the ghosts flitting about her. What had their agony to do with his own?

And yet visions flocked around him. Dismembered bodies calling out *WHY?* Whole ranks of Grinders with their heads pulped to no purpose because it was easier to work them into a frenzy than to harness them to some rational strategy. Ghosts reaching their fingers into him in vain search for the purpose that once animated them.

Scenes from his life, evoking Arvada's scorn.

Arvada.

PAIN.

Sinews stretched till they began to unravel, while hammers pulverized his knees and elbows. Fire crisped his eyeballs, and electroshock convulsed him, causing the red-hot stake on which he was impaled to dig deeper into his bowels.

The agony filled him till he could think of nothing else.

Almost.

Yet somehow he still willed himself after the aura of suffering that marked Mirai Allan's passing, even as the PAIN fought to rob him of his mind and his will.

Fear, never far distant in the holobrain, stabbed into him. Feeling himself start to dissolve into oblivion, one cell at a time, terror seized him and shook him dizzy.

But the PAIN dissipated, then ceased.

Why?

Oh.

He was entering the Terror Barrier. Where even the Group Mind feared to tread.

He feared it too. But the Evolved could not follow him here, so he resisted the urge to try and fight his way clear. Presuming he still could.

He sensed the source of the suffering he'd followed close ahead. An agony that made the PAIN seem not trivial — nothing could do that — but shallow. Limited to individual horizons, while he passed into a far broader realm, courting an agony with truly existential scope. Transcendent, though not in the way he had once sought.

The thought evoked a compassion in him Sahan marveled to behold.

The cloud of pain and need ceased drifting away. It hovered, waiting for him. Sahan froze.

But now the suffering again came floating toward him. Sahan forced himself to remain still. The cloud began to transform. Within it he saw a human outline. A woman.

Mirai Allan.

She reached out for him.

Pull out! pull out! Once she gets her hands on you, her suffering will become yours. Her terror, her endless scream, will become yours. Forever.

Sahan backed away. Using his mind, not his limbs, which fear had severed from his brain.

The woman's spirit halted. He caught suggestions of black hair, clenched teeth and wide, agonized eyes, but when he tried to fix those eyes in place, trying to communicate with whatever remained of her humanity, they floated in and out of the churning dark gray cloud of her face.

But her hands kept beckoning. The presence of a fellow-creature in this terrible place revived some core of awareness within her, long buried beneath her own demented screams.

Was it Innocence he sensed calling for release? Nobility? Sacrifice? All? Certainly something much larger than Sahan Kotori ever aspired to.

Now he sensed other voices also calling out for release. Each one alone in its pain, locked in its own discrete quantum of agony, its own tight-wound universe of terror.

These were the ghosts that had seeped from Mirai Allan into the Terror Barrier. The lost voices of the Christians being crucified, their inner screams as bit by bit another piece of their connection to faith, to each other, to life, was excised out of them. The transcripts she'd tried to absorb into her own mind, then hide in the Terror Barrier, that the truth might someday be known.

Now their loss amplified hers. All their separate screams joining in hers, transcending the agony any single soul could hold within itself, even here in the badlands of the Terror Barrier.

So badly did Sahan want to free her of her burden! And free the lost spirits crying for release within her.

But there existed only one single way. The ghosts had already found him, more than once. He alone could take her burden onto himself.

It was too much.

Here, finally, he learned the absolute limit of his courage.

Such a sacrifice would rob him of his vengeance against Arvada.

He tried to pull back. The wraith, once more reduced to a gauzy cloud enclosing a boundless universe of suffering, started to follow.

Panic seized him. He floundered, beating wildly against the insubstantiality of the holobrain. Compassion faded; only fear remained. The cloud drew closer.

In his terror he cried out a single word.

ARVADA.

And flew into—

PAIN.

Squirming and screaming, seeing in vivid depiction all the cruelty she had visited upon him, he seized onto it and held it close.

Chapter 20

"I AM NOT SO naïve as to expect the truth," said Arvada, blowing the steam off her coffee, "but just for the record, what did you think would happen when you agreed to help guide me into the holobrain?"

Sitting across from her at the Captain's table Beck did not reply with the insouciance she expected. Instead he worked his lower lip against his teeth as he stared down into his cup.

"You may recall, Captain Sattar, I did advise against such a venture. But you were your customary intractable self. In fact I even seem to remember a *possible* hint of a threat. I don't remember which particular threat this was, because I cannot recall a single conversation we ever had that did not include some dire warning."

"Sorry 'bout that," she said. "I fell into the habit with Sahan. It never worked on him either."

"But I did in fact obey your orders."

Arvada stared around the blank pastel blue walls of her quarters. She'd wanted to call up some scene or pattern to assert something of herself, but in the end this represented the limit of her imagination. By bringing Beck here she hoped to relax him with a less coercive setting than in their previous talks. Now her quarters differed little from the prison cell of his first abode, except for the blue tint. Apparently the best she could do.

"Do you have any idea what happened in there?" she asked.

For a long time Beck didn't answer. Then he put down his cup and lifted his eyes to hers.

"I have some. You met Sahan Kotori. I'm fairly sure of that. Whatever you expected, the meeting turned hostile. Extraordinarily so. The turbulence in the holobrain exceeded anything in my admittedly limited experience. By orders of magnitude. Frankly, Captain, I myself was not unafraid. Did I catch a whiff of the Terror Barrier?"

"I believe so."

"And is that not enough to convince you never to attempt such a desperate venture again? Or if you must, to at least leave me out of it?"

"Correct me if I'm wrong," she said, "but I am not aware you made any attempt to help me."

Swiveling, he shot up out of the chair. He took two steps to the wall and spun around.

"*Help* you? How? By diving in after you? Perhaps straight into the Terror Barrier? Even assuming I *could* have helped you, an idea itself grossly naïve, what consideration have you ever shown me that would suggest I should *help* you? As I have several times mentioned, and you have frequently made starkly clear, we are not friends, but enemies."

He had a point.

"I'm sorry," she said. "Here, don't go all askew. Sit down."

He did so, with pronounced ill grace.

"On the positive side," she said, "if you actively did anything to further imperil me, I am not aware of that either."

"If I had," he said darkly, "I think it highly unlike you would be aware of anything. Except terror." He shook his head. "That was an absurd risk to take. At least now you know."

"*Could* you have made it worse for me?"

He stared out at the ersatz universe in the false window behind her head.

"Beck?"

"Once Sahan Kotori found you? Don't be absurd. At that point any power I might have either to help or harm you became irrelevant. Captain Sattar, did you learn nothing? One more such encounter, and your powers of self-expression will be reduced to a dribble. Or a scream."

"But before Sahan found me?"

"Maybe. But I did not. Neither to help nor to harm you. Why would I?"

"Because you don't like me. And because the Evolved have made me a priority target. Flattering, if a bit puzzling."

He gave a scornful laugh. "Come now, Captain. You are endowed with sufficient unpleasant qualities without adding false modesty to the list. How many other Alliance officers have taken an Evolved battleship? Let alone two?"

"That first fell to Sahan."

"Who has now been neutralized, at extraordinary cost. Leaving you. Together the pair of you violated a host of deeply calculated and eminently reasonable projections. Or so we thought. Randomness, Uncertainty, Chaos theory, the theory of large numbers, these things we understand. Loaded dice are something entirely else. To the Group Mind, you're cheating."

Though secretly pleased, Arvada affected indifference. "If their precious projections turn out to be so much swamp gas, why don't the Evolved just call it a learning experience and go the hell back where they came from?"

Beck shook his head with an oh-if-it-were-only-so-simple *triste*. "Because having drawn attention to themselves, now they're afraid you'll follow. That is our founding legend, don't you see? And yours. How the *Stephen Hawking* fled the persecution of Earth, which has been pursuing us ever since."

"That's bullshit. You know it's bullshit. Earth is only recently emerging from a couple of centuries of muddling through."

"You did not even know we existed. Yet both your spheres keep expanding ever further into space. And ever more heavily armed. Leaving us to flee before them, as always. We are barred from ever attempting to terraform a stable planetary base because the time frames stretch too far. We cannot have a true Homeworld. This was what the Group Mind wished to secure. The underlying purpose of this war was not conquest, but the desire to secure a lasting peace with the Peregrine Alliance."

"*Peace?*" she echoed incredulously.

"Yes, peace." Beck's indignation broke through his smirking self-righteousness "What was so outlandish about our terms? Accept certain limits on your technology, just for a trial period. Until we could be confident of good relations between our people."

"Beg for your crumbs, you mean. And meanwhile go to war against Earth for you."

"Not necessarily. War with Earth was one possibility, but—"

"One possibility *hell!* Either you or your precious Group Mind has got some synapses crossed in your memory circuits.

Peace?" she shouted again. "Why the hell do you think I'm here?"

"Pure bloody-mindedness, as far as I can tell!" Beck shot back.

An urgent knock came from the guards stationed outside.

"Leave us the fuck alone!" she shouted toward the door.

They gave each other Medusa stares for close to a full minute. Only instead of one of them turning into stone, they both broke out laughing.

"You — are just — so full — of shit," she gasped.

"And you've been looking for a war to get into ever since you played your first space video game."

"There may well be something to that," Arvada admitted. "But here's the thing. What I find really creepy about the Evolved? It's the dead ruling over the living."

"You can hardly call the Group Mind dead," Beck protested.

"I do call them dead. They died. That's my personal definition of dead. Idiosyncratic as it may seem."

He waved a hand at the window, as if all human history was spread across that pastiche of space. "Oh, and we can see what grand utopias living humans have created throughout history. They—"

"They? You're not dead yet, friend."

"But I am an Evolved, and what you see is but my infancy. My true adulthood will arise once I am incorporated into the Group Mind. Yes, right now you and I and all other humans are included within the same *we*. We are by the very nature of our birth lone barbarians. Wanting everything, fearing everything. Happy only when taking from each other. Building our monuments on a pile of skulls. And yet, Captain Sattar, you Peregrines have at least had a glimpse of something greater. Even you, crude, violent creature that you are. Look how far you have progressed in Tai Chi. That requires sensitivity to the infinite. Does transcendence hold no lure for you at all?"

"Maybe someday. Right now I'm busy fighting a war against the dead."

"The Group Mind is not *dead*."

"Anyway, Sahan had a deeper interest in transcendence than I do. Pure white light sorts of things. One of the few things he brought with him from the Dainichi."

"Sahan Kotori," Beck said grimly, "may get his glimpse of the infinite in a form he won't find so pleasant. You too, if you venture back into the holobrain. Your former lover keeps wading into parts of the holobrain even the Evolved avoid."

"You cannot understand Sahan," she returned, though the prophecy chilled her. "Or his capabilities."

"Thankfully. But the point I was trying to make, Captain, is here you Peregrines have stood so close to the borders of the transcendent, only to turn away. How did you allow your sense of wonder to atrophy? Have you no memory of Maeda Rao?"

"We venerate Maeda Rao," Arvada said uneasily. Like all Peregrines she'd learned what were purported to be the sayings of Maeda Rao and their significance. But also like most Peregrines, she remembered few and understood fewer. The only times she or anyone in her circle had ever used them were in one-upmanship contests or thankfully brief essay questions at the Academy.

"More in the breach than the observance, it appears," said Beck. "Look at yourself, Captain. You claim to harbor this epic love for Sahan Kotori. But you humans have no conception of the true nature of love. You cannot experience the totality of it, because you are mired in your own individuality. No matter how noble you feel, greed is still at the root of your emotions." He raised his hands in a gesture of concession just as Arvada was contemplating hitting him.

"Not your fault," he continued. "You are as evolution made you. But there *is* something beyond. Something where the bonds of isolated existences are dissolved, and love, real *love*, is made possible. And yes, I say this knowing that in this stage of my existence the full experience is denied as much to me as to you. But I have had glimpses, the merest glimpses, into the Group Mind. The sort of love I tell of *does* exist. I assure you of this, Captain. And we offered it to you. Only to be rejected."

"Oh, you *offered* it to us. You mean, when you told us we could find love only by making war on Earth? I see your point. We Peregrines *are* limited, not to grasp such a simple concept as that. Such a tragic thing, to have to live among the, ah, living. I'm sure you'll be much happier with the dead."

"Jejune sarcasm doesn't become you, Captain. This war you insist on fighting is creating death and suffering, for no other end than to condemn your race to a continuation of the death and suffering that marks all human history."

"I bury the dead. I don't live by their dictates."

"The Evolved are so much more alive than you."

"Then let them go back to their precious little Garden of Eden and leave our world alone! We no longer bow down trembling before the gods. We are definitely not going to bow down trembling before the dead."

"They do not claim to be Gods," Beck said calmly. "They do not have the power to create or manipulate objects through will alone. Though someday, who knows? Would you not want to live, centuries perhaps, to behold something so magnificent? Or even laugh to find it a pointless exercise? But until you join us in the Group Mind or something like it, you condemn yourselves to true death. The dark specter of humanity through the ages. Along with all the pain and fear it brings. Death has always made humanity its slaves. Forcing you into worship of things you could never see, leaving you to prove your faith through the slaughter of those who fashioned their gods in different fashion. It is this curse of *death* the Evolved would free you from."

Arvada sagged, sick of the whole argument.

Beck considered her. And for a moment, looked sympathetic. She had no idea why.

"Your love for Sahan Kotori is noble, Captain, in its way. But it is in vain. The Sahan Kotori you knew can never exist again. He died plunging into the sun at Harrar's Reach."

He stared down at the table, then looked back up at her. "I hesitate to tell you this, Captain Sattar, because I don't know if it will bring you comfort or distress. My sincere hope is the former. In his last moment of life — the last as the man you knew — Sahan's ship broke up around him, leaving him staring at the sun. Even as the light burned out his eyes and the radiation destroyed his body, he cried out at the glory of what he saw. And the word he used to express his wonder was, *Arvada*."

She sat stunned.

"The Evolved recovered the memory. I very much regret it no longer exists. But the *man*, the man who loved you, died seeing your face in the sun."

Hot tears rolled down her face. Let them.

"Thank you," she said.

Beck nodded. "Enemies do not have to hate each other. They can will it otherwise."

"Yes. Then let us will it so."

He bowed.

Oh Sahan. So your final call was to me. To our love. I knew it.

No, I didn't know it. I had no way of knowing it. But I thank you.

Now here is my oath in return. I know that despite what Beck says, the Evolved will never rip that cry from your mind. Even they cannot dig that deep. Not against you, Sahan. Never against you.

I will find you. *You*. And I will make that cry of love live again.

Chapter 21

ARVADA PILOTED HER APPOINTED "Captain's barge" over to *Dysis*, Solange O'Grady's flagship.

Before the war each heavy actually had a dedicated landing craft with the ship's logo and the Captain's name emblazoned on the outside, and numerous VIP amenities on the inside. Even some of the more vainglorious cruiser Captains sometimes made up a special craft for themselves. Since the war, the "barges" had all reverted to type. All you'd know them by was an occasional flash of color below hastily slapped-on paint, and forlorn bolt holes where the luxury loungers used to reside.

Following the victory at Rione, Arvada had found some of the crew emblazoning a very colorful and martial eagle, her increasingly popular nickname among the public, onto one of the landing craft. She took a moment to admire the fiery eyes, vicious beak, and curved talons, then with heavy heart chewed the perpetrators a new asshole. She'd sparked jealousy all her life; she didn't need to fan the flames now, when she was hoping to avoid backlash from the senior Captains and the Citizens' Council.

So while the offenders covered over all traces of their work on what would have been their off-duty shift, Arvada took one of the sleds over to the *Dysis*. Solange had emphasized that this talk must be private. She would not trust ship-to-ship transmissions, no matter how chopped and scrambled.

"We're receiving a new source of intelligence from Harrar's Reach," Solange told Arvada, as the two sat down over coffee in the sumptuous Captain's quarters. Sumptuous in terms of sheer space, a precious commodity aboard a fast cruiser. Yet here in this line of battle ship Solange kept the two rooms so plain as to approach severe. The wholly unadorned walls were set to a dim, deep lilac color Arvada found slightly claustrophobic.

"Or," Solange qualified, "what *may* be a new source of intelligence. That's always the question with these things."

"Ugh." Arvada had her own painful experience of faulty intelligence, both inadvertent and deliberate. She looked around at the four toadstool-like devices transferring the room into something of an obstacle course. Sound dampeners. They created a soft pressure in her ears.

"It was picked up by one of our drones orbiting close in to Thais' solarsphere. Every time we try to float one further out, the unmanned defenses pick it off. Despite the radiation that close to the sun, this message required almost no reconstruction. Which suggests it *might* be a military source. The officer in charge took one look, then sent the whole package straight to me. Ultra coding. It looks like we have a decision to make."

"My vote is. don't trust it. And I don't even know what it is yet."

"I tend to agree with you. But the consequences either way are huge."

Though they'd last seen each other scarcely over a week ago, Solange appeared to be aging into her rank. Her once porcelain-white freckled skin had lost some of its luster, and tiny lines spread from the corners of her mouth and eyes. Nor did her flagrant red hair shine quite like it had just a short while ago. Arvada made out a few incipient streaks of gray she hadn't noticed before.

It all came as something of a shock. Solange always seemed so formidably energetic that any sign of aging approached sacrilegious. The stress of command. Arvada made a note to check her own face more closely in the mirror. When she got up the nerve.

"Haven't we always," said Arvada, "had sources within the Reach?"

"Yes, here and there. Shipping movements, where Catalan's ships berthed, conditions in the colonies, the sort of low-level info we'd easily pick up for ourselves if we could just work some drones past the defenses. Civilian sources, all of them. This is the first time we see decidedly military fingerprints on the information. And listen."

She looked over both shoulders, as if there might be spies lurking in her bedroom. "It provides the coding sequences for two quadrants of the stationary defenses. The defenses that would tear most of the fleet apart if we tried forcing our way into the system."

"I see where this is going," said Arvada. "Like all buy-now hustles, we have to act fast or watch the opportunity disappear, right?"

"Exactly. The defense codes are changed on a regular basis. Our source might or might not get the new codes to us. They might or might not still be alive by then. And of course they might or might not be on our side. Obviously we're not going to rush right in with guns blazing. But it does for the first time raise the possibility of an invasion of Harrar's Reach. The three Evolved heavies stationed there will be a tough nut to crack, but not impossible. Not if we can bypass the fixed defenses. As for what's left of Catalan's fleet, I am increasingly of the opinion that for every ship that fights against us, one more will join us and two will run away."

"I feel the same." Arvada sniffed her coffee. The aroma spirited her away to freshly-plowed fields ringed by tall, thick-foliaged trees. She sipped. Dark, richly textured; strong but without any trace of bitterness. And possessed of a bite that elevated the light-headedness induced by the prospect of final victory even higher. Before she left *Dysis* she simply must pry some of this brew out of Solange, if she had to trade a cruiser for it.

"So I take it," she said, "we face the usual dilemma. The more extensive effort we make to determine the source's authenticity, the more we risk exposing it. And time is not on our side."

"As you say. Like the coffee?"

"I'm about ready to give up eating. Where did you get this?"

"Would you believe it? From the *Druga*. That bitch Catalan did herself proud, before she decided treason was safer if she never poked her own nose out of the Reach. So she turned her so-called flagship over to J'Ayla Sul. Who naturally surrendered it a little more quickly than decency required."

"Didn't we forbid looting?"

"RHP. But the source. The intelligence, I mean. What do you think?"

"It could of course be authentic. There must be many, many naval personnel looking to build up some brownie points should the war turn against them. Or they may be genuine patriots. On the other hand … it's just exactly the sort of thing Sahan would do."

"Sahan?" Solange did not hide her skepticism. "Whatever the Evolved must have done to his brain to weaponize Sahan against you, I find it hard to believe there'd be enough left to put him in charge of strategy. Sorry. I know it's painful."

Whatever the Evolved must have done to his brain.

"But he would have to be capable of strategy, for the Evolved to pit him against me."

"Yes, there is that," Solange acknowledged.

"No one in this fleet ever realized just what Sahan was. Solange, please, I know I don't rank as the most objective observer in the world, but I do know Sahan. Don't think of him as some kind of mummy in a Grinder body, lurching and flailing around. Is he sane? No. Is he still dangerous? You have no idea."

Solange stared at her suspiciously. "You're talking like you have first-hand knowledge. Arvada? Talk to me, dammit. You can't ask me to trust you at the same time you're holding back information. It doesn't work like that."

"No, you're right." Arvada took a preparatory breath, trying to separate out her emotions from her experience. "I've been inside the holobrain. And I met Sahan there." Further words backed up in her throat.

"You met him," Solange said grimly. She bit her lip at the effort of keeping herself under control. "Okay. Then what?"

"And then, well…." How to put this? "He came very close to, ah, killing me. Or something worse."

"Worse than killing you? Arvada, what the hell is going on here?"

"It's all right, Solange, I got away." To bring up Hypatia Wren and Mirai Allan would only add more eldritch elements to an already bizarre tale.

Solange rose from her chair, walked to the opposite wall, and stood with her back to Arvada. After a long precarious moment she returned to her chair.

"You are violating the trust I put in you when I gave you command of your own task force. Arvada, you can't just jaunt off to … some whole other reality, whenever the mood takes you. I need Arvada Sattar. What I *don't* need is another Sahan Kotori."

Arvada bowed her head, chastened. "Just one more thing. I have some reason to believe that the Evolved's control over Sahan may be less than complete. Less than they believe."

"How? Arvada, what the Evolved haven't replaced or discarded they've mapped in eight dimensions. What do you mean, their control may be less than complete? Any part they *may* not control is the part that wants to do something 'a little worse' than killing you."

"That's probably true," Arvada conceded. In fact it was most perceptive.

"Now you're making *me* crazy." Solange put both hands to her temples to ensure her head had not wandered off into other realms. "But look. There's an aspect of this new intelligence we have to decide on right now. Apparently the Evolved mean to reinforce the colony of Aulaire."

"Aulaire? Why? There's nothing there but a few Grinders."

"The report indicates that the reinforcing fleet will include not just additional Grinder infantry, but settlers recruited from various colonies within Harrar's Reach. We know that the Evolved have had increasing problems with the workforce, ranging from inefficiency to outright sabotage. Whether they're marooning some of the soreheads or trying to establish a genuine beachhead, I don't know. Strategically, if they can make Aulaire productive again, it could supply many of the shortages within Harrar's Reach."

"Those shortages," Arvada announced, "are deliberate. Another tactic of Sahan's."

Solange gave her a sour look. "You have Sahan Kotori on the— Oh, forget it. Normally the problem with putting serious work into Aulaire would be to keep us from taking it back. Catalan's navy can no longer be trusted to stand and fight at anything approaching equal odds. However, the same source of intelligence suggests the Evolved intend to station one of their own line of battle ships off Aulaire."

Arvada was dumbstruck. An Evolved heavy was certainly formidable, but by itself not necessarily invincible, should the Alliance commit to risking the six or seven heavies necessary to overcome it.

"But that would leave only two Evolved heavies inside the Reach," she pointed out. "It's not like the Evolved to cut the odds so fine."

"Maybe they're more concerned with just how desperate conditions inside Harrar's Reach could get. If the people turn against Catalan, the Evolved can hold a couple of large habitats with Grinder troops. Maybe even three or four. But no more. It would meant their material base could no longer support the war."

Arvada mulled it over. She kept circling back to the same conclusion. "I'm having a lot of trouble with this. Right now there are three Evolved heavies holding Harrar's Reach. Even if we could get through the fixed defenses, that's one bloody battle. Only, all of a sudden one comes sailing merrily our way. Why? To alleviate the food shortages aboard the habitats inside the Reach? Does that really make sense to you?"

Solange looked uneasy. "It might, if the shortages are turning the whole population against Catalan."

"But why would there be shortages in the first place? Sure, before the war Harrar's Reach concentrated on high-end production. Even so, whole habitats existed dedicated to nothing but food production. Massive resources must remain."

"Unless the labor force is staging what amounts to a low-level revolt, using sabotage or even dedicated inefficiency instead of open protest."

"Humor me a moment. Assume that this whole operation, the shortages, the intel, and the plan to reinforce Aulaire, is some plan of Sahan's."

Solange looked away to the dark lilac walls of her quarters, as if more sense was to be found in their calm blank expanse than talking to a self-evidently monomaniacal Arvada Sattar.

"So I'm humoring," she said sourly.

"Sahan is sending us what amounts to an irresistible target. He knows we'll attack it. And he knows just how. Because it's what we've done before. We'll hit it coming out of Jump, deep into the sun."

"That's what *you've* done before. There is a body of opinion, of which I am by no means dismissive, that holds that battles deep in the sun, especially against an Evolved heavy, are an authentic nightmare scenario, and that you, Arvada Sattar, are close to exhausting your luck."

"That's why I want to use some of our damaged ships as shields. Our other heavies can establish a fire base. Behind the shields we'll send cruisers close as we can. We'll clamp on and blow our way into the hull. Just like we did with Beck's ship. If the mission really is to activate Aulaire, we'll find Peregrine settlers inside, along with a suitable escort of Grinders. But what I'm really expecting is a whole bunch of Grinders. And Sahan. Because that's what I believe this whole operation is about. A chance for Sahan to...."

Her voice faltered.

"To kill you 'or worse'? Arvada, I can see why you're thinking that way. And maybe you're right. After all, Sahan Kotori was crazy in a number of ways, but not least was his love for you. The whole fleet knew it. Now the Evolved have transformed that passion into a lust to destroy you. So your scenario about this all being one carefully coordinated trap, okay, it does have a certain plausibility. But does that make it a good idea to give him what he wants?"

"Kill Sahan, and I believe the Evolved will turn a lot more amenable." Arvada's heart felt two hundred years old.

"And if he kills you?"

Arvada remembered the fanatic hate, that would lead Sahan to pull her down into the Terror Barrier with him just to feel her agony.

"He will still die." And when Solange looked dubious: "Solange, this is not speculation on my part. If Sahan kills me, he will not survive the battle. He does not intend to."

Her certainty left Solange appalled. "Is this anything to do with the 'worse than death' scenario you brought up?"

"Yes."

"Jesus Christ, Arvada. What the hell's going on?"

Arvada raised her cup, near empty though being several times refilled. She stared into the black remains as if trying to transform them into a crystal ball.

I *have* to reach Sahan. He may kill me or I may kill him or we may kill each other. Or somehow, *somehow*, we may....

She didn't know. She might preach *somehows*, but she didn't see any.

But it was clearly their destiny.

Why fight it?

"It is what the war's come down to," she told Solange.

Chapter 22

Once more into the sun.

Arvada sat in the Captain's dais on the bridge of the fast cruiser *Natessa*. Ligea Romero sat in the XO's chair to her right. Tarika Okada, now Second Officer, ruled over the stations curving around the front of the bridge, with the viewscreens above.

They showed yellow. Magnesium-bright, marked by streaks of red and blue, rolling upward from Aulaire in searing tongues of flame, occasionally parting to reveal glimpses of the starfields beyond.

You could almost smell the heat. Though in reality that was the sheen of sweat starting to form within Arvada's suit as the cooling system, nudging unsustainable levels hard, topped out.

She commanded the largest force she'd ever led on such a venture. Of course officially, Solange O'Grady was in charge. And Arvada swore to herself she would defer to any commands Solange might issue. Within reason.

It was still her plan, her action.

And her enemy. Because for the first time in this war, Sahan would be fighting directly against her. This time she could not count on the man many called her "familiar" to conjure up some weird-ass miracle in the face of disaster.

She tried to suppress her uneasiness at the thought. Of course she'd always known how capable Sahan was. How dangerous. That's why she cultivated him at the Academy, when so many were trying to cultivate her. And in the years since she'd seen his capabilities grow.

But so had hers.

And really, looked at a certain way, she was fighting only part of Sahan, while he must do battle with all of her.

Familiar metallic groans surrounded her as differential expansion, and to a lesser degree gravitational distortions, strained the hull. Generally the bridge crew performed their tasks smoothly, in the low, competent tones of professionals well-drilled to their task. But sometimes, when a gravity wave suddenly sucked the cruiser deeper toward the heart of the sun, or a hiccup broke out amid the strained roar of the engines, everyone turned to stone, as if Aulaire had reached up and locked them in stasis.

All so familiar. The threat from the sun, the tension of waiting for battle. Arvada felt as though she'd spent half her life in such a tableau. Why not, when the seconds dragged by so slowly?

In contrast, her heart raced madly.

Deployed around the *Natessa*, another fifteen fast cruisers and six heavies moved as slowly as they could in order to maintain orbit while staying within the boundaries of the Jump point. In addition, two heavies damaged in the battle of Rione, the *Argo* and the *Parthenia*, had been repaired sufficiently to move under their own power. Crammed with weapons systems in place of life support and crew quarters, they were remotely guided by technicians aboard Solange O'Grady's *Dysis*.

The enemy drones had already come and gone. Most of them. Some were destroyed by Alliance drones, which also jammed electromagnetic transmissions in an environment already clouded by radiation. The enemy fleet should not find this suspicious. With the colony occupied by Grinders, the Alliance would naturally maintain close surveillance of Aulaire and its Jump points, hiding possible ambush sites as a matter of course in a routine game of chicken.

Much planning had gone into such considerations during the War Council. Arvada paid little attention. Sahan wanted a battle. She knew it, sure as if she could read his mind. The Alliance fleet could shoot off flares, and still he'd come.

"Perturbations," Tarika announced.

"Helmets on," ordered Arvada. The crew was already suited up.

Solange O'Grady transmitted general orders to the heavies. "Let the Collaborationist ships pass through. Do not engage unless forced to defend yourself. Our target is the Evolved line of battle ship. Nothing else. Commodore out."

"Objects starting to materialize inside the Jump zone," called Tarika. "Signatures indicate enemy ships."

"Climb!" shouted Arvada. "Climb, climb, climb! Climb like your ass is on fire." Over ship-to-ship she heard variations being issued throughout the fleet.

Though the enemy vessels remained invisible, her own force shimmered into view as they rose into altitudes of lower radiation and the Alliance ships dropped their blurring fields.

At the forefront the drone ships *Argo* and the *Parthenia* rose on flaring engines. Close behind followed four Alliance heavies, led by Solange in *Dysis*. Completing the finger-four formation came the *Megara*, the *Druga*, and Ayama Cleves' *Leya*.

Two more heavies spread out on either side. Each served as a shield for eight fast cruisers clustered close behind. The *Natessa* led the starboard flank.

Now Arvada could see the enemy ship. Not literally; the distance was too great, the speeds too fast, the clouds of radiation and defensive chaff too disruptive. Nevertheless the *Natessa's* sensors gleaned enough information to project the enemy's image onto the screen: the slab-sided cliffs of the main hull, the tripartite engine complex outlining the stern, the aggressive plow nose of the forward section, like an ancient Greek trireme built for ramming. The hull stayed smooth. The gun turrets would only bulge out once battle began.

Hello, Sahan.

Would her heart *never* settle? Combat always jiggled the pulse upward, but this was ridiculous.

The rest of the Collaborationist fleet, three heavies and five cruisers, cut through the solarsphere well above the Evolved ship.

Solange saw them too. "What do you think?" she called on Arvada's private channel. "Will they wait until we've engaged the Evolved, then swoop down on us from above? Do you think we should deploy a screening force?"

At one point it would have been remarkable, a fleet Commodore asking a fast cruiser Captain for advice on dispositions at the commencement of battle. This war was breaking so many conventions. Probably all wars did, for those trapped inside them.

"Certainly not much of a one," Arvada replied. Don't sound too peremptory; Solange is in command, after all. "I believe they're no more than decoys to lure firepower away from the Evolved. They'll threaten, but probably do no more than make a pass at crippled ships."

"Still," said Solange. "If they do come down on us, I'd like some time to meet them. I'll station one of the reserve heavies between them and us." A moment later Arvada heard her ordering *Haimati*, into position to screen out the Collaborationist ships. John Two-Vests' command. To get past John, the enemy would have to mean it. Arvada wondered if any of Raisa Catalan's Captains still had the stomach for that kind of pounding.

The simulation of the Evolved ship gave way to the real thing. Heavily magnified, it appeared largely as a blue-gray blur, but her shape gradually firmed against the squirming backdrop of Aulaire.

A few minutes later the fighting commenced.

The two shield ships, *Argo* and *Parthenia*, veered around the Evolved at bow and stern, then bore in toward the port side with their newly reinforced batteries blazing. From below, Solange O'Grady's four heavies began weaving while firing every gun and launcher they had and surrounding themselves with clouds of chaff. The heavy *Oringo*, which had shielded Arvada's line of cruisers, took position off the Evolved's bow. The eight cruisers zoomed past, looping around to station themselves behind the *Parthenia*. The opposite eight, coming around the stern, took up a similar position behind the *Argo*.

The drone heavies didn't directly shield the cruisers. But as they closed at top speed, threatening to ram, they forced the Evolved's port guns to concentrate on stopping them. And the explosions against the Evolved's hull as the guns of the *Argo* and *Parthenia* pounded her distorted the aiming systems, further lowering the payoff for attempting potshots at the more distant, fast-moving cruisers.

The Evolved ship, outlined in fiery, brief-lived tattoos from heavy fire on all sides, bulled forward as if meaning to complete her Jump into the Aulaire system despite Arvada's predictions. She gave at least as good as she got. Explosions danced all along the bluff bows of the shield ships, and missiles looped around to attack their engines. But that roundabout trajectory made the rockets vulnerable to counter-fire from the sixteen cruisers closing behind.

As for the rams themselves, the lack of crew and life support had made it possible to reinforce the forward sections till they were practically solid steel. Though what had been their bows now looked to have been eroded by a few centuries' worth of asteroid strikes, they kept coming.

Which was all very well. But Solange's four heavies were taking a beating. As Arvada watched, the *Megara's* stern slowly imploded, inward-crumpling sheets of steel revealing quickly smothered bursts of flame through rents in the hull. Arvada resisted the temptation to listen in on what she knew must be happening: frantic orders as the crew tried to abandon ship, even more frantic cries for help from members trapped in collapsing sections of the hull, and screams cut off, not fast enough, as walls imploded or flame hot as a welder's torch broke through. A flurry of life craft and escape pods puffed away like seeds blown from a dandelion.

Scarce a minute later the *Parthenia* disintegrated into a brief-lived fireball, then a storm of shrapnel spinning off into space.

But the remote-controlled *Argo*, once Everson Brooks' pride and joy, made it through. The chewed-up remnants of her bow struck the Evolved midships with such terrific force that the gigantic enemy vessel was knocked sideways several times the length of her own hull. Another quickly curtailed sheet of flame flashed along her side, obliterating the *Argo* and shivering the Evolved's whole hull.

"Attack!" cried Arvada, throwing off her seat harness and jumping to her feet. "Everyone, in after her!"

The cruisers dashed forward. If any of the Evolved's port guns were still functional, the impact had knocked their aiming systems offline.

First in was Wayland Takedi's *Keyna*. Though the hole blasted in the Evolved's side by the *Argo* looked easily big enough to fly into, he followed the plan, flaring out his cruiser as he came in and belly-whomping into the wounded ship's hull. Arvada heard a muffled blast over her phones as a hole was blown in the enemy's hide, then a screech of metal as bay doors slid open.

"Boarders away!" cried Takedi, causing Arvada to wave her fists and loose an involuntary yip of excitement as she all but shouted *fix bayonets!*

Next in were *Usagi* and the ever-dependable *Bhimadevi*, followed closely by *Lyngheid*. Arvada was limiting the initial attack to four ships, so that depending on what they found she could choose where to concentrate the attack with her remaining twelve.

Within a few seconds Marines and Riggers were streaming into the Evolved ship, looking for trouble. The *Natessa* held back while Arvada assessed the situation. The Evolved ship was huge, and she wanted to know where Sahan would be. Not fight her way through hundreds of battle-mad Grinders to reach him.

Was she maybe just a little bit scared?

She tried to tell herself that her nervousness sprang from reluctance to be forced into kill-or-be-killed combat with the man she once — still — loved.

But he was also Sahan Kotori, and no matter how much Arvada dominated him through the years, a part of her had always been a little afraid of him, too. With Sahan, you never quite knew where the limits were.

Something was wrong.

The attack parties from the cruisers moved through dark and empty corridors. Many of the hallways were bent and twisted, some collapsed from the *Argo's* impact. Some compartments had their ceilings bowed to scarcely a meter above the floor. Dust constantly clouded the vid feeds. Drones sent on ahead saw more of the same.

Tarika stood still as a statue over the forward monitors. Ligea Romero, phlegmatic as they came, glanced at Arvada in concern.

It all made sense, Arvada told herself, as the tension in her heart spread down to her stomach and up into throat. Sahan knew one of the shield ships might get through. The shock and damage on that side would be fearsome. So he withdrew the Grinders to more secure positions. Now he waited for the Alliance forces to walk into his defense zones.

Oh, this was going to be a charnel-house.

Unless maybe....

Unless I lead our forces in person. Sahan is not going to risk me getting cut down by some anonymous Grinder. Where I go, there will he be. And that is the true battle.

"All boarding crews, this is Captain Sattar. Hold in place. I am entering with reinforcements."

There. He'd hear that. And wait for her. He'd always wait for her. She'd known that from the first. That if she went on frustrating him for a thousand years, at the end of it she'd still find him waiting. Though maybe not necessarily with love.

God, I'm scared.

Ligea Romero stood in front of her, forcing Arvada to acknowledge her.

"Captain, you are operation commander. Boarding the enemy is a job for your Number One. The same way you always let Sahan Kotori handle off-ship operations. Or else assign one of the other Captains."

"Your request is noted, Number One," Arvada replied, touched by both Ligea's concern and her courage. "But this time it doesn't work like that. It's me Sahan wants."

And he would kill his way through the whole fleet to get to me. Oh Sahan, Sahan, Sahan. How did it come to this? Was hatred the bedrock of our relationship all along?

"You have the bridge, Number One. Here is what—"

She broke off as a low urgent beeping reached her ears on a seldom-used channel.

Beck.

Should you listen? Do you trust him? Could he somehow be in league with Sahan?

She couldn't afford not to hear him out.

"Beck?" she acknowledged, securing the channel so no one else could listen.

"There is something badly wrong here, Captain Sattar." His voice was perturbed. Genuinely, or was he acting? Why would he tell her the truth?

"Explain."

"As you ordered, I've been trying to use our holobrain to enter into the one aboard the Evolved ship. I hoped to find Sahan Kotori for you."

"Thank you." Dangerous work, if he meant it.

"I couldn't find Sahan," he said. "That in itself is not alarming. If he chooses not to be found, his abilities in the holobrain far exceed my own. But I find no sign that the holobrain is controlling Grinders, either."

Her heart kicked out against her chest.

"Are you sure? Could Sahan be shielding them somehow?"

"A force of Grinders sufficient to battle your forces? The holobrain would be hyperactive trying to control them. No, Captain Sattar. There are no Grinders aboard that ship."

She killed the channel. Went wide.

"All personnel invading the Evolved ship! Evacuate at once! Emergency protocols! Bridge crew on *Keyna*, *Usagi*, *Bhimadevi*, and *Lyngheid*. Be ready to redline away the second the last of your crew is taken aboard. Screw the engines. Move, people! Move for your lives!"

She collapsed back in the Captain's chair. A store of barf bags were tucked in a compartment along the flank. She fished one out, was very nearly sick as her shaking fingers tried to pry the mother-fucker open.

"Captain?" asked Ligea, worried.

As always, as soon as you got the damn bag open, you'd either already vomited all over yourself, or the impetus passed, leaving the nausea still threatening your stomach, nose, and throat, like a sneeze that demanded to be loosed but wouldn't quite come.

The *Lyngheid*, last ship to disgorge her crew, was the first to recover them. Arvada watched the cruiser shudder with the force of the sudden acceleration.

God, God, God.

Half a minute later the *Usagi* lifted off from the scarred hull.

And was just beginning to accelerate away when the Evolved ship exploded with such force as to engulf her.

As Arvada watched, pieces of the wreckage rattled hard against the hull of the *Natessa*, six kilometers away.

Chapter 23

THIS TIME IT WAS Arvada who requested a private meeting with Solange O'Grady. Despite some reservations, she had no other shoulder to cry on.

The post-battle review, attended by all the Captains — the surviving Captains, Arvada thought bitterly, those from the cruisers *Keyna*, *Usagi*, and *Bhimadevi*, in addition to the heavy *Megara*, being painfully absent — had judged the battle at Aulaire a victory. For the first time an Alliance force had engaged an Evolved heavy in a fleet action and destroyed her. In addition, one of the Collaborationist heavies and two of their fast cruisers had surrendered rather than flee back to their supposed master Raisa Catalan.

Yet though material considerations justified calling the battle a victory, the loss of the Riggers and Marines from Arvada's cruiser force, as well as most of the crew of the *Megara*, would visit personal tragedy on almost every colony in Peregrine space.

Nor could they readily be replaced. More Riggers kept volunteering every day. They came in already adept in power suits, but training them in the effective use of weapons, then instilling unit discipline, these took time.

Still, the direct Evolved force in Harrar's Reach now consisted only of two heavies. Which though still imposing, no longer appeared anywhere near so impregnable as it had before Aulaire. Speculation rose about the possible "endgame" of the war: the invasion of Harrar's Reach itself.

That conversation got so ebullient during the Captains' post-battle debriefing that Solange O'Grady finally had to shout it down. When someone came up with the means to neutralize the fixed defenses around Thais, she declared, *then* planning for an assault on the Reach could commence.

Arvada noted that Solange did not reveal the secret source of intelligence claiming to have the codes.

Throughout the Alliance, Aulaire was hailed as a great victory despite the losses. Another Evolved heavy, believed all but vulnerable after the disaster at Demeter, had fallen.

The Eagle had struck again.

And was sick with remorse.

"Oh God, Solange," she said, settling into the swivel chair across the table from the fleet commander, "I really screwed up. All those people, all those dead ... I was so *sure*."

As always, Solange radiated sympathy. "Aren't you getting a little full of yourself? It was a battle. We won. People died. There's always the butcher's bill to pay. And while I know you have a tendency to forget this minor ancillary fact, *I* was fleet commander. I owned the plan the second I signed off on it. So stop acting like I was such an idiot, because it doesn't sit well with me."

"I would never say that. Or think it. You trusted me. And I totally—"

"You know, I really wish you'd find some middle ground between wild exuberance and total self-abasement. It's like living with a teenager. Why aren't you drinking your coffee? Don't you like it anymore? That was Catalan's personal cache from the *Druga*. There's not so much left I'm going to waste it on some dilletante incapable of properly savoring such a delicacy."

"No, no, it's wonderful, as always." Arvada took such a large sip it burned her lower lip. She gave no indication. She'd studied never to show physical pain. Sahan never did, and he could get quite insufferable about it.

She'd made him show pain, though. Time and again. He always tried to hide it, but she always saw through.

And God help her, she sometimes — maybe more than sometimes — let it be a source of pride.

Now it was Sahan's turn.

"He beat me, Solange. I thought I knew just what he would do. I'd seen his hate. *Felt* it. I thought it would drive him to seek a final reckoning right then and there. I thought I could finally read him better than he could read me. Hubris, that's what it was."

"Just don't ask for a refill," said the Commander, eyeing Arvada's cup sourly. "We want any more of this, we're going to have to break into Harrar's Reach and take it."

Arvada took another quick but more modest sip. Which still scalded the raw spot on her lip.

"Really, it's delicious." It tasted like one wet hot utterly neutral mass trying to force its way down her tension-narrowed throat. "But all those people, Solange. They died needlessly. I sent them into a trap. I knew so many—"

Solange's green eyes glared. "Don't tell me how many you knew. I knew some myself. Deharon Lendahar, the *Megara's* Captain? We were ... close friends, once. Now I keep seeing his face in the walls. What of it? We're *soldiers*, dammit. Stop feeling so frickin' sorry for yourself and concentrate on the job. Which is beating the enemy."

"*Can* I beat him? Sahan knew just exactly how I'd react. I thought he'd finally lost that overwhelming self-control he used to have. In truth he's measuring out his revenge. He wants to draw out my suffering, like he believes I did to him."

"Was he so completely off base?"

"No!" Arvada cried despairingly. "I feel sick admitting it, but no. I'm looking at him and me all the way back to the beginning, and you know? I think Sahan may understand all that happened between us better than I do."

Hardly strange," said Solange. "Considering how all those years he was undoubtedly looking at you a lot harder than you were looking at him. And let's face it. He's probably smarter than you, too. Smarter than me, maybe smarter than anyone. People always found him a little scary, and not just in the Decahedron. You basked in that, didn't you? Your own personal tiger on a leash. Only you never stopped to consider that a man resourceful enough to be of so much use to you, you were bound to lose control of him eventually. Even if by falling in love with him."

Arvada felt herself under a magnifying glass in the sun, the concentrated rays drying out her tissues, withering her heart.

"Solange, why are you doing this to me?"

"Because I'm trying to help you pull your head out of your ass. Look, you got beat. It happens. Logistically it counted as a victory, but just between us, *you* got beat. Not used to it, are you? It's been just one victory after another for Arvada Sattar. The Eagle. Well, in dark times people need a hero. We can't afford to see that statue toppled. So count it as a victory, and let the dead bury the dead. We've got a war to fight."

Arvada's breath squeezed out of her tightened chest. Solange was right. Arvada had to drop the self-pity. It wasn't her that got killed when the Evolved ship exploded.

But the fear, that was harder to dismiss.

With a weary sigh Solange rubbed her palms across her eyes. "I was never taught about this kind of war. Trafalgar, Actium, Midway, these I understand. But here it keeps on coming down to you and Sahan Kotori. And that son-of-a-bitch is standing between me and my coffee."

The shift caught Arvada wrong-footed. "Excuse me?"

"My *coffee*, dammit. The only place to get more is from Raisa Catalan's private stores. And they're in Harrar's Reach. If I run out, it's going to put me in a very, very, bad mood."

"I rather thought you were always in a bad mood."

"That's me in a *good* mood. Change it at your peril."

"I suppose that given time we might—"

Solange glowered. "Given time? Didn't I warn you not to put me in a bad mood?"

"Are we on some timetable here?"

Solange's fist slammed the table. "Every moment that passes, that misbegotten affront to humanity Raisa Catalan is drinking more of *my* coffee!"

"Well if you put it like that."

"Besides," said Solange, reverting to a calmer state, "I'm getting pressure."

"From the Citizens' Council?" asked Arvada, rather guiltily. She'd been following events with at best half an eye, while the other eye and a half stayed on Sahan.

"From the *new* Citizens' Council. Elections having been held, it was sworn in aboard the *Kepler* five days ago."

"Oh, right."

"They're a damn sight more promising than the last lily-livered crew, I'll give them that. Only now we have the opposite problem. Instead of urging unilateral disarmament, this lot are fire-eaters. Half of them are Riggers who lost parts of themselves fighting Grinders. Well maybe not half, but they do stand out. Now they're on the vengeance trail, and they refuse to acknowledge anything can stop us. Not with the intrepid Arvada Sattar leading us into battle."

Ooops.

Solange shrugged philosophically. "That's the way of it. The unpalatable truth is, I spent too long sitting on my freckled ass obeying orders like a good little girl, while you and Sahan Kotori ... well I'm still not entirely clear just what you two renegades got up to. It certainly impressed the hell out of the Evolved, though. Not to mention our own populace. Remember the days when the Council wanted to prosecute you as a war criminal? This lot, they want to build you a statue. If you live long enough to go into politics, your mother will be just a footnote in your biography."

"I didn't want this."

"No?" Solange looked dubious. "I rather thought you did. You never exactly hid your light under a bushel. And now here you are. You don't rule fame, Arvada. It rules you. Didn't your mother ever teach you that? Or did she never admit it?"

Arvada couldn't remember her mother ever admitting anything. But now that it came up, she could better understand how she had ever deluded herself into casting Solange O'Grady as motherly. It was all relative.

"The upshot is," Solange went on, "the Council wants to see me drinking, no, bathing, in Raisa Catalan's coffee. The feeling throughout the colonies is we've finally gained the upper hand, and all it will take to be rid of the Evolved forever is one final push."

"But that push can only be against Harrar's Reach. And if we try to break through the fixed defenses, we'll lose half our ships before the battle even begins. At least."

"But to the Council, and pretty much the people at large, that's a military problem. We're the military. We're supposed to solve it. And the pressure keeps increasing because conditions in the habitats keep getting worse. Those aren't our enemies any more living under Raisa Catalan's domination. They're *us*. And the people of the Alliance want to set them free. Or rather, they want us to set them free. Also, we do have to be a little delicate how we treat the Council these days. We did after all throw the last one out."

"We demanded new elections, due to wartime conditions. The elections were honest. We didn't coerce anyone."

"Good for us. But if we are to be seen *respecting* the people's voice, at some point we actually have to *listen* to the people's voice. Which is calling on us to free Harrar's Reach. We can resist. Up to a point. Beyond that point, and it is a *very* slippery slope, the Council is going to *order* us to relieve the citizens of the Reach. And if we tell them to get stuffed, then we're starting to look an awful lot like a military dictatorship. Specifically, you and I look like dictators. And here's the thing. *You* might get away with it. You're the darling of the people. Only once we go down that path, it might be harder than you suppose to turn back. A delay for this, a postponement for that, an emergency declaration over here, sooner than you know, you're absolute ruler. Just of course until the situation settles, then you'll restore full democracy. Shouldn't take more than a decade or two." She wiggled her hand in the air. "Maybe three."

"Solange...."

"I'd like to be remembered by history as one of those who repelled the alien invaders. Not the chief enabler of the woman who smothered Peregrine democracy."

Arvada was about to protest she wasn't a dictator, didn't want to be a dictator, would never under any circumstances serve as a dictator.

Then she remembered her mother, a radical firebrand who would declaim against military authoritarianism when Naval Command did no more than say they lacked the resources (partly due to her) to provide logistical support to her latest scheme to colonize some wandering asteroid parsecs from the nearest functioning colony.

You could never *suspend* democracy. Because within that atmosphere of suppression passions on all sides would heat to boiling, until there was nothing left but disparate groups maneuvering — or killing — to achieve absolute rule. Then call *that* the Peregrine way.

To avert that, she might *have* to assert power.

Did she just say that?

Solange nodded at Arvada's dawning look of comprehension. "We're not there yet. But the point's approaching."

Arvada sipped her coffee automatically. And wished she hadn't. Now lukewarm, it had grown even more tasteless. But she had to swallow or Solange would be offended.

"If we can't find a way around the planetary defenses," she said, "then I have to find some way to lure Sahan out of the Reach. And hope to hell I do better next time."

"Well, work on it. Frankly, this holobrain stuff, I find it spooky. So as commander of the fleet, I'm going to do what responsible authority always does in the face of crisis. Hand that responsibility off to someone else. With the proviso that if their scheme works, the credit goes to me, and if it doesn't, they take the blame. Bet you can't guess who I have in mind."

Solange looked so insufferably full of herself she might have swallowed a hologrammatic projection.

"Thanks, Solange."

"Look. Sahan Kotori loved you. That love might have been sick—"

"Don't say that!"

"— but no one can argue it wasn't all-consuming. So maybe the Evolved have turned that love to hate. The obsession remains. *That's* his weakness. It's always been his weakness. You have to find some way to make use of it."

"It's not like he's not aware of that."

"Of course he's aware of it. He was always aware of it. But you kept him wrapped around your little finger anyway."

"You make it sound so cold!" Arvada protested. "It wasn't like that."

Not really. Not most of the time.

Dammit, it's not like she ever lied to Sahan! Maybe she denied her own feelings, to him and herself both, but that wasn't lying. Sahan was a free man with all the relevant information plainly available.

SAHAN, I'M SO SORRY!

"Well however it was," said Solange, not seeming to notice Arvada's remorse, "work on it. Humph. Weirdest officers in the navy, the pair of you. But *work* on him. And don't look at me like I'm asking you to airlock your dog. He's the enemy, remember? And it's hardly like you never hurt him before."

Arvada fixed a neutral expression on her face. That last remark hurt. It was cruel, and meant to be.

But motherly, in the manner Arvada had grown up knowing such things.

She would have to return to the holobrain. She saw no other way. The place she'd hoped never to visit again. The place where she risked—

Try to put it from your mind. That was the way to deal with danger. Concentrate on the task at hand, executing each step properly, in their proper order. Block out the consequences, win or lose.

"I'm on it, Solange. I'll get you your coffee."

The stern façade crumpled. "Arvada, I'm sorry having to ask this of you. And despite appearances, I am *asking*. If it gets, you know, too hairy, abort. Please. Okay?"

"Of course." It's not so easy as all that.

The two of them fell into silence.

No more guilt, Sahan. No more pity. Love, well, let's just table that until after the war, okay? I'll keep pictures of the *Keyna*, the *Usagi*, and the *Bhimadevi* on my wall so I don't forget.

Oh Sahan, how could you do that to me? How could even the creature the Evolved made of you do that to me?

Solange said you're smarter than me. Well, maybe. But you demand me for all eternity. While all I now ask of you is your death.

And that shouldn't take but a moment.

Chapter 24

HE FLED MIRAI ALLAN, fled the agonized plea in her eyes. He fled the ghosts that swarmed about her, reaching for him as if he could somehow free them from their scorching hunger.

He fled through wavering mists of purple. He fled through yellow curtains of electric discharge, jerking at the shocks but tearing through them like spider webs.

Wandering zombie-like through the holobrain, Mirai Allan embodied Sahan's one true fear; that he would be robbed of his vengeance against Arvada. From seizing her in his embrace and dragging her down to the Terror Barrier with him. There to spend centuries, millennia perhaps, knowing, *experiencing*, her every torment. As she would know his own.

PAIN.

Sahan found himself writhing on the floor of a plain gray corridor.

The pain stopped. He looked around. He could not distinguish this corridor from any of one hundred, two hundred, maybe three hundred others in the Evolved ship. It didn't matter. Only one location mattered: wherever the holobrain wanted you to go.

Sahan got to his feet and began to walk. His destination too was predestined, though unknown to him.

A bubbling sensation swelled in his mind. It grew in intensity, squeezing on all sides. He could no longer think. He wanted to stop and scrub the sensation from his head. But he kept walking, because the holobrain directed him to and he lacked the capacity to resist.

The bubbling grew worse. He felt lost. Not inside the ship, but within the universe. He possessed one discrete existence. But who was the being that filled it? Any attempt to anchor that effervescence to a Self dissolved at once.

A plethora of voices began to filter through the bubbles. Incoherent, further dividing his already vaporous awareness.

Some panicked core tried to huddle in on itself, only to find its center vanished.

His body lacked the mechanism to whimper. A frayed mental screech zig-zagged off into the void instead.

Still the body kept on walking. Finally it slammed face-first into a wall. Its legs kept on trying to march forward, compressing his nose and cutting his lips against his jutting Grinder teeth.

The bubbling thoughts calmed to little more than a simmer, irising down to a stream narrow enough to elicit comprehension.

A VOICE arose.

From on high. Radiating displeasure.

To make this lesser being understand the gravity of its transgression, the VOICE restored identity to it. The figure marching into the wall recalled that it was Sahan Kotori.

More or less.

His offense: consorting with the enemy. The concept was at first unclear, but gradually began to straighten into something like a narrative.

The Evolved had not brought Sahan Kotori back to life to indulge his fantasies about Arvada Sattar. Mutual torture in the Terror Barrier was all very romantic, but a diversion from his ordained existential purpose. Utterly misguided, in fact. They'd fashioned him to *kill* Arvada, not play cat and mouse.

For them, his ordained existential purpose was to remove Arvada Sattar's individual quanta of unpredictability from the time stream. Simple and straightforward. Meanwhile, to have their chosen weapon flitting about the Terror Barrier did not eliminate unpredictability; it enhanced it.

DO NOT TRESPASS THERE AGAIN.

Or, some deep sense implied, you will never leave.

Which sounded reasonably aversive in itself. However, the VOICE was given to redundancy. So since the creature currently referenced as Sahan Kotori had persistently exhibited learning disabilities in this regard, it would aid his retention of said proscriptions with a mnemonic device.

PAIN.

At last Sahan stopped trying to march through the wall. He fell flopping and kicking to the floor instead. The worst part was the spike penetrating from his anus to his heart, sprouting gang hooks every few centimeters. Bad enough if you lay perfectly still, but the way the electric shock made him shake and writhe around like that—

The PAIN stopped.

He crawled back to his knees, all he could manage at the moment.

And, the VOICE reminded him, you lost one of our ships for an insignificant return. You knew all along Arvada Sattar would spot the deception before she ever boarded, didn't you?

How could I? I'm no friggin'—

PAIN.

I'm setting her up for the kill, he moaned, when at last the agony ceased. Locking revenge uppermost in her mind.

Simple and straightforward, the VOICE reminded him.

Simple and straightforward, he agreed. To hear is to obey.

This time he managed to claw up the wall all the way to his feet. Where he stood gasping and crouched around the lingering pain in his guts.

Will that be all? he asked hopefully.

NO.

Vishnu on a stick, what the—

PAIN.

I'm listening! he screamed, having returned to the floor as a new element joined the repertoire: a sort of electric noose fastened around his testicles while the shock bounced him about.

The Grinders are *not* your soldiers, declared the VOICE. They are *our* soldiers. Train them, lead them in battle. But do not, repeat do *not*, try to make them yours.

Understood, he acknowledged.

When nothing else happened, he rose in stages.

Understood, perhaps, came the VOICE. But internalized? Most humans have a most murky perception of reality. You, on the other hand, see it with exceptional clarity. Yet you do not *accept* it, because you always believe you can shape it to your will.

I admit I was just that way, he moaned. But that's all in my past.

WE will now present you with a certain reality. One you are familiar with. One you have already tried to turn to your own ends. Succeed, and WE shall have to reevaluate your capabilities. Fail, and WE will hope the lesson will prove salutary.

Couldn't I maybe just swear an oath instead? On my mother's head, say? Her eternal soul?

But he was already walking. Through corridor after corridor. Toward one of numerous training halls aboard the Evolved ship.

He came to a wheel-lock door. Opened it, though his hands were loathe.

Before him stood maybe a couple of hundred Grinders. Unarmed, but looking most perturbed. Even enraged. Looking in particular at him.

He dropped his gaze.

There stood the human body of Sahan Kotori.

Now he heard the low collective snarl, edged with saliva, that his appearance evoked. And felt the throbbing sensations from the holobrain as it worked the Grinders into ever greater fury.

***

THEY CHARGED IN A solid wall.

When Sahan first took in the Grinders' hostility, fueled by his human form and the holobrain pumping in as many stimulants as their well-conditioned hearts could contain without spouting blood out their ears, he had a brief thought of exerting his own will against that of the holobrain to halt them.

But in the one and a half seconds available before the first Grinder smashed into him, his influence did not cross their threshold of perception.

That particular individual died from a punch to the chest, but Sahan could not evade the body's momentum because he was hemmed in by more bodies on either side. He slammed against the door under the collective impact of at least a dozen onrushing Grinders. He hadn't even room to fall.

Over the next few minutes, though his distorted sense of time was not to be trusted, every Grinder that could find space to fit its prognathous jaws onto some part of him gnawed and gnashed right through the tough outer fabric of his "skin." At first tearing loose in patches, which the Grinders clawing from behind grabbed and chewed further, the fabric eventually frayed and turned to saliva-sodden green lint. Below it lay the striated mesh forming his motor system. That proved a tougher nut to chew. But not impassible.

He didn't bleed, of course. Spurted, leaked, drained, but did not leak. But his pain receptors seemed to have been boosted past the conventional evolutionary standard. The combination of crushing, ripping, and tearing induced by the body-wide chewing was aggravated by the fact that it took so long to sever the interwoven material of his artificial musculature.

But after some time those consigned to the outer ranks grew impatient. Squeezing through, they grabbed his arms and legs wherever they could. Pulling with all their might, less by deliberate strategy than just the imperative of hanging on as the whole pile of bodies, with him at the center of it, staggered this way then the other, they began to pull him apart.

This is a test, Sahan told himself. It was the fallback line he'd developed somewhere around the age of eight.

Finally the Grinder tug-of-war resulted in the popping-loose of his arms and legs. It was not quite so bad as he'd anticipated. Even a relief, in some ways.

He was still just as glad he couldn't see it. One eye had been pounded into jelly, the other chewed and spit out by a Grinder.

As they yanked the muscle-strands of his body apart, it imparted an almost ticklish sensation, in addition to the feel of having your sinews ripped apart. Rather bouncy, as if his innards were composed of rubber bands. Which they about half were.

Finally the Grinders got around to pulling off his head. Which did not kill him, of course. They bit and clawed their way right down to the protective oblong shell containing his brain.

That stopped them. They chewed on it, kicked it, hurled it against walls. All of which together induced a sensation of sea-sickness, but could accomplish no further harm. All other pain had ceased, having lost its means of transmission.

The brain within the shell normally received its main nutrition from a complex housed within his body. The Grinders must be splashing fluid across the floor from ripping apart the tubes joining head to "vitals," but left on its own, his brain could still survive for weeks, perhaps, on small recyclers mounted inside the casing.

At last some enterprising Grinder came up with the idea to build a fire and roast the contents of the brain casing. Sahan didn't know this at the time, as all his external sensory apparatus had been torn away. Nor did he know that at that point he and the Grinders alike succumbed to a deep sleep.

From which he did not wake for quite a long time, to find himself in a new body, a duplicate of the old.

Still aching in places few people ever knew they had.

And though the VOICE did not visit him again, from time to time Sahan thought he detected an overwhelming hint of smugness in the air.

Chapter 25

Arvada leaned cross-armed in the doorway, looking down at Beck lying on the lower bunk. His current crew quarters were no great cut above his accommodations in the brig, but Arvada did want to show some element of trust.

Why, she wasn't sure. That trust did not include removing his monitor or dismissing the guards outside his door. But she did wave them to the end of the corridor.

"Why did you warn me the Evolved ship was a trap?" she asked Beck.

He did not bother to shift his eyes from their contemplation of the upper bunk. "If I hadn't, you might have been so slow to catch on you'd clamp us onto her hull. And I'd have been killed."

"A good reason," Arvada acknowledged. "But you could have waited longer, gotten more of us killed. I had no intention of going in myself until I had Sahan located."

"Now you tell me."

"I am trying to work myself up to thanking you." If for just one minute you'd stop being such an insufferable smug bastard.

Finally he looked her way, a sardonic grin lifting his bored ascetic face.

"Not necessary, Captain. You were close to catching on. Sahan Kotori had your reaction timed down to the minute. He did not want to kill you so quickly. And not outside the holobrain, most of all. Did he really want to take you with him into the Terror Barrier? I sensed his rage, but only in a general way."

"He did."

To her surprise, Beck gave a little shiver. "To face the Terror Barrier voluntarily, just for such an intimate expression of revenge ... that is quite beyond my imagining. What stopped him?"

She was certainly not going to tell him about Mirai Allan. Or Hypatia Wren.

"Perhaps he had second thoughts."

"That demon? When you make enemies, Captain, you admit of no half-measures."

"It was your kind did this to him. This precious Group Mind you reverence so much."

"Yes, and that somewhat disturbs me. I thought we'd put such manipulations behind us."

Before Arvada could question what he meant, though she believed she had a pretty good idea, Beck swung around to sit on his bed, though having to lean his head forward to avoid the bunk above. The posture looked uncomfortable; clearly he meant to distract her before she could press him about his last words.

"Credit where credit is due, Captain Sattar. You yourself laid the groundwork for Sahan's transformation. Only slight distortions of your mutual history were necessary to turn love into hate. Pain provides a most fertile bed. Whatever he's become, the Group Mind couldn't have done it without you."

"You lie."

"Oh?"

He did lie. Sahan could hardly avoid having some stores of resentment. But the kind of insane self-destructive fury she'd felt in the holobrain, that was strictly the creation of the Group Mind.

Wasn't it?

You provided fertile ground.

"I loved him!" she cried.

Beck stared up her. "An assertion, or a plea?"

Arvada held herself firmly in place, shoulder against the doorway, arms still crossed over her chest. Any display of temper would only affirm his accusation.

"Captain Sattar." Beck leaned forward to look up at her, his neck bent at an awkward angle. "You and I have both done or excused things that were better not done. Whatever divides us, remorse lies heavy on both our hearts. May we not for the moment let that bond supersede our enmity?"

Arvada could not gauge his emotions. He seemed sincere, but how would she know?

He stood, looking her directly in the eye, shorn of his customary smirking air. "I know we will not achieve any meeting of minds, but if some better understanding could take place between us, that would surely be a good thing."

"Would it?" She trusted his insults more than his professions of comradeship. "I still have to fight this war. Not empathize with the enemy."

"But if peace is ever to happen? Can you not imagine you and I at the forefront of the process?"

"I'm struggling."

"Try, just for the moment. The Group Mind. It is *not* the rule of the living by the dead, as you say. It is the next, inevitable step in evolution. And both Evolved and Peregrines are taking the same path. We are both leaving natural evolution behind. My people may have advanced further down the path. But the end points coincide. They must. No other culmination exists but collective consciousness. A fuller expression of life and thought than individual existence can ever achieve. The final dissolution of the barriers of individual existence, freeing us from the isolation and fear of death it condemns us to. Ultimate liberation. *That* is what you call 'the rule of the dead.' And you are so, so wrong."

Arvada found the vision seductive. Her immediate future struck her as something she'd rather wake up on the other side of. She could dredge up no other emotion about it than dread.

But that was where fate had stuck her, and she'd just have to make the best of it.

"Sides are drawn," she told Beck. "Maybe someday we Peregrines will come to where you are. But only by our own path. We will *not* be coerced into yours, no matter what wonders you wave before us."

Then she stated her core refutation of his vision. "And when we find our path, we will not carry the blood of the *Hawking's* Christian colony on our hands."

Beck's face had carried appeal. Now he retreated behind his customary smirk, once more addressing not a simply a social, but a moral inferior.

"My, aren't we ... holy? Suitably aggressive, Captain, as fits your style. Only" — he held up an admonitory finger — "wrong. All of you who now call yourselves Peregrines, all are descended from the Riggers aboard the *Hawking.* Same as me, same as all the Evolved."

"But we left in protest. We went out to colonize Harrar's Reach despite all the dangers."

"Is that what you've been told? The great Peregrine myth? Perhaps, a few of you did protest. As no doubt some of those who are now Evolved did. The decision did not rest easy on anyone. But such 'protests' never reached the stage of, say, actually *doing* anything. By the time your forebearers decided to take their chances in Harrar's Reach, the whole matter had passed into the realm of philosophical discussion."

"So why did they leave? Survival in the Reach for the first two generations was touch and go."

"And half the systems aboard the *Hawking* at that time were bordering on failure. You think the Riggers exorcised the Christians just for fun? That enclave represented a genuine threat to the ship. But your Peregrine fable of moral protest, that was invented after the *Geniah* expedition. Officially you never had any knowledge of any repression at all. And that, my dear Captain, was a lie. In reality your ancestors were no more than rats running from what looked to be a sinking ship."

Arvada tried to marshal her thoughts for a refutation. Beck's accusations undermined everything she believed about her heritage.

Unfortunately, the conviction came upon her that his account might all too easily be true. Tales of your ancestors' heroic self-sacrifice seemed quite plausible when you weren't called on to make such sacrifices yourself. Once forced to fight for survival, you began to marvel at how upright your predecessors must have been, that they could so steadfastly rise above all the compromises and downright brutality inherent in the messy business of self-preservation. Morally they'd been far, far, above today's debased generation. Superhuman, even.

Or just maybe, the old stories had benefited from a touch of, oh, refurbishing.

"At a loss, Captain? It appears you cannot so easily wash the blood off your hands after all."

"Maybe not. But it wasn't us who made Grinders."

Beck had the grace to flinch. "That much is true." He extended his palms in a gesture of resignation. "We needed soldiers to defend ourselves. Given the possibility of immortality, who is going to volunteer to die? As to their form, that was a deliberate attempt to—"

"Make them less than human. Expendable. "

Beck gave a perplexed frown, as if trying to forge a convincing progression from an array of thoughts that upon examination were linked not by reason, but expediency.

"How I am coming to see those events, Captain, is as a religious war. The Christians had their God. We had our own Godhead — the promise of humanity transcending its animal origins. Of overthrowing all previous visions of God, if you will."

"The Group Mind."

"Whatever you want to call what was done to the Christian community—"

"Genocide?"

"You accuse your own ancestors in the same breath. Because they were there when it happened. Yet managed to deny it in all their accounts and records, so you still believe, though perhaps not quite so much as formerly, that their hands remained unstained by blood. Or neurons.

"But enough." he said, attempting a less accusatory tone. "In such religious conflicts there can be no half-measures, no compromises. Since no god or panoply of gods can ever be proved, faith counts for all. If anyone is left alive to utter any contradiction, then the possibility exists that somebody else may listen. And spread that idea, and on and on. And then then the whole house of cards may collapse. Because since the whole house of cards is erected on nothing but belief, take away one certainty, and the whole edifice becomes open to question. In the end, one side had to eliminate the other's entire way of thought. Which unfortunately in this case meant removing much of the mechanism for that thought."

"And us? Are our two peoples fighting a religious war?"

Beck sank back upon his bed. "I would hate to think it, Captain. And yet after a certain time, don't all wars lean more and more toward a belief in absolute good and evil? We can only hope we have not quite yet reached that point. Though hope itself is nothing but another form of faith, albeit considerably more subject to disproof."

In that note of resignation, Arvada caught her first real sign that she might yet infect Beck with doubt.

Chapter 26

THE FLEET HAD GATHERED around the twin cylinders and drydocks of *Kepler* to complete refitting and hopefully impress the freshly-elected Citizens' Council with its bright shiny readiness for the final stage of the war. Which no one had any actual plan for.

Right now the strategic situation looked discomfortingly like a stalemate. The Captains themselves did not speak such a word where it might be heard outside their own planning sessions, but they had little to offer the Citizens' Council beyond manly smiles and bold assertions.

Two Evolved line of battle ships protected Harrar's Reach, the final bastion of the enemy forces. The Collaborationist fleet still possessed what might be a formidable force on paper, but few believed even half its ships would contest an Alliance invasion, or that most of those who did would contest it very hard.

On their own the two Evolved heavies could still inflict heavy losses. Right at the limit of the Alliance fleet to absorb and far more than would have been thinkable before the war.

But there remained the fixed defenses girdling Thais, the main system sun. The estimate of fifty percent losses breaking through was regarded by some Captains as optimistic. As for the mysterious source that claimed it could reveal the codes to those defenses, since Sahan's deadly ruse at Aulaire, Solange had come around to Arvada's opinion that it was a trap.

That would definitely restore the upper hand to the pair of Evolved ships. And encourage the faint-hearted among Catalan's commanders to pitch in.

Thus the stalemate.

And thus the increasing pressure on the fleet to break it. Advocates of a near-future attack among the Citizens' Council and a fast-growing segment of the general population were not so ignorant as to write off the planetary defenses. They did, however, point out that if the two Evolved ships currently holding Harrar's Reach should be reinforced by two or three more, then any prospect for the *Reconquista* effectively vanished. So waiting brought its own risks.

Such was the situation when Arvada told Solange O'Grady she intended to make a reconnaissance-in-force inside the solarsphere of Thais.

The difference between "telling" and "asking" created something of a sore point. But they'd agreed Arvada would command the cruiser wing of the Alliance fleet. And as Solange herself pointed out: "If you ask the average citizen who commands the fleet, you'll hear a lot more Arvada Sattars than you will Solange O'Gradys."

To enter the solarsphere of Thais itself, ostensibly for close observation of the fixed defenses, Arvada would take only six of her cruisers. But her whole wing would be stationed near a Jump point near Aulaire, ready to make the leap into Thais should some target make itself available.

Somehow, once in the Aulaire system communications got crossed up. So that Solange never received notification that Arvada had stripped the other twelve cruisers under her command of close to every Marine and combat Rigger aboard, and stuffed them into the six cruisers of her deep penetration force.

With a peremptory knock on the door, Arvada pushed into Beck's room. The prisoner had been given access to the gym and every entertainment venue the ship possessed. Should he try to press further into any computer than this, one of several microchips implanted beneath his skin would cause very loud alarms to sound.

Arvada had even several times invited him to join her in the dining hall, hoping to render Beck and the crew less alien to each other. But he preferred to take his meals in his room, formerly assigned to a petty officer, where he spent his time lying on his back staring at the upper bunk. Which was how she found him now.

"Bestir yourself," she said. "I need to reach Sahan. You are going to help me."

He did not bestir. "That is a very bad idea, Captain, as your previous experience should have informed you. Classically bad. Epochally bad. A mistake for the ages."

"Your objection is noted. Of course there is no way I can force you to help me. That is, no way I am willing to employ at the moment. This precise moment."

"Leaving the possibility open?"

"Sahan always used to say, resist collapsing the probability cloud as long as possible. In your case the possibilities cover quite a wide range. A bigger question is knowing if I should trust you."

Still he did not divert his gaze from the bunk above. "Given that a state of war exists, and we are on different sides of it, I should think the answer would be self-evident."

"You'd think so, wouldn't you? Only I'm not so sure. I'm thinking that once inside the holobrain, if we actually do find Sahan, we'd be a lot smarter to stick together for mutual support. And if we don't find him and you decide to get tricksy, well, I know I cannot defend myself against Sahan. But I may be approaching the point where I can defend myself against you."

That got him to swivel his head. "Beware hubris, Captain Sattar."

"Beware me, Beck. And beware Ligea Romero, if I or my mind don't come back. Next to her, I'm positively anal-retentive about observing the rules of war. All my First Officers have been that way."

"I am not surprised." He got slowly to his feet, stretching ostensibly, though having practiced Push Hands with him, Arvada could not believe such a supple body could ever stiffen up. "They do say pets come to resemble their masters. Or is it the other way around?"

Arvada had never been wholly sure just what "insouciant" meant, but she was willing to bet the look on Beck's face qualified.

"Fun and games are over, Beck. Move it."

"Ready or not?"

"If you *ever* feel ready to meet Sahan in the holobrain, you're crazier than I am." The brusqueness was intentional. Arvada wished to hide Beck's uncertainties from himself.

She believed he still regarded himself as a relatively loyal Evolved. That all his images of his personal afterlife, good or bad, involved the Group Mind and the holobrain. And that he might even seek some good deed to make up for not going down with his ship when Arvada took it.

None of that looked promising.

Yet Arvada also believed, without daring to analyze it closely, that Beck was falling prey to divided loyalties. Not to the Alliance versus the Evolved; that was too straightforward, too ingrained for him to challenge.

More about the ultimate morality of his cause, and hers, and the whole twisted chain of circumstances that had brought him here.

And it was after all Arvada who'd gotten him his holobrain. And provided his only companionship. The same Arvada who'd taken his ship and held the power of life and death over him. Which while he might resent, might also strike something of a conciliatory spark.

Bring them to the surface, and he'd shut down all doubts at once. He was an Evolved. End of story.

But let his doubts about the war simmer some, let his hopes to stop before hostilities reached the same stage of genocide-or-nothing that doomed the Christians aboard the *Stephen Hawking*, and who could tell?

Chapter 27

A few months ago M'Dari would have rushed straight in with a wild slanting slash of her practice sword. And Sahan would have casually slipped to her left and back-handed her on the noggin just hard enough to see stars, that she might contemplate the probable outcome should she attempt the same wild-assed idiocy against a Rigger armed with a battle-saw. Let alone, Vishnu help us, a Marine.

Now, though, she made two darting feints with the tip; one to his forearm, the second to his leg. Sahan knew damn well they were feints but blocked down with his own mock battle-saw anyway to lend her encouragement. Whipping the tip aside, M'Dari slashed him across his wrist. With real weapons, he'd now be short a hand.

She giggled at her success, as the others around them laughed and stomped in appreciation. Grinders did not giggle often or attractively, their mouths not being well suited for it. And their laughter resembled trying to clear something firmly lodged in your throat. But Sahan found any amusement from them rewarding.

He bowed, acknowledging M'Dari's victory. Who knew? Now that she had faith in the move, she might practice till she actually became good at it.

Immediately he clamped down on his pleasure. The Evolved might not like it. They might think he was bonding with the Grinders again. They might remind him of the rules with PAIN.

So he scowled, invited the next challenger forward, and rewarded their sudden attempt a low sweeping attack at his forward shin with a firm thump from his saw, leaving them sprawled and twisting on the mat. The atmosphere turned more safely somber.

But not hostile. Or even apprehensive. The Grinders showed no more sign of their last little contretemps, when they playfully tore him to pieces, than his new body did. From time to time Sahan thought he caught them avoiding his eye, but he said nothing and neither did they. They remained eager to learn. Of course their lives depended on honing these close-combat skills. But he also felt, or thought he felt, some of that very bond the Evolved were determined to eradicate on both sides.

They preferred fear. So they'd orchestrated Sahan's integration with the Grinders so that from the first they feared him.

But fear was not true respect. The Group Mind had lost sight of that, since they were so far from their own origins. Fear bred obedience, but only up to a point. When other fears competed, such as was inevitable on the battlefield, then the Grinders would just bounce around in a panic among them. Instead of having enough true respect for Sahan to trust to his orders as their best survival option.

Lately, he thought he detected the Grinders beginning to accord him at least the beginnings of that respect.

Of course the Evolved discouraged that. Someone other than the holobrains leading their slaves? Who knew where that might end? So they tempted Sahan with visions of near-transcendence, then punished him by having his budding allies literally tear him apart.

Once again they confused fear with respect.

Even that, though, failed to broaden the gap between him and the Grinders. In fact Sahan thought their fondness had increased since they chewed through his outer layers, unraveled his insides, tore off his limbs, pulled off his head, and meant to roast his brains. Didn't everyone want to beat up their parents/teachers? He always did. Hell, the Dainichi would probably say he should welcome such acts of self-actualization.

And his sacrifice, if you just looked at it as such, dove-tailed in symbolic ways Sahan couldn't fully trace out but sensed, with their own creation myth.

And so the bond grew between them. Sahan did find his own low-key but palpable fondness puzzling. The Grinders had been robbed not only of all purpose beyond the next few minutes, but all qualities of civilized social behavior. Even Sahan could not pretend to be charmed by their rough but authentic primitivism. Rough it certainly was, but nothing authentic had happened to these people since their ancestors got half their brains scooped out of their heads back aboard the *Stephen Hawking*.

On the other hand, no one had ever liked Sahan much, either.

As for his attempts to teach them more advanced concepts of combat, learning came hard for the Grinders. But once they grasped a technique, they clung to it. And being free of squabbles over competing theories, they exhibited a facility for communicating physically what they'd learned.

Which deserved his respect in turn. Along with satisfaction that he'd reached these proto-humans in a way no one else, not a single soul in the whole of the universe, ever could.

Only he had to try to bank such emotions beneath his customary surface layer of anger, because the Evolved kept riding herd on his mind. So Sahan taught them what concepts he thought they could learn, while constantly telling himself his sole purpose was to forge them into the weapon that would deliver Arvada to him.

So when he felt some outer force probing at his mind, Sahan winced. Then tried to harden himself against any feelings at all. If the Evolved detected no emotion emanating from him, they might glide on by, thinking that whatever they'd detected was a false positive, or else an aberration suppressed almost as soon as registered.

Only the probing didn't stop. Though not increasing in intensity, it groped around the outer layers of his consciousness, seeking admittance.

Not the Evolved, then. They'd just bull on through.

Hypatia?

Don't even think it!

Only it wasn't Hypatia. She was never so clumsy.

Arvada.

Could it be?

Yes, now he recognized that touch. Probing for weakness. Where does it hurt the *most*? Having once found her way into the holobrain, the witch-avatar just had to return to make sure Sahan hadn't forgotten her enough to experience, say, a moment's peace.

She thought she was so clever, finding her way into the holobrain.

Let's see how clever she is at finding her way out again.

He'd give her a lesson she'd *never* forget. Not for a hundred or a thousand or a hundred thousand years. Or ever. Then it would be Sahan laughing. Laughing so loud she'd hear it even through her screams. As he still heard her laughter rippling through the worst of the PAIN.

Easy, easy. Throttle down. Start nursing sweet dreams about Arvada and the Terror Barrier, the Evolved would plunge down on him like a hawk. They didn't like him indulging his private fantasies. Quick and dirty, that was their way.

"Faster!" he roared at the Grinders. "Two at a time! Prove to me what you've learned. The more you've practiced, the less it will hurt."

The Grinders cast nervous glances at each other. Sometimes during these two-on-one drills Sahan could get rough.

Then finding assurance in numbers, or perhaps recalling the last time they ganged up on him, they started coming. Sometimes two, more often three or four. They weren't great ones for rules, the Grinders. Or counting.

They were also more skilled than they used to be.

Which helped. Because having blades, even practice ones, sweeping in from several directions at once emptied Sahan's conscious mind remarkably well. What he'd learned in life through effort and pain now repaid him in reflexes. Sahan glided across the floor, frequently bulling his way through onlookers or hurling them at the others to keep as many of his attackers as possible in a ninety-degree quadrant to his front, and hopefully tripping over each other.

Yet even when he succeeded, this tactic did not provide the same protection as when he first started training the Grinders. At that time a pair to his front would invariably both attack him directly, funneling their strikes toward a single point. Now, on the other hand, as one engaged to the front, the other would step to the side, then attack his flank, forcing Sahan to defend two points. Or more, as all pretense of order broke down.

Draw your attackers into a line, was the standard advice. Only this became harder as more of the Grinders ended up sprawled unconscious underfoot, forcing him to leap over them rather than step. Sahan hated leaping. A discerning attacker could predict where you'd come down.

He could have called an end to it, then lined the Grinders up to make sure they only attacked in pairs. But that would detract from his real purpose.

For as the exercise became more and more of a free-for-all, Sahan left other considerations far behind. All his will focused on the moment. He fought without conscious thought.

So powerful was his concentration, so direct his actions, that even under this wild attack by the Grinders a segment of his mind could float free. Something far deeper than conscious thought brought inner and outer worlds together. Combat became a dance, a cosmic dance, in which geometry and physics twined with blood and fury in a complex interaction straining toward a theoretically perfect conclusion. The fluctuations of the entire universe momentarily fixed in a single place and time.

Now a slice of that concentration, or madness as many had believed it, wisped down to the Terror Barrier.

Arvada could follow him here if she dared. The Evolved could not.

He waited. Around him, tenuous as ghosts, swirled the twist and turns, the cuts and parries, of the combat in the training hall. His eyes saw not the purple mists and lightning-strike weavings of the holobrain, but the grimacing jaws of Grinders and the after-images of their weapons streaking at him. Too many, too quickly.

He abandoned all restraint in his counter-strikes. Such calculation would pull him back to the surface.

The Grinder attacks slowed as more and more crashed against floor and walls.

Come, he urged Arvada. I cannot hold here long.

She joined him.

Not in the visual landscape of the holobrain, though that was in fact where they met. He saw her face shifting like a will o' the wisp from one Grinder to another. Though she should not have been able to reach out beyond her own small presence within the holobrain, somehow every face she took over attacked him on the moment. Now the combat whirled ever faster as Sahan took the offensive, trying to smash that face shifting so tantalizingly from target to target before him.

She spoke to him. Despising him because he was too slow to shatter her image as it flitted about the room.

Let us finish this, said the face. Her face. Her hated, wretched face. *You and I.*

No order remained in the training hall. The Grinders swung at him or fled from him soon as he came close.

And still he could not reach her.

I will be in the solarsphere of Thais, the face said. *With my cruisers. Meet me there. Just you, and your ship, and these bug-eyed minions of yours.*

Now he was taking blows. Lots of them. A few bites, but he moved so fast the teeth ripped loose before they found purchase.

Meet me there.

A flurry of Grinders flew through the air before him.

If you love me, meet me at Thais.

He screamed, a throaty, braying Grinder scream, choked with fury and pain.

And came back into the training hall.

All around him Grinders lay still, or writhed on the floor, or crawled away, or cringed along the walls. Moans and frightened mutters filled his ears. Most of his teeth and one eye were gone.

Sahan fell sobbing to his knees.

"It wasn't you," he called to them, his voice bubbling through the chemicals in his mouth that substituted for blood. "It wasn't you."

They only cowered further away.

Still on his knees, hands outspread, he turned his face to the ceiling, calling on the Evolved.

"I love them!" he cried. "See!" He waved one arm over the bodies lying still or trying to crawl away. "And I went back to the Terror Barrier. I disobeyed you. Give me pain!"

He braced, but nothing happened.

"Give me *pain!*"

Silence.

Falling back on his haunches, Sahan sagged forward. He watched the the vaguely mauve-tinted fluid that circulated inside him splatter on his knees.

If you love me, meet me at Thais.

He went on sobbing. Just sobbing, without tears, because those too had been taken from him.

Chapter 28

Would he come?

Could he?

Or would the Evolved drill into Sahan's mind deep enough to uncover Arvada's challenge, and turn it to their own ends?

In which case she just might lose her whole force. Six fast cruisers, their crews, and the nearly nine hundred Marines and combat Riggers she'd crammed aboard them. That would end the stalemate, alright. In favor of the Evolved.

Or would Sahan come, but trick her one more time?

The legend of Arvada Sattar.

Held motionless in the Captain's chair by the gravity of her own thoughts, Arvada stared at the main screens. As she'd done for hours now. The *Natessa* floated amid a simmering backdrop of stars, distorted by the heat beyond the screens' ability to correct. Around her the cruisers *Nerissa, Lyngheid, Kalki, Anata,* and *Mahamari* hovered nose up, engines fighting off the gravity well of Thais while rolling pillars of flame lanced up from the white-hot furnace below.

Though badly distorted, with max magnification and computer correction almost half of the largest habitats and colonies making up Harrar's Reach could be seen. Would they be free tomorrow? Or....

The bridge crew stared similarly transfixed. And not a little mystified. They'd been told to watch for an Evolved line of battle ship materializing out of Jump. They'd also been told the six cruisers of the task force would board it. Supposedly the enemy would not open fire on the attackers, just sit passively waiting for the combat troops to blow their way into its hull.

The proposition seemed extremely dubious on the face of it. As for the reason the Evolved ship would be so obliging ... none had been given. Just a warning that if the Evolved *did* start firing on them, they were to flee for the Jump point, opening up new frontiers for the engineering manuals.

From time to time Ligea Romero cast sidelong glances at Arvada. No doubt wondering if her Captain had gone as crazy as that other explorer into the holobrain, Sahan Kotori.

Earlier Arvada had called Ligea into the main conference room and tried to explain.

Before Ligea arrived, Arvada sat staring at a picture of Sahan displayed on the far wall. And herself. Taken back in their Academy days, it showed the two of them during a stroll amid the great forest of Maeda Rao Park, out of uniform and shockingly young. Not laughing despite the rare free time, nor peering up in wonder at the mammoth trees, some nearly as big as a hunter-killer.

Instead their pose — had they ever really been so young? — was much more typical of those days. They'd paused to face each other. Sahan was trying to explain some concept to her. The edge of pain and anger that gave his face rather a predatory cast even then, had opened into fascination with the idea he was trying to convey, and the fact that she was hearing him out. His spread fingers formed a bowl in which like an alchemist he tried to gather disparate elements into some at least arguable elixir.

She couldn't remember which wild theorem he'd been advancing. She'd forgotten too how blond his hair once was; stress had threaded it with silver over the years. Though graceful and well-proportioned, he appeared too slight and too young to establish himself as the terror of the Decahedron he was coming to be known as even then.

Arvada could not remember what they'd been discussing. Some conjunction of concepts everyone else had disregarded or dismissed or never imagined in the first place; she could be pretty sure of that. Sahan always bristled with ideas about things you could do with a starship. Or sometimes a universe.

If you were crazy enough.

But, also quite typically, he did not appear wholly sure of himself in the photograph; his eyes fixed on Arvada as if trying to convince her by force of emotion as much as argument.

And in the picture her twenty-year-old self stared back at Sahan in fascination; not like she believed him, but that he could even come up with a concept so fruitful of wonders. She held her head cocked slightly to the right, her mouth parted on one side in an incipient smile as if to ask: are you *serious*?

And yet her fascination was evident. Dooming him.

Or both of them. For what she looked like to her older self was a young woman involved far past the point she realized. A woman getting glimpses of future possibilities nothing else in her life suggested could exist. A woman who without any conscious romantic overlay had already begun to join her future with this wild man. Committing herself to this ever-flowing font of strangeness; a confederate who for wild-ass escapades, improbable adventures, and hair-breadth escapes no one else could ever match.

If she was crazy enough.

And somewhat to her surprise, she had been. They'd both been.

Only they hadn't known the half of it.

If you want to accomplish anything different, her mother once told her, anything that means anything, you have to dare yourself. Stay scared. Because as soon as you aren't rising to some challenge, you're losing ground.

Even at the time this picture of her and Sahan was taken, Arvada must have realized that her ... partnership, call it, with Sahan, would be one long dare. And that she'd spend a lot of her life obeying her mother's dictum, staying scared.

After all, what mother could possibly object to a nice young man like Sahan Kotori?

God, it hurt to see the two of them so young. So full of hope and playfulness.

But here the tale must end.

And yes, she was scared.

Ligea Romero's knock on the conference room door shocked her abruptly from her reverie.

"Come." She switched off the picture of her and Sahan, leaving a plain blue wall in its place. She stood as Ligea approached. They didn't bother with salutes.

"I issued a challenge to Sahan Kotori," Arvada told her. "Through the holobrain. I know this is difficult to understand—"

"With respect, Captain," Ligea interrupted, "it's impossible to understand. I will carry out whatever orders you give me. You know that. But I cannot promise to comprehend any of this weird shit — ah, I mean, anything to do with the holobrain.”

“No, of course not. My apologies. These ... people, the entity we’re fighting, the Group Mind, their world is so completely different. I understand very little of it myself, and I’ve been there. I just hope....”

She let it trail off. She wasn’t sure what she hoped.

“Arvada, listen,” said Ligea, invoking a rare familiarity. “I trust you. That’s all either of us needs to know. Whatever happens here, I’ll never question you, and you need never question me.”

“Thank you, Ligea. It’s been such a source of strength, knowing you have my back. The situation is this. I challenged Sahan to meet us within Thais’ solarsphere. In one of the two remaining Evolved ships.”

Ligea blanched a bit at that, stalwart soul that she was. “Six cruisers against an Evolved heavy?”

“We’ve done it before,” Arvada pointed out.

“Yes.” Obviously Ligea was working hard to fulfill her promise not to question her Captain.

“The enemy ship will not fire upon us.” Fingers crossed.

“And may I ask the Captain why that is?” Formality had restored itself quickly once an Evolved heavy entered the conversation.

“Because Sahan wants to get to me. Personally. To kill me.” And worse, but no need to tell Ligea that. “I will be leading the boarding party.”

Ligea’s lips pressed together, holding back the suggestion that she should be the one to lead the attack against the Evolved vessel.

“Understood, Captain.”

"Sahan doesn't want you. He wants me. I know this sounds grandiose. But the battle, and the war, will not end until either Sahan or I kill the other. Or we both do."

Ligea grimaced. Her own bet in such a contest was discouragingly clear. She'd known Sahan on and off through the years; sometimes liked him and sometimes not, but always held him in a bit of awe. Hardly likely that would decrease now that Sahan had in effect risen from the dead and been refashioned into a purpose-built weapon against Arvada.

"There is also a chance," Arvada said, "that it will be the Evolved themselves who turn up."

No. We have to prepare for that, but … no. Sahan won't let them. He won't let them reach me. And no matter what they've done to his mind, no matter how strong they are, I refuse to believe they can stand between him and me.

"We'll know," she said, "if they start firing on us. In which case, we run. Every ship for itself and devil take the hindmost. Since we're holding near a Jump point, hopefully we can enter grayspace before they get target lock."

And pick off all six of us.

"Understood, Captain," Ligea said with less than overwhelming conviction.

"Even if everything goes according to plan, it's going to be one bloody operation. Sahan will bring every Grinder he can get his hands on. I'm thinking that may be around four hundred. Five at the outside. From the way the Evolved have kept them out of sight despite all the disorder in the Reach, I don't think they have all that many left. And Sahan can't get his hands on all of them. We'll have close to nine hundred suits, though there's a couple of half-trained Rigger units I'm reluctant to throw in unless I absolutely have to. So we should have numbers on our side. I'm still expecting a bloodbath. But I say again, Ligea. Win this one, and we win the war."

"Yes, Captain. Ah, Captain?" Ligea looked pained; her eyes struggled to meet Arvada's.

"Yes?"

"Does Admiral O'Grady know where we are and what we're doing?"

"The fleet commander knows approximately where we are. She has not yet been informed of our plans."

"I see." Ligea took a deep breath, while Arvada wondered how this was going to come out. Then gave a rueful laugh.

"Well, I guess we better damn well win, then. The Evolved may be bad, and I always thought Sahan could be a little scary even when he was on our side. But piled on top of each other, they still can't be as bad as Solange O'Grady in a foul temper."

***

ARVADA MEANT TO FOLLOW Ligea to the bridge, but found Duncan Mallory waiting outside the council room.

For the past several months she'd assigned him to training combat techniques to the Rigger volunteers. Not really a job for the Earth observer, but Marine trainers were in increasingly short supply, and he certainly possessed the skill set.

Plus it kept him further away from her.

For the poor Earther was in love with her. He concealed his longing behind a mask of propriety, but every now and then an incipient warble crept into his voice when he looked her in the eye.

Arvada was not wholly without temptation herself. Since losing Sahan she'd been lonely in a way nothing in her life, even command, had ever prepared her for. Not that Duncan could ever fill even a fraction of that space. Her heart had hardened into a mace with bristling spikes. Memories of Sahan moved her. Thoughts of revenge against the Evolved moved her. Nothing else.

Her body, however, was not quite so exclusive. Arvada longed for even the momentary relief sex could bring.

And Duncan was the only person in the fleet she could indulge it with.

Arvada never even considered it. She'd seen too far into Sahan's nightmares, and knew damn well she'd played too far into them in life. She would not bring any to reality now.

Still, she could make such discipline easier on herself by not having to see Duncan's eyes fixed on her every move whenever she stepped onto the bridge.

Now seeing Duncan waiting for her, she knew just what he would ask. Previously Arvada had told him she wanted him to stay aboard the *Natessa* during the battle. As a representative from Earth, she was responsible for his safety.

He'd protested, of course. Volubly. So she'd cut him short, reminded him who was in command, and dismissed him still fuming.

Now with a profound feeling of resignation she sat back down and gestured him to a seat across the table from her.

"Captain Sattar," he began, "I must ask you to reconsider your position."

"Really."

"Captain...." Breaking off, he steepled his fingers against his temples. "*Please* do not ask me to stand around doing nothing while you board against God knows how many Grinders.

And Sahan Kotori, whatever he is now. What purpose can I possibly serve here? I'm not even in the chain of command."

"But you are an *observer*," she reminded him, even as she felt herself already losing this argument. "My responsibility to Earth is to see you do not get killed. Just being aboard during this mission is incredibly dangerous."

He snapped so stiffly upright in his chair you could all but see the ramrod projecting from his mouth. "As an observer, then, may I respectfully suggest that given the operations I have already experienced, you are full of shit *Captain*."

"I shall take it under advisement."

"I've been training these Riggers for months," he protested. "Though I'm an Earther, as you folk say, I fully believe I have gained their respect. More, I believe they have come to regard me as one of them in this war."

"I believe so too," said Arvada. "It speaks well of you."

She could not help notice how handsome he was. You might say boyish good looks, and that was what she'd seen when Duncan Mallory first came on board ... a year ago? But war had ironed the boy out of him. The less bounteous Peregrine rations had chiseled his jaw into a new angularity, and close-up examination of just how narrow the gap between life and death could be had focused his gaze into the slightly absent, slightly predatory look of those for whom life was just how you passed time between battles.

For he'd not just trained the Riggers, he'd fought alongside them. Leaving his official role behind, and with it, his official loyalties. Now everyone aboard regarded him as just one more of the crew. Except that they hoped his adventures might create some stir on Earth, and bring it faster and more whole-heartedly into the war.

Arvada suppressed a smile, recalling how Duncan, holder of some title or other on Earth, once asked her for permission to meet Sahan in the Decahedron. Fearing Sahan might already be tending toward jealousy, and not wishing to explain to Earth how their representative got killed in a friendly bout, Arvada refused.

If Sahan might have killed him then, he certainly would now.

"Captain?"

"Yes. Duncan." She'd been daydreaming. "I will tell you the truth as best I can. I have been able to get a glimpse into Sahan's mind."

He looked horrified. "How?"

"By entering the holobrain."

"The holobrain? But you never told ... sorry, Captain."

"The Evolved have turned Sahan against me. They have turned him into a monster of hate. They have filled his mind with images of me mistreating him. Laughing at him."

"Please let me come with you. To face him alone—"

"*You* are one of those images. In fact, you appear in several. Right now Sahan believes I betrayed him in order to, ah, conduct an affair with you. If he knows you're among the boarding parties, he'll head straight for you. He'll want to kill you first, just to taunt me with it."

"He may not find that quite as easy as he thinks."

"Oh, but he will. No, Duncan, don't protest. *I* know him. I know you both."

"Sorry. Captain. But even so, it still must be better for us to face him together."

"If I allow you to come," she said, "knowing what I know, then I am responsible for you." She held up a hand to forestall his objection. "You don't feel that way, but I do. I will have quite enough to deal with meeting Sahan. I just can't afford to worry about what's happening to you."

"Then don't." And when she started to object: "You've deliberately been avoiding me. I respect that — Captain. It may not be what I hoped, but after all you've been through, all I could do was offer support where I could and stay out of your way otherwise. I hope I have acted decently."

"Your behavior has been impeccable." Another good man she'd brought to pain.

"So I went to train the Riggers, as you assigned me. Only it's become much more training *with* the Riggers. I have learned so much about your people. And ... respect is the wrong word ... it has *moved* me. So much and so deeply. Same as I have been moved by you. Sorry about that last bit. But this is the time for truth if there ever was one. I cannot be a Peregrine. But right here I have the chance to make myself part of your story. And nothing matters so much to me. If I fight here and die, I die for a cause I" — he looked away from her — "I love. I die knowing I have made myself part of your heritage."

She was touched. And yet it was still murder.

"But if I sit this one out," he said, "while men and women I care so deeply about, who I would share my life with, go on to fight and die, then what is left to me? A life of regret and guilt. A life in exile from the cause and the people whose quest I want more than anything else to be part of. And if you, Captain, should die, God forbid, while I sit here, maybe watching it happen ... then every breath I take thereafter will be bitter with shame. Would you condemn me to that? If your cause isn't worth dying for, then how can you call on all these others to fight?"

She could not leave another man with nothing but bitter memories.

"Choose a platoon of Riggers," she said, before she could think better about it. "You will serve as my headquarters defense." After all, how could you know who would live, and who die?.

"Thank you. From the bottom of my heart." He hesitated, then leaned forward, earnest as a man could be.

Her body stirred. Days of fear accelerated other bodily impulses.

"Arvada...."

"Dismissed."

The last private conversation Arvada had before ensconcing herself on the bridge was with Beck. She found him contemplating the holobrain. The golden sphere repulsed her. She could not trace her distaste to any specific thought.

Had she truly contacted Sahan? She believed so. She could not have mistaken that blast of hate. Had he understood what she meant to tell him? Could he carry it off, in the face of the Evolved? Could—

Stop it. The die is cast. Remember the challenge Sahan used to taunt you with: You are Arvada Sattar. Now prove it.

If you love me, meet me at Thais.

And what about Beck? Would he try to warn his masters through the holobrain? Arvada might detect such an attempt. More likely she would not. Even if she did, it might be too late.

She could have him sedated. Heavily. So heavily he couldn't even dream, and possibly give away information indirectly. Of course since she had no idea what degree of sedation might be necessary to still his mind, she'd have to err on the side of caution. For her, not him.

It was the smart thing to do. The only thing to do.

"You may return to your quarters," she told Beck.

"Captain Sattar. I would talk with you."

"Go on," she said, thinking: *don't press your luck.*

"Understand, this is difficult for me." No insouciance now. His eyes, usually so direct and challenging, engaged hers only through main force of the muscles tightening from mouth to forehead.

"Speak. But understand. I have just challenged Sahan to battle. Whatever you have to say, I want it quick, I want it direct, and I want it truthful."

"Yes, Captain. What the Evolved — what we — did to Sahan Kotori, is wrong. Just wrong. In thus subverting his humanity the Group Mind went too far. As it did with the Grinders, and the Christians before. Perversions. All of them perversions. In doing this, we have defined ourselves as something other than I believed us to be."

Arvada struggled to order her conflicting emotions. A perversion? A puppet? Yes, but it hurt her to hear it declared so openly. She still hoped to save Sahan. Somehow. She had no plan. Not beyond killing him, should luck favor her. And to hear Beck assert out loud what she had tried to hide from herself, destroyed at a blow her stubbornly persistent fantasy that love would still somehow find a way.

"There were reasons for what was done," Beck stated, obviously struggling to maintain his composure. "There always are. But not good enough. Not for me."

She felt no triumph. Perhaps because this show of humanity lowered the barrier that always allowed her to think of him simply as the enemy, and expendable.

"Captain?"

"I'm listening."

"We underestimated you badly. You and Sahan Kotori in particular, but your whole people. We acted like your lives were nothing but a minor prelude to the destiny we planned for you. We held individual life to be unimportant, even among ourselves. We held that any belief in anything but the Group Mind was no more than a primitive superstition to be eliminated through the most direct means possible. We held the human form itself to be so arbitrary we could do with it as we chose. And worse, we showed the same contempt for the human mind."

"In other words," said Arvada, "you declared yourself gods."

"Not gods," he returned hurriedly. "Not...." He stared at the holobrain, as if it would answer all questions. "Maybe gods," he conceded. "Certainly something so far beyond human it excused all lack of humanity."

"Does this mean you will help me?"

"I cannot fight the Evolved, Captain Sattar. That is far beyond my abilities. Even Sahan Kotori can overcome all my efforts. But should you enter the holobrain, I will help you in any way I can."

"Be more specific."

"I can't. You are a human being, going to fight something that doesn't bleed, or fear. You go to fight a monster, Captain. A monster that to my vast regret and shame, represents my people."

He swallowed. "I can only hope you slay it."

Chapter 29

"Suit up!" Arvada called, first over shipwide, then ship to ship. "All personnel suit up."

She did not need to add that this was not a drill. Everyone aboard all six cruisers had been waiting in apprehension for the Evolved line of battle ship to mirage into sight.

Since there'd been no telling when it might appear, Arvada ordered everyone to keep their suits and weapons close at hand. Now before Sahan's great blue-black plow-nosed ship, warty with weapons clusters, could even settle into solidity, pairs of Marines, Riggers, and crew helped each other fairly dive into their suits, plugging in each other's pigtails and cross-checking oxygen and fuel lines. Those growing up in environments separated from space by nothing more than a thin shell tended to cultivate alacrity in donning suits.

Then all hung still as the force of six cruisers waited for Arvada's next orders.

Hello, Sahan. So you kept faith.

If you love me, meet me at Thais.

Well, here we are.

A sudden squeezing of her heart startled her. Did she, could she love the monster, in Beck's words, in addition to the man?

Even as the thought ran through her mind Arvada scanned the readings on the monitor before her. If the Evolved ship opened her weapons pods or bracketed the cruisers with targeting beams, every Captain was under instructions to flee toward the Jump point at all hazard to the engines, and not wait for Arvada to signal the retreat.

"She's just hanging there," Tarika Okada's voice sounded within Arvada's helmet. She stood behind the workstations curving around the front of the bridge, in command of sensors and weapons.

Arvada had planned this all out beforehand. Or thought she had. Now, with over fifteen hundred people's lives depending on her next move, she wavered as she could *swear* she felt Sahan probing at her mind.

Or could it be Beck, betraying her?

No. The sensation, though faint, all but screamed of Sahan. That overwhelming yet patient urgency. That mocking familiarity, as if he knew Arvada better than she knew herself. Which all too often he did.

"Beck?" she called over their private channel.

"He is here, Captain Sattar. And full of rage."

Very well. Ignore the sensations of your body. Enact the plan.

"Captain?" asked Ligea Romero.

"Attack! All ships attack! In after her!"

Inertia pushed her gently back in her chair as the *Natessa* accelerated toward the Evolved ship. Still no fire came from the heavy's batteries.

Arvada unstrapped herself from the Captain's chair.

"She's all yours," she told Ligea.

"Captain, I'd still like to go with you."

"Permission denied." And more softly, on the XO's channel: "I want you there too, believe me. But Ligea, if this operation goes nova, I need you to save whatever can be saved."

As she said it Arvada realized that in her heart she did not truly expect to come back.

Never go into battle presuming defeat.

But getting killed did not necessarily mean defeat. Not if she took Sahan with her.

Giving Ligea's arm a quick squeeze, Arvada walked toward the elevators at the rear of the bridge, leaning slightly against the acceleration. She hardly felt her feet touch the ground. Nerves.

She rode down alone. The bridge held only essential personnel. Everyone not considered absolutely necessary at some shipboard station had been assigned to the boarding party, the med teams, or damage control.

In order to squeeze in more infantry, not just the cargo bays had been converted into staging areas, but the hangar bay as well, the task force having left nearly all its auxiliary craft beyond the last Jump zone. In both cargo and hanger bays a second deck had been jury-rigged to double the space.

Arvada took the rail car to the central bay. The lower staging area was crammed with white-suited Riggers and a lesser number of blue-suited Marines, all hooked to lifelines running fore and aft in case the *Natessa* went into sudden gyrations the inertial dampers couldn't handle.

She should give some kind of inspirational speech. Should have thought of something beforehand, but she'd had too much on her mind.

She called up General Address to speak to the entire task force. She felt pins and needles running all through her.

"This is Arvada Sattar. I won't lie to you. The coming battle is going to be one tough mother. But if I didn't believe we will win, I would not take you into it. I also believe that today we have the best chance since the war began to defeat the Evolved once and for all. I am proud to stand among you. You all know your jobs. Let's go do them."

She fell silent. Rather to her surprise, the deck before her erupted in cheers. Whole-voiced and prolonged. Through her earphones she heard muffled echoes from other troops arrayed in other hangars.

Hear that, Sahan? That is *me*. Because I am one of them. One among the living. And I am coming for you.

A pang hit her, though she kept her face suitably determined for any of these cheering fighters who might be able to see through her faceplate.

Coming to free you at last.

Closing on the Evolved ship, the six cruisers fired off salvos of rockets to breach her hull. On screens overhead or on feeds to their faceplates, Arvada and the waiting soldiers watched areas on the Evolved's hull flash yellow-white. The flashes hit in succession, clearing almost instantly except for whirling fields of debris. As the salvo ceased, half a dozen gaping cavities ringed by petals of peeled-back steel formed a ring on the Evolved's hull. Storms of debris still blew from the holes. Pebbles rattled all along the *Natessa's* hull as, approaching the enemy, she deaccelerated.

This time the attacking ships would not clamp directly on. Should Arvada once more prove wrong and fall into a trap, at least the cruisers would have a chance to escape, along with the infantry reserve.

But those fingers groping at her mind told her Sahan was indeed here, and eager to finish this once and for all

The cruisers swung belly-forward to the Evolved's hull, holding fifty meters off. Arvada waited for the shrapnel bouncing off the hull to quiet. Eight seconds, nine, ten ... good enough.

Elation finally obliterated apprehension.

"Boarders away!"

***

THEY FLEW THROUGH SPACE, headed for the six metal-toothed cavities the cruisers had opened in the side of the Evolved ship. Hundreds of them, the white suits of the Riggers stark against the black of space, the blue-suited Marines all but invisible on visual, though the exhaust trails of their jetpacs showed bright red.

Arvada flew toward the rear of the first formation. Somewhat guiltily, but she meant to kill Sahan, not die in the initial assault. She kept waiting for her helmet siren to warn of incoming fire, along with streaks from her radar and motion detectors and possibly a violent lurch from the suit's autopilot.

Nothing happened. Sahan did not choose to defend the beachhead.

But so deep in the solarsphere were they that for open space it was hot, damnably hot. The moment Arvada flew out of the yawning cargo bay her suit had whined to signal excessive heat, and the temperature reading throbbed in eye-straining scarlet across her faceplate. She issued the mental command to kill the display.

The suits could handle the heat for the short distance they had to travel. But in addition, everyone's jetpac was maxed out, tilted down at nearly forty-five degrees as they struggled against the gravity of Thais. Instead of fading centimeters from the nozzles, the infrared exhaust trails tailed out seven or eight meters amid the ambient heat.

Below the swarming invaders the fusion zone glared white even through the faceplate filters. The magnesium-yellow tongues of flame erupting from Thais appeared intent on gobbling the swimmers up like a superheated whale. Lose power, and you wouldn't float, you'd sink. Straight down into the flames.

So disregarding caution as to what might lie within those holes, Arvada, along with everyone else, crossed the gap as quickly as she could.

Her boarding party arrived inside the Evolved ship without casualties. The space they occupied had been thoroughly chewed up by the cruisers' missiles. The Riggers and Marines fanned out along twisted beams sticking forlornly into space, and thirty-meter sheets of bent and rippled deck plating.

Arvada saw her people primarily outlined in red, in the center of which flashed small flashing silver transponder signals to fend off friendly fire. The jackstraw landscape itself glowed faintly red through the green outlines of radar. This close to Thais the material had absorbed so much heat that even gaping open to space it did not dissipate at once.

The inertial dampers in this section had either been destroyed by the missiles or deliberately shut down. Of course there were no lights, not from either side.

Holding to a section of beam by her toes, Arvada communicated with the leaders of the other boarding parties. All fared the same.

Why? This would have provided excellent defensive terrain from which to pepper an incoming force.

Could it be a trap after all? Did Sahan really have to be here for Arvada to feel him trying to claw his way into her mind, as she did even now? She wasn't in the holobrain, but—

Or was she? There would be a holobrain in this ship. Could Sahan pull her into it against her will? Maybe even without her knowing?

"Captain?"

It was Duncan Mallory, at her side and concerned about the sudden stiffness of her body.

Pull yourself together, woman. If you're going to see ghosts at every turn you better get these people out of here right now.

"Move out," she said. Then repeated the message on her command channel. She checked to make sure that sniffer drones, both flying and creepy-crawlies, were sent out ahead to check for whatever they could find, including caches of explosives. Who knew what Sahan might do? Judging from the scratching at her mind, he knew damn well where she was. He might be perfectly content to blow up as much of her force as he could, helping guarantee a more private rendezvous for their final reckoning.

Was this whole operation a bad idea?

What the hell are you doing?

Sahan had gotten into her head. Soon he'd be running this operation, if she let him.

Make your mind one-pointed. What are you here for?

To kill Sahan.

Get to it, then. And let nothing stand between you and him. No matter what it looks like.

Chapter 30

Arvada's force, divided into six detachments, probed cautiously into the Evolved ship. They entered a dust-choked landscape crumpled in on itself, dimly outlined to their night vision in vague traceries of gray-green, out of which sudden glowing red figures flew at them like demons, leaving a wake of blue and yellow lines.

Sahan must have blown up half the ship to create a terrain so well suited to the Grinders. Wherever line of sight exceeded ten meters, favoring fire from rocket launchers and flechette rifles, the Peregrines saw only vacancy, daring them to enter. Where they crawled on their bellies amid clouds of ash through torn bits of metal effectively imitating outsize barbed wire, with their sensors clouded by dust and their shoulder-mounted weapons nothing but an encumbrance, there the Grinders were sure to pounce.

At least a short way into the ship the inertial dampers reasserted themselves. Otherwise the air, already thick with ash, would have been nothing but a prickly metallic soup.

Bodies, both the silver-green suits of Grinders and the blue or white of Peregrines, littered the ground more and more thickly as Arvada crept and duck-walked through the wreckage. She kept her best estimate of twenty to thirty meters back from an illusory "front line." Often, crawling through the tight stuff, she could see the bootheels of the advance troops ahead of her.

Grinder bodies outnumbered those of her own troops, but not by as much as she'd hoped. Nowhere near. Reports from all six attack groups indicated that the Grinders were fighting more effectively than previously. Less blind fury, more calculation. And more skill with their weapons.

One other thing caught her attention. The Grinders' heads no longer exploded as they died.

Sahan.

He'd not only taught the Grinders how to fight more effectively, he'd disabled the holobrain's influence, that by stimulating them with chemicals, drove them into a frenzy. He'd also somehow suspended the mechanism that signaled their heads to explode in the moment before death, so that their primordial fear would not fly directly to the Terror Barrier, adding to its strength.

The Grinders still fought with ferocity, but they'd added cunning.

Arvada discovered this for herself moving her "command post" — Duncan Mallory and a bodyguard of four to twelve Peregrines, depending on how broken up the terrain — down a slanting forty-meter slope of ruptured deck. Explosives had pockmarked the rippled surface into a checkerboard of pits and protrusions covered with a thick layer of ash. Twisted beams arced overhead like the bones of dinosaurs.

With the gray-green blurs of radar so blurred by the dust, Arvada ordered a couple of flares tossed ahead. In general it was thought that dark favored the Peregrines, since their implants made them more efficient at reading and reacting to the sensors. But amid all the metallic ash the sensors themselves were operating at diminished efficiency.

Besides, too much of her concentration went to maintaining communication with the other attack groups. The increasingly abstract landscape, slippery with ash underfoot, was too treacherous and irregular to navigate on sensors alone.

With the flares providing a spluttering light full of dancing shadows, she started down the slope with her escort spread around her. The "ceiling," varying anywhere from one to fifteen meters overhead, was nothing but an irregular expanse of metal masticated beyond all guess of what function it once served. At intervals high-pressure steam shot up or down from buried and ruptured pipes. One suddenly erupting spout, bright red in her infrared sensors and hissing like a snake, missed Arvada by less than a body length. The pressure covered her suit and faceplate with moist hot metal ash her helmet blowers could not entirely clear.

So thick was the dust she had to supplement the existing air with oxygen from her tanks. The dust itself was fine and sharp-edged, abrasive to faceplates and clinging like burrs to suits and sensors.

The air filters could not douse the scent of burnt plastic and metal. Or her own sweat. Or of the eviscerated bodies scattered across the slope.

She worked her way down, weaving around the areas where the irregular mass above almost touched the deck. She kept crouched even when space opened overhead, because the ever-present ash lying thick across the slope constantly threatened to slide away beneath her boots. In some places she slid along on her butt. Like the others, her uniform soon became covered with a film of metal dust, black to steely gray. Presuming the same would be true for the Grinders, she tried amping up her magnetic sensors, but the whole area became just one blur, so she shut it down.

And all the time Arvada kept receiving and responding to a constant stream of messages. Each of the six cruisers had inserted around one hundred and twenty soldiers into the Evolved ship, holding some back in reserve. Though all six forces still moved forward in distinct clusters, they kept their flanks linked at all times.

Arvada wanted to keep the Peregrine force coherent, but moving on a broad front. That way if any section got halted, the others could execute flanking maneuvers around it, hopefully encircling and eliminating the attackers. A second reason was that despite the sniffers, the terrain ahead remained uncertain. She did not want to bunch up her force only to find it trapped in a box canyon of wreckage, dust, and Grinders.

But for all her fine intentions, keeping the separate columns of her force in supporting distance of each other proved increasingly difficult. The wreckage through which they fought their way was not uniform. Some areas were so badly collapsed and ash-choked as to be wholly impassible. Soldiers might wriggle through in single file, but aside from ripping their suits open on metal barbs, the danger of being picked off one by one as they crawled with their bodies cramped into near-immobility was too great.

Other areas had not suffered the same degree of collapse. Here movement was slow — and almost invariably opposed by Grinders — but progress could be made without losing formation altogether.

Yes, the Grinders were exhibiting a skill surprising to those who had fought them before. Casualty reports squeezed Arvada's emotions like a fist. But at any given point the Peregrines still maintained a local superiority of numbers. If not, the idea had been that they could hold until support came from the flanking units.

But the time lag for such support was increasing dangerously.

Arvada knew that at all costs she must avoid another localized massacre, as had overtaken Sahan aboard the *Enodia*. That was simply unthinkable. And just the sort of maneuver Sahan was likely to try in order to thumb his nose at her. Let her know what it felt like.

Yes, yes, he must have something like that in mind. She must pull all the groups together. Bunch them tight as possible. They *must* outnumber the Grinders. Keep them bunched up and....

She'd done what she had to do! Sahan's leg, the calls of WHY?—

Where was she?

Arvada froze, trying to reorient herself to the here and now.

That probing she'd been trying to shut out had broken through.

Sahan.

Voices in her earphones called for instructions.

Beck! she cried inwardly.

Duncan was at her side, holding her elbow to steady her. She shook him off.

Beck!

And he was there, in her head. Arvada did not know how. Maybe it had something to do with the holobrain aboard the Evolved ship.

Beck steadied her. Held forth measured, even pulsations, slowing first her heart, then her brain rhythms. It did not shut out the urgency or the worry. But it enabled her to resist them.

Arvada fell back on a time-tested formula: Screw you, Sahan.

Mental tricks aside, though, Arvada could tell from reports she was getting about the landscape that Sahan was trying to shepherd them. How could he have staged a series of explosions so precisely as to spread out the approach points?

Because he was Sahan. And now he offered Arvada the choice: either let each attack group venture so far from each other as to become effectively isolated, or gather them up in one bunch, forcing the formation into a snake-like configuration with a narrow head dragging behind it an exceedingly long tail. So that at the foremost point the Grinders could batter the advance with equal or superior numbers. Or else attack the flanks at a multitude of points.

Progress would be slow. More like glacial.

Arvada was not at all sure time was on her side. She did not believe the Evolved had authorized Sahan's action. Otherwise they'd be here already, happily blowing up her, Sahan, Peregrines, and Grinders alike. He'd slipped the leash, but for how long?

The Evolved don't have half the control over him they think they have.

But even Sahan couldn't make an Evolved line of battle ship plain disappear from Harrar's Reach. Sooner or later the other one would be along, visiting fire and brimstone on both sides.

Sahan would know that.

But would he care? All he wanted was time to meet Arvada and take her with him into the Terror Barrier.

But he had to split off some of her forces first. Arvada had been right; he'd never had much more than four hundred Grinders to start with. And he had a whole lot less now.

The risk to getting her forces too spread out wasn't a massacre. The numbers didn't run that way. On the other hand, if they did drift beyond any quick mutual support, Sahan would have evened the odds at the point of conflict.

She called Torrance Severin, first officer of the *Lyngheid*. His detachment was furthest out on the left flank, with the terrain pushing them further in that direction. He'd called for instructions a few minutes ago, and Arvada, still trying to wipe Sahan from her mind, had told him to wait.

"I don't want you drifting any further out," she told him. "Contact Jessamin Fauré with the *Anata's* advance. Work out coordinates for the closest spot behind you where you can cut over and come in behind her. Together your forces will form our left flank."

"Acknowledged. And if the terrain opens up again, should I still keep my people in support of *Anata*, or move left to widen our front?"

"Contact me when the situation presents itself. Until—*Shit!*"

"Captain?"

But Captain Sattar was otherwise occupied. Because as she half walked, half slid on bent legs past a depression on her right, a steel-gray figure coated so thoroughly in dust that its infrared signature was no more than a dull amorphous blur sprang up out of the ash and swung a vibra-sword at her near leg.

The leg bent to take her weight as she half slid, half stomped down the slope, her foot buried in thirty centimeters of ash.

Chapter 31

As the Grinder swung its vibra-sword at her knee, Arvada threw herself sliding down the slope, only her right leg got mired in the same ash that had concealed the pit from which the creature sprang. She held her battle-saw in her left hand, too far to bring around in time.

On instinct she performed two actions simultaneously. One was to utter a shrill little whimper. The other was to utilize the only movement available to her. Even as the sword swept forward she did not drop so much as *pull* herself into a deep squat.

ZWANG!

With a shower of sparks the sword glanced off the flechette rifle projecting down from its shoulder mount, three millimeters short of the muzzle.

Arvada fell on her back as her heels shot out from beneath her, wrenching the trapped knee. A sheet of ash blew up around her like a steel-gray shroud. The Grinder was a red blur above her.

Twisting left, to strike again.

Once more Arvada did the only thing she could do. She rolled, or rather bounced, straight into the Grinder's legs, holding the battle-saw above her.

ZWANG!

Glancing off the circular blade of the saw, the vibra-sword slid along her helmet.

Zwiiiiiitch!

But the angle was wrong, the Grinder was already starting to fall, and the blade scraped by without penetrating.

Arvada kept rolling, bumping her foe's sword-arm out of the way with her helmet and partially burying the Grinder's head in the ash of the pit from which it had sprung. Legs folded, she used the full power of the suit to bounce to her feet.

The Grinder rolled in the other direction. Thinking it was trying to give itself room to jump up as she had, Arvada crow-hopped forward to cut it in half. The Grinder was barely more than a blob in both visual and infrared.

But she did not miss the whip-like streak of dull red sweeping toward her ankle.

Good idea, but not quite good enough. Arvada lifted her forward foot. Barely in time, as the underlying ash sucked at it. The vibra-sword swept past and before the Grinder could reverse the stroke Arvada swung the battle-saw with her falling weight behind it into the Grinder's back between the shoulder blades. A torrent of blood, its heat wisping upward like a departing ghost, gurgled through the suit.

But the Grinder's head did not explode.

Which almost made Arvada strike again before she could convince herself the foe was well and truly dead.

Oh Sahan.

Why had he suspended whatever mechanism exploded their heads at the imminence of death? For the Evolved would never make such a change. They'd blocked the Grinders from the final microsecond of death-knowledge to keep the primordial terror from accumulating in the Terror Barrier. The Grinders themselves being isolated from the Group Mind, they would not be affected. But all those motes of panic in the face of death would build up over time, rendering the Barrier even more impenetrable.

Sahan was trying to sabotage the transition from Living Evolved to the Group Mind. He'd gone rogue. Again.

Arvada could not suppress a moment of admiration. Even after rebuilding his brain, the Evolved showed no more luck in controlling him than she ever had.

No wonder he believed he could carry Arvada down into the Terror Barrier. He'd even redecorated their crypt.

Fear replaced admiration. Death, okay. She was a soldier. But to be trapped in hell with a madman laughing at your every torment?

Shake it off. Think you're scared? So is every man and woman who followed you here. So go kill the bastard.

Duncan was at her side. He did not ask if she was all right; in a fight with battle-saws and vibra-swords wounds were immediately and grossly apparent. And her mind didn't show, though Arvada felt it must be screaming loud enough to alert everyone aboard.

"I never thought to check the depressions," he told her. "So obvious, too, with all this ash all over everything. I'm sorry."

"I didn't think of it either." She saw several fresh Grinder corpses lying across the slope, blood still pumping from the dreadful cuts inflicted by the battle-saws.

And one dead Rigger. She did not want to know who.

"It is your function to coordinate the battle," said Duncan. "Mine to see you aren't killed doing it."

He sounded so abject.

"Well, just see that it doesn't happen again," she told him. "Like you say, it's not my function to get killed."

Not until I meet Sahan. Then we'll see.

Incongruously, she laughed. She had no idea why. Duncan stared like she'd just gone barking mad.

"Move out," she ordered, as overtaking them, the rearguard stared at the bodies. And at their Captain. Who wore a wide sash of blood and glittering metal ash across her front.

As they reached the bottom of the slope Arvada made a mental call to Beck again.

Are we moving in the right direction?

He did not answer in words; the two of them were not linked that strongly, or perhaps her ability was lacking, because he understood her questions well enough.

But a small irritation in her brain, like sand forming into a pearl, pointed out a direction, though she could not say just how.

There lay the holobrain. Shut that down, and you shut down the Grinders. So she believed Beck was telling her.

Of course his knowledge, valuable as it might be, came from a time before Sahan had ensconced himself among the Evolved.

Arvada felt no surprise at all when the direction her brain told her to go matched the most accessible path through the wasteland Sahan had made of the ship.

He was inviting her in.

***

SLOWLY, ONE HARD-FOUGHT METER at a time, the Grinders were driven back.

Because they'd suffered so many casualties? Or because Sahan was pulling them in for a final counterattack?

Losses were horrendous on both sides. Over two hundred and fifty Grinders confirmed dead. Among the Peregrines, the number was a little under two hundred, though forty-eight wounded were being evacuated to the cruisers still standing off the Evolved's hull. Wounds in fights with battle-saws and vibra-swords were pretty grim; if half survived that would count as good fortune.

Ominously, a still unknown number were missing, indicating that the Peregrine formations were breaking down.

It was far from the almost two-to-one kill ratio the Alliance had come to expect.

But Arvada still had nearly four hundred and fifty fighters under her command. She doubted Sahan had half that number. Plus she had a reserve.

Which she several times considered calling up, then cancelled the idea.

In truth, she feared that Sahan — or the Evolved, emerging suddenly from Jump — might yet destroy the ship. In which case why lose two hundred souls she did not yet know were necessary?

So the Peregrines advanced against only spotty resistance, closing in steadily on the holobrain. Arvada had consolidated the original six groups into three, each around one hundred and fifty apiece. Otherwise they'd get hopelessly spread out. Parts of the ship had been all but fused together.

Even thus reduced, the three prongs were still forced to fan out further and further. While Arvada's central force met virtually no opposition and a relatively clear approach, if you didn't mind crouching and crawling.

Sahan was rolling out the welcome mat.

At last she ordered the two flanking forces to try to come in behind her. Then she tried to establish contact with Beck.

Instead, it was Sahan's presence that boomed forth.

She did not see his face; that is, the Grinder face he now wore. His words came across as a mumble, clouded perhaps by her not being in the holobrain. Not wholly. Not yet. But his anger, that rang like a warning siren as she filled in the garbled message from her past knowledge of him:

You called on me to meet you. Here I am. Obedient as always. What now, Arvada? Our destiny stares us in the face.

His rage, and his confidence, sucked at her nerves like undertow.

She tried to answer him: Sahan, this is not you. This is what the Evolved have made of you. I loved you. Always. I tried to hide it, and that cost us both. But try to see past what the Evolved have done to your memory. Can you not feel anything of the love we shared?

But in answer there came only that same withering blast of hate she'd come to expect. No memories remained to him of their love. No more than their God remained to the Christians who'd also had their beings altered by those who went on to call themselves the Evolved.

You'll have to kill him.

I know.

"Captain? Arvada?"

Duncan again. And again at her side. Blurry in the light of the flares glinting off the steel dust heavy in the air.

"Are you all right?" And when it became obvious she wasn't: "Is it him?"

Now Arvada wished she'd granted him a private channel. They couldn't take off their helmets to speak privately. With so many steel particles floating in the air they'd be blinded in minutes.

She didn't want to offer him up to Sahan's vengeance. But if she tried to order him away, at this point might well refuse to leave her. She couldn't have the others confused and worried over her problems with discipline.

And he'd earned the right. His dream lay here. And if the price was his life, he would at least die living it.

"Move out," she ordered. "The holobrain lies close ahead. There we will find the rest of the Grinders. Along with Sahan Kotori."

What is your plan for victory?

To fight. Nothing more. What more could be worth planning, against Sahan?

She wanted to retreat. Not for herself, but these others. Only they'd come too far. And maybe, just maybe, the war really could be won here.

Besides, some force she could not resist pulled Arvada toward him.

As it always had.

Chapter 32

They moved forward uncontested.

Though Arvada had lost contact with Beck, she hardly needed his guidance. The maze of destruction they'd fought their way through ceased, leaving an open passage through corridors and halls.

Arvada did not believe Sahan would spring a trap without some grand flourish. She nevertheless ordered a halt while the last of the sniffer drones were deployed.

Though the drones had exhibited a high casualty rate, this batch returned unscathed. With pictures of several entirely passable routes forward. Beyond that, the probes indicated an indefinitely vast and apparently open area amid the crazy-quilt chaos Sahan's demolition had left of the ship. Here extensive jamming had caused them to turn back.

Just to be sure, Arvada sent patrols ahead while waiting for the last of the flanking forces to report in. The extra troops would assure her of superior numbers, though this was somewhat illusory because confined in such narrow quarters she could not deploy most of them. Still, they would be there in support if through some deviltry Sahan forced her lead element to fall back in disarray.

Arvada briefly tried to determine the numbers facing each other, then soon discarded the effort. She did not think that at this point the battle would come down to Peregrines versus Grinders.

The patrols returned to report they could go no further than the probes due to a large screening force of Grinders blocking the way.

The holobrain?

A throbbing sensation began to invade Arvada's skull. It had been there since she first entered the ship, but now it grew steadily stronger.

Sahan again.

She expected mocking laughter. That challenging air he so often had, even when you did not know just what the challenge was about.

Not now. The presence grew in her mind till she could practically imagine him standing next to her.

But not in laughter. His passion exuded a wave of heat even through her suit. Of course it would; it was psychological, not physical. Thank God, or he'd burn her to a cinder where she stood.

Desire. That's what she felt. Not sexual, or rather not primarily, though Arvada felt his presence probing her body, trying to clutch her close, to force his mouth — his human mouth, not the Grinder mouth he now wore — upon hers.

But his desire far transcended the physical. He wanted *her*. Every aspect of her being, her mind, her life ... and most of all, her eternity. He wanted to fuse them all together in one eternal scream. To which he would join his own. That was his idea of victory. His lust for vengeance was risen to superhuman heights, that he would inflict such suffering even on himself.

Turn.

And.

Run.

"Troops from the flank forces reporting in now, Captain," said Duncan.

She stared in confusion, momentarily lost in another realm. As reality settled into place she knew she saw a dead man walking.

"Thank you, Commander. Bring your force" — what was left of it — "forward with me. I will lead from here."

Chapter 33

AGAINST ALL CONVENTION, AGAINST all Duncan Mallory's objections and her platoon leaders' as well, Arvada strode at the head of her troops into the cavernous area that held the holobrain.

The Grinders stood bunched at the far end of a central corridor close to fifty meters high. At the sight of Arvada's force they advanced in a slightly bunched but still discernable matrix formation. The Riggers and Marines formed a phalanx to meet them. Though scarcely more than a third of the suits available to her, Arvada could see that her force still outnumbered the approaching Grinders, if not by much.

"Hold!"

The voice resounded in her skull.

Arvada knew none of her own people heard it, since it came through the holobrain. But the Grinders received Sahan's order clearly, and stopped at once.

"Hold positions!" she commanded.

The two sides faced each other from thirty meters away, silver-green suits on one side, blue (but dismayingly few) and white opposite. They'd been slaughtering each other for a good two hours, but instead of wearying them toward any inclination to truce, the urge to finish off their enemies showed plainly in both sides' strained, half-crouched postures and quick bee-hum bursts where over-eager fingers tightened on the triggers of battle-saws and vibra-swords.

The imminence of the holobrain remained strong in Arvada's mind. Though she saw Sahan nowhere, she felt him pressing her right here in her head.

Would she really have to fight him?

Though she'd risked so much, and expended so many lives for the chance, here and now the prospect became something she would have preferred to leave for later. Much later.

Beck had told her that the holobrain on this Evolved ship would be much more complex than the captured specimen aboard the *Natessa*.

In fact there was no single holobrain, but rather a multitude of them, lining both sides of the corridor from front to back. Each holobrain lay shielded within its own opaque sphere, which flashed various colors, most tending toward the red end of the spectrum. The spheres were suspended some twenty meters overhead within a network of pliable cords stretching from floor to ceiling. So numerous were the holobrains that the webs blocked any view of the walls beyond.

One aspect of Arvada's surroundings nagged at her, but took a moment to parse out: metal dust no longer filled the air. Finally her nostrils could dispel the stink of powdered steel and fresh-spilled blood.

On a raised platform at the far end of the hallway, Arvada saw a machine fluted as a church organ, flashing colors like the spheres, but much more brilliant and ranging through all known shades and some her suit might possibly read but could convey to her only in indistinct and shimmering shades. The ever-flowing patterns were incredibly intricate, combining sometimes into fractals, sometimes into flowing abstractions.

Onto this platform walked Sahan. Of all the soldiers in the room, nearly two hundred on Arvada's side and what looked like around one hundred and fifty for the Grinders, he alone wore no suit. Just a pair of dark green pants.

Did he think to fight her without a suit? Artificial body or not, Arvada could hardly believe Sahan would dismiss her skills so contemptuously.

His presence swelled in her mind as he stepped down from the dais before the flashing lights and came forward in a slow, stalking walk, the Grinders parting before him. A battle-saw drooped casually from the long tendril-like fingers of his right hand.

Arvada told herself to go meet him, but the savagery of his appearance, along with the pressure of his presence in her mind, glued her feet to the floor.

Passing through the Grinders, Sahan stopped some ten meters away. Even without a suit, he stood taller than anyone in the room. His face was gaunt, skull-like even for a Grinder, and emphasized by the way the jaws stuck forward, lips drawn back over two white, outsized, deadly rows of teeth. His eyes were great dark ovals, set perpendicular in his head and reflecting light like a cat's. His skin, which Arvada knew to be no skin at all, glowed in shifting shades of golden green, darkened or brightened by the pulsing lights of the surrounding holobrains and the machine at the back of the hall.

Arvada felt herself sweating under the strength of his rage. Her suit's cooling system, designed to preserve her in far more extreme environments, could do nothing to lessen that heat.

Fight him. You must fight him.

She stood frozen.

More than fear held her back. This horror in front of her, perverted in body, mind, and soul, still held all that remained of Sahan. Seeing him, feeling him, Arvada knew she would never turn him from his wrath.

Even so, the thought of truly fighting him, of killing *Sahan*, sorely cramped her heart.

The field created by the holobrains rippled strongly through her head.

"Sahan," she called. One last appeal torn out of her.

"You should not have come."

"I had to. Like you."

And with that Arvada stepped forward, hoisting her battle-saw to port arms, and sick at heart.

Duncan Mallory ran out in front of her, his own saw raised. "Duncan, no!"

It almost seemed that Sahan, his eyes fixed on her and his saw still hanging down from his hand, would not even acknowledge the attacker. Then Duncan made an evasive leap to his right, carrying him past Sahan as his saw swept down.

Sahan sank and twisted. The movement brought his own saw around loose and blurringly fast. Arvada exhaled hard enough to jar her solar plexus at the terrible familiarity of that style.

The blade ripped through Duncan's suit at nipple height. The harsh rip of the suit parting around the blade did not quite drown out the wet plash of Duncan Mallory's heart being cut in two.

Duncan buckled from the knees as a high-pressure gout of blood painted the green of Sahan's body with red lines and splotches. The blade of Duncan's battle-saw glanced off Sahan's shoulder. If the Earther, who'd always wanted so badly to fight Sahan, had remained conscious just a quarter of a second longer, the saw might have cut off Sahan's arm. But the nerve signals to the finger had stopped instantly, and as Sahan straightened, no more than a shallow cut in the sheath and underlying bands that made up his body constituted Duncan's final legacy.

Arvada struggled to recover her breath. The scent of blood again filled her nostrils. For several seconds it bubbled in a scarlet fountain from Duncan's chest, but such a flow could not long maintain itself.

I let him come. All the time knowing it must end this way, I still let him come. Well, he is most surely one of us now.

Sahan's curse, sent through the holobrain, crowded all further grief and guilt from her mind.

"*That* was the man you betrayed me for! The two of you together sent me to *this*." He pounded his Grinder chest with his long-fingered Grinder fist. Wiping a hand down his blood-stained chest, he held forth the reddened palm. "Now *this* is my answer to your treachery."

Too late, she thought dully. Too late for Duncan, too late for all of us. Our fate has brought us here. Now that fate must be fulfilled.

Arvada stalked forward to kill or be killed.

***

WATCHING DUNCAN DIE, ARVADA finally fixed her mind on killing Sahan. Anger and shame drowned all regrets, and all fear.

But her attempt at single combat was frustrated. This time by every single Rigger and Marine advancing with her.

Sahan laughed. A deep, grim, smoldering sound, yet not wholly without that familiar note of caustic disdain she knew so well.

"Halt!" she commanded. Her people did so, with a shuffling reluctance.

Oddly, ominously, the Grinders never stirred.

New impressions afflicted her brain. The stench of Duncan's pooling blood filled first her head, then her entire body, with a shivering nausea.

Which almost immediately changed into ... an aphrodisiac?

Blood. She Craved more blood. *Lusted* after more blood.

Sahan had no blood. But whatever circulated through him, that would do. Arvada advanced on him hungrily.

Only to be paralyzed by another sensation. Echo-location bounced off the surroundings directly into her brain. As was supposed to happen, but only when she turned it on. Which she hadn't. It hit her with the force of a punch.

Her whole visual field perceived nothing but glaring yellow spider webs surrounding her, while at their centers throbbed the predatory spiders themselves — the holobrains, in bright, bright red, because now infrared too had cranked itself past levels the sensors were ever meant to transmit, or the brain to absorb. And neither her mental nor her verbal commands could turn it off.

Then the motion detectors started jarring her whole surroundings. Already blind to all but the yellow webs from which glared glowing red spider eyes, Arvada's sight began darting about involuntarily, trying to track motions darting by faster than either eyes or brain could cope with.

"Out of your helmets!" she warbled into her control channel, as nausea threatened to make her vomit. "Everyone, out of your helmets! Help each other detach your pigtails!"

She worked to unclamp her own helmet but the procedure, practiced thousands of times at emergency speeds, eluded her as her fingers turned spastic as her eyes. By the time she finally plucked the helmet from her head she bled from several torn fingernails and was screaming from sensory overload.

And still the ordeal continued. Detaching the pigtail that transmitted the sensors' inputs to her brain was awkward at the best of times. Now with her fingers pecking disjointedly while her eyes and stomach and ears quailed under fusillades of inputs her brain couldn't process, it became impossible.

Arvada knelt by a Rigger rolling helplessly on the ground, clawing at her helmet instead of unclamping it. The responsibility of command steadied her just enough to fumble the woman's helmet loose, while her own helmet jerked painfully at her pigtail, further jarring the storm of inputs. Finally she managed to detach the Rigger's pigtail. The woman swiveled to her knees, wide-eyed and panting hard.

"My God! What just—"

"My pigtail! Snap it loose!"

The woman stared uncomprehending, her brain not yet steadied into the real world. Arvada slapped her, watching four herky-jerky hands sweep across to slap four herky-jerky faces. The Rigger gave a start, then with much fumbling and painful yanks detached Arvada's pigtail.

Arvada held her hands to her temples to try and fix her head in place. Now she understood.

The implants. Brain structures transcribed from sharks to pick up scent and magnetic resonance, infrared from snakes, echo-location from bats and dolphins, motion detection in part derived from frogs.

Reports from the *Geniah* expedition warned that the holobrain had turned their own implants against the Peregrines. But the claim had been glossed over, partly to avoid conflict with Earth, and partly because these conclusions came from Hypatia Wren, the sole survivor among the Peregrines, and were dismissed as an attempt to disguise her own culpability for slaying half the crew.

And now Sahan, Hypatia Wren's only ally, had found a way to use the same tactic against the Peregrines here.

Grabbing her saw, Arvada tried to stagger to her feet. Instead she bounced, slammed an arm against the floor, leapt into the air, and made three hopping attempts at landing before finding a precarious balance.

Without the pigtails, the suits were crippled. Though they could respond to the pressure of the limbs, without any direct connection to the motor sensors of the brain, the logarithmic mechanism could not be properly controlled.

Forgoing the massacre offered them, the Grinders still held in place. Did Sahan enjoy the spectacle too much to bring it to a close?

"Out of your suits!" shouted Arvada, as a number of Peregrines, though free of their helmets, still bounced around dazed and uncoordinated.

Finally the Peregrines shed their powered suits. And stood with weapons clutched, gathered not into any fighting formation, but clumped together for the false impression of support.

Sheep to the slaughter.

Sahan had beaten her. Only not just Sahan. In fact it was Arvada's own hubris that brought her here. Her ridiculous illusion that some fugitive remnant of love might yet inspire Sahan to the worship he'd long held for her. No doubt because she was Arvada Sattar, and the universe but a red carpet rolled out beneath her feet. The role her mother groomed her for, and Arvada's own vanity had grasped at.

Now that vanity had rendered her the self-deluded commander from hell, leading those who trusted her straight to their doom. If Sahan did after all manage to take her into the Terror Barrier, would she hear their dying cries there, as he still heard the dead of the *Enodia*?

Sahan stood watching her from black, cave-like eyes. Kneading her mind with his intensity, his hatred enclosing her like a vampire's cloak. Without taking his gaze from her, he waved his free hand behind him. The Grinders, who had bunched up behind him as the Peregrines revealed their helplessness, once more parted, opening up a corridor to the sparkling machine at the back of the hall.

He beckoned to Arvada.

"It is time."

She did not even think to refuse. Grabbing her battle-saw, she followed Sahan down the passageway, up onto the dais, and into the arc of reflected, ever-shifting light forming a shell around what must be the Evolved ship's central, coordinating holobrain. All along the platform the lights writhed like maddened supplicants before the great machine.

Near the fluted base of the structure Sahan swung around to face her. His presence throbbed in her head.

Arvada knew she had entered deeper into the holobrain. She could see beyond the enclosing field of light, see the hallway where her armed but unsuited troops, having followed her as far as they could, bunched together, uneasily eyeing the Grinders who having let them through, now flanked them on both sides, still immobile, with the lights of the machines playing over their faceplates.

Could her people see her? Arvada did not know. They couldn't pass through the arc of light; their futile pushing and pounding gestures revealed that.

She and Sahan had stepped into a separate realm. His realm. If he defeated her, as now seemed inevitable, he would share with her in eternal torment the joining he had failed to share in life.

He raised his saw to middle guard.

"Sahan, wait. We—"

"You will never laugh at my pain again. Because from now on, our pain will be one."

Resigned, Arvada raised her saw.

Chapter 34

AT THE BASE OF the great machine, its variegated lights twisting like a ball of snakes, Arvada advanced on Sahan.

They circled each other, battle-saws held forth, just beyond range without some preliminary movement. Sahan's green-gold skin slithered from near-black to near-white beneath the shifting lights. His black eyes too reflected the hypnotic patterns of the machine.

He would not kill her outright. Not if he could avoid it. That would rob him of his full revenge. First he meant to cripple her. Then while she lay bleeding, physically helpless and mentally weakened, Sahan would exercise his strength within the holobrain to pull her down with him into the Terror Barrier.

Arvada tried to press down the queasiness that image inspired. Too abruptly. She had to pull back quickly as her body tightened. Sahan slid forward in response. Arvada felt the pressure of an impending attack. Then he thought better of it. Once more they circled.

Arvada told herself she needn't think of winning. That was too great a challenge. She need only kill him. If she died in the same moment, she'd achieved what she came here to do.

She resorted to the merest hints of footwork, trying to draw him into a premature reaction. Sahan ignored them. His black eyes, with the colors from the holobrain weaving patterns across them, never wavered from her own.

The Grinders and Riggers pressed up against the light barrier had gone still. Perhaps they too felt the weight of eternity hanging over the scene.

She and Sahan had become locked in a battle of sheer concentration. Which she must surely lose. Committing herself to the attack, Arvada lunged left and forward, leaving her head open because he'd be reluctant to strike such a fatal blow. Her battle-saw darted toward his forward leg.

Only where she meant to set her foot down, there was suddenly no floor.

Metal jaws clamped down hard on the Evolved ship and shook it like a flag in the wind. The thunder of metal fusing under heat and pressure bulged Arvada's eardrums.

Dizzied, she staggered downhill, easy prey for Sahan.

Except that he, with his battle-saw poised to take her arm off, was backpedaling frantically down the same slope. Beyond the cave of light from the main holobrain, the webs holding its lesser fellows shivered, snapping hard enough to launch nearby Grinders and Peregrines through the air.

The ship steadied.

What was going on? That impact hadn't come from any weapon ever mounted aboard a fast cruiser. Had Solange O'Grady penetrated Arvada's duplicity and brought her heavies through Jump?

Where was Sahan?

Instead of cutting her down he'd run to the base of the machine. Dropping his battle-saw, he pulled open a panel invisible to her. He plunged both hands inside.

Her chance! Arvada strode toward him, trying to suppress all guilt at striking from behind — it *was* still Sahan, sort of.

Only before she could reach him a second shock, along with its Doomsday clatter, sent her skipping sideways as once more the deck lurched.

That wasn't Solange. Even the Alliance heavies couldn't jolt an Evolved line of battle ship that way.

Arvada saw no screens to tell her what was happening. Without her helmet she could get no feeds from the cruisers.

Then she realized. The firing hadn't come from any Alliance ships. They would not fire on their own troops.

But the Evolved would fire on Grinders, and Sahan, without a qualm if it meant destroying Arvada along with such a large force of Peregrine infantry.

In order to meet Arvada's challenge Sahan had gone AWOL, taking one of the two Evolved ships still in Harrar's Reach with him. That he could master the holobrain enough to accomplish such a feat must have come as a profound and most distressing surprise to the Evolved.

A surprise they now must terminate at all costs.

Even as Arvada searched for a way to avoid this doom and came up empty, she could not escape a trill of pride that she and Sahan between them had driven the Evolved to such desperate measures.

But all satisfaction fled as a third shot sent ear-piercing reverberations into the room from every direction. The glowing machine intensified its colors to blinding intensity. The holobrains vibrating in their webs issued a monstrous groan.

Fainter vibrations came to her through the deck. Arvada recognized the slithering hiss of rocket tubes, and a more ratcheting progression of ... a rail gun?

Sahan was returning fire.

Incredible. He could still master this ship's batteries with the Group Mind doing everything it could to stop him?

What *was* he?

Even so, this ship could not possibly match the enemy's firepower. Not after the way Sahan had smashed it up. At best it might force the attacking ship to longer range. diminishing the accuracy of its barrage this close to the sun and its blurring radiation.

Sahan, Arvada realized, was trying to buy time. Because time was all he cared about. Enough time to pull Arvada down with him into the Terror Barrier.

He stood no more than four meters away, his hands still engaged inside the alien machine. His mind was working so hard to master this ship and its defenses his whole body quivered with the strain.

Kill him, kill him.

What held her back?

Kill him, or spend eternity screaming.

This ship would be destroyed, and all her people with it. But that would happen anyway.

Raising her battle-saw, Arvada charged Sahan's naked back.

Chapter 35

In the moment that she ran forward with her battle-saw upraised, Arvada fully meant to cut Sahan's green Grinder head off. He stood with his back to her, his own battle-saw at his feet, his hands engaged within the machine that generated the dancing lights.

Did her resolution falter before she could strike? Did some stubborn bond of love misguide her feet at the last moment?

Or did her attack fail simply because another crashing jolt from the second Evolved ship knocked out the inertial dampers, launching her off the deck so that her battle-saw bounced in a shower of sparks off a glowing semi-circular tube half a meter above Sahan's head?

The force of Arvada's blow knocked her away from the fluted columns. She windmilled, instinctively hunting for some resistance to bring her against either the floor or the machine.

Chaos enveloped the chamber as the inertial dampers, reeling from the shock, blinked on and off, assigning up and down at random. Riggers and Grinders floated jammed together in drifting mats. There was some rough warding off with untriggered swords and saws, but remarkably, no streams of blood sprouted from the ungainly knots, probably because no one on either side dared start such a carnival of blades while thus locked together.

The dampers steadied. Only horizontal to their original orientation, smashing Arvada shoulder-first into one of the fluted surfaces, two meters above Sahan's head.

The shifting gravity forced him into a push-up position to keep his hands active inside the panel. Arvada registered the faint sounds and vibrations of rockets and what she presumed to be rail guns.

Eternity hung in the balance.

Arvada lunged down, or across, the rippled surface with all the power of her legs.

Only to have the inertial dampers suddenly reorient themselves to normal.

Shooting straight past Sahan, she pointed her battle-saw down to break her fall. She hit the deck clenched as tight into a ball as she could get, taking the impact on her shoulder-blades with a force that launched a solid kick to the back of her neck.

Still she managed to use the momentum to continue the roll, slamming her feet down to lift her as she spun around. She landed facing Sahan, battle-saw held in middle guard before her.

He stood facing her, much closer than Arvada expected. His saw dangled in one hand at his side. She thought his pose oddly laconic.

She lunged, directing her saw straight at his chest.

He cut her left hand off.

It took Arvada a moment to accept what had just happened. Despite the pain, the spurting blood, the emptiness beyond her wrist bone, and the battle-saw drooping in her other hand, it was still quite a large adjustment to make.

Even as her mind tried to catch back up with reality she swung the battle-saw with her right hand, hoping to catch Sahan by surprise.

With the extra power of the suit she might have had a chance. Now the blow was clumsy, and he caught the weapon's stock in his hand. Twisting it from her grip, he tossed the saw to the side, followed by his own.

Arvada thought of kicking at his knee, but why look silly? This was Sahan, and her balance was already queasy from loss of blood. She must face whatever fate awaited her with whatever dignity she could muster.

Her knees slammed against the floor as Sahan grabbed her left forearm with his right hand and levered her down. She stared fascinated at the stump of her wrist, the way the white bone washed in and out of view beneath the blood bubbling from the welling flesh.

Riggers beat and lunged against the arc of light enclosing her and Sahan. It remained impervious, an impenetrable wall of sliding light.

Would the spurting blood have time to kill her? Or at least deplete the oxygen to her brain sufficiently for her to sink below the threshold where Sahan could conquer her mind?

That would be nice.

Damn, she was tired.

She winced as Sahan squeezed her forearm like a vice. Arvada thought it needless brutality.

Oh, a tourniquet. Of course. Even demented, Sahan retained that irritating pragmatism.

But acting as a tourniquet did not allow him sufficient freedom to move. Arvada caught the scent of burning. She stared around, confused, then saw it came from Sahan's left hand. The skin or whatever substituted for it was starting to smoke. And beneath that, to glow red.

How did he do that? Amazed, Arvada looked into his eyes. Big black pools. Steady and workmanlike, no more. Pain was no more than a goad to Sahan. A sweetener for his revenge.

She screamed as Sahan pressed his left palm over the stump of her hand; she couldn't help that. She gagged, halfway between choking and retching, at the scent of burning flesh and blood. Her flesh and blood.

Pull yourself together, woman. Is this Tai Chi?

She took one look at her wrist and quickly turned away. You could serve it on a plate. But now that the wound had been cauterized, there was no chance she would die or lose consciousness before Sahan dragged her down into the Terror Barrier.

Damn. Now her only hope lay with the Evolved.

Who obliged with another volley, rattling the ship from its plow nose to its tripartite stern. The vibrations beat against her knees. But Sahan, the room, and the machine making the lights were all still here.

When was that cross-eyed AI in the other Evolved ship going to pull its head out of its electronic ass and blow this wreck into muons?

Apparently not soon enough.

Sahan's left hand, black and misshapen, still gave off wisps of smoke. He released his grip on her left arm. Arvada clutched the stump to her chest.

Sahan laid his right hand against the side of her head. Arvada started to pull it away, but of course that did no good. His mind was already flooding into hers; it wasn't strength that failed her, but will.

In quick succession she witnessed the images fueling Sahan's hate. In particular the one in which she and poor slain Duncan forced him into the hunter-killer, in effect surrendering him to the Evolved.

Speech lay paralyzed. Otherwise Arvada might have protested that these scenes were not her. They had nothing to do with her. They were all fabrications of the Evolved. That a wholly different reality bound her and Sahan.

Only she was no longer so sure. Seen from a distance, and Arvada felt increasingly distanced from herself, the falsehoods did contain a certain rough logic. Love or hate, or both together, the force that twined her and Sahan about each other surmounted their individual lives. They could live a thousand times over, and each sequence, from tragedy to joy, love or hate, would be no more than a permutation on an immutable theme.

But the consolation of philosophy fell short. Fear invaded her. Fear of dissolution, a terror that could not be fought because it began with the corroding away of the Self. Will and courage shrank to very tiny motes within a very large void.

The searing pain from her burned hand spread through her body. Then beyond, so that even as she dissipated into the universe, Arvada knew she'd find that pain waiting to claim each separate molecule.

She stared upward. Where a moment before had stood a Grinder, she now saw Sahan in the human form in which she'd always known him.

The holobrain? Or Sahan further dominating her fragmented mind?

Forever, she heard Sahan's voice echo in the vacant spaces of her consciousness.

Forever.

Forever, she acknowledged, surrendering up to him all that remained of Arvada Sattar.

Chapter 36

Forever, Arvada heard herself repeating, in answer to Sahan's call.

Spiraling down into pain and terror, but still following where he led because this was Sahan and she knew that wherever it ended, they belonged together.

Forever.

Then the fear and the pain and the hypnotic fascination of *forever* faded.

Arvada Sattar returned. Still kneeling, she knew not whether her eyes were open or shut. Within the holobrain, it did not much matter.

Sahan was stepping back. Slowly, reluctantly. Still in his human form. Still with the antic lights of the great machine lighting up the conflict quivering across his face.

Arvada lurched to her feet, heedless of the pain as she used her left hand to push off the floor, forgetting it was no longer there.

She stood facing Sahan. Such agony in his eyes! He appealed to her, the urgency of his plea resonating within her as if they shared the same soul.

But for what?

She held out her good hand to him. Trying to project outward the love that might save him from whatever danger approached.

He took a step toward her.

Then halted.

"Sahan," Arvada called. "Come to me."

Though shaky on her feet from shock and loss of blood, she took another step toward him.

Then she too froze in place.

From the background of light a figure began to emerge, come walking. Then another.

The first figure emerged from the haze of light into not-quite flesh. A woman black-haired and ethereal. Very tall, very slender. Beautiful, in an angular, slightly disjointed sort of way. But with eyes that seemed to shine out from within a different universe.

Hypatia Wren.

Arvada recognized her at once. Not from the pictures she'd seen of Hypatia in her star-crossed youth, but from the force of personality she carried with her within the holobrain.

And the figure trailing her?

As it gained shape from the light Arvada recognized her as the same woman Sahan had fled from the last time they met in the holobrain.

Mirai Allan.

Looking like a sixteen-year-old girl, though she'd lived through a full career.

Then Arvada understood. This was the Rigger girl who'd fallen in love with a Christian boy. Whose own heart had stopped when the purge robbed him of his mind. Leaving her emptied of all but the crusade for truth.

In the same way, Hypatia Wren appeared fixed in age at the time when she would have suffered the loss of her own lover during the *Geniah* expedition. Following which she descended into a coma to seek out the holobrain, and embark on her quest for revenge.

Arvada wanted to fall to her knees in reverence. These two women had made sacrifices literally unimaginable.

For love.

And for truth.

But Arvada found their appearance here most ominous.

Though in appearance a girl, Mirai limped along with a hunched and dragging gait that bespoke immense pain, inner and outer.

Hypatia, in contrast, approached Sahan in a long-legged graceful stride. With obvious reluctance, he turned away from Arvada to face her.

"Sahan," Arvada called, trying to will him back.

The ship shook to another salvo. The lights that formed Hypatia Wren and Mirai Allan jiggled, then settled back in place. Corporeal once more, Hypatia reached out a hand. Tenderly she touched Sahan's face.

"It is time."

Sahan hunched, head down. There followed a long trembling moment in which Arvada thought, hoped, he might turn back to her. In love or hate she did not know, but she could not bear the thought of being parted from him.

Sahan raised his head.

"I know."

Hypatia caressed his face with both her hands. "Sahan Kotori. Born to love, born to pain." She kissed him.

"Sahan, please," Arvada moaned.

Sahan did not turn.

Hypatia stepped aside. Sahan walked toward Mirai Allan. Who reached out her hands, beseeching. Pain screamed across her face.

Arvada started forward, but Hypatia checked her with a hand on her shoulder. Though seeming a creature of light, her touch could not be resisted.

I'm losing him. This time forever.

"Sahan...."

He took Mirai Allan in his arms. They embraced.

And Arvada was hurled backward by the force of their touch, and the years of agony suddenly bursting free. She slammed against the great machine, then crumpled to the floor, a vast hollow ringing in her head.

She still called *Sahan!*

Where he had been, she sensed only a coalescence of agony far beyond her comprehension.

Then the universe tore itself apart.

Chapter 37

Dɪᴅ ꜱʜᴇ ʀᴇᴀʟʟʏ ꜱᴇᴇ ghosts?

Later Arvada would strain to recall if the figures ever assumed an actual image as they winged from the space where Mirai Allan had just dissolved into a swirl of colors. Though her mind sought such solidity, memory failed to recreate it.

But at the time, cowering on the floor at the foot of the great machine with its fluted columns of light, shielding her face with her good hand, *ghosts* was the word that came to her.

For their emanations fairly screamed of the Terror Barrier: fear, emptiness, a degree of isolation beyond the realization of any living being, and of which Arvada understood even a fraction only because she herself had been dragged through the boundaries of that realm.

The ghosts' naked desperation pressed her down like a physical force.

Then she saw Sahan writhing and stuttering out gasps from the pain he'd taken into himself to release Mirai Allan.

Arvada crawled to him, pushing through the force of the ghosts, pushing through the fear, pushing through the pain in her burned and severed wrist.

But as she reached out, Sahan too began to transform into light, as Mirai Allan had done.

"Help him!" she pleaded to Hypatia Wren. But Hypatia herself was fading fast.

"Sahan!"

Hold him hold him hold him. Hold him here.

I can't!

"Take me with you!" she cried.

Then she lay alone, clutching air.

Only not quite alone. Because all around her there still flew the ghosts or spirits or wraiths released from their entombment within Mirai Allan. Arvada cowered away from the long-compounded hunger the years in the Terror Barrier had bred into them as they searched for faith, for certainty, for love, within a realm that contained only fear and emptiness and pain.

Lost souls indeed.

Lost souls now swarming like bees toward the nearest source of life that might possibly regenerate them, and at last ease their loneliness.

Not the Grinders and Riggers jostling about outside the arc of light. These minds, these souls, were impervious, and anyway existed outside the holobrain.

Not Arvada. She could not possibly encompass them.

Only the Group Mind offered refuge. Because only it possessed the scale of transcendence that promised to make them whole.

And so they flew straight toward it.

Carrying all the horrors of the Terror Barrier with them.

Chapter 38

As ARVADA WATCHED THE ghosts freed from their long gestation within Mirai Allan fly deeper into the holobrain, seeking the Group Mind, walls the Evolved believed would stand for all time fell in a moment.

The great machine whose cavern of light still encased her began to tremble. An unearthly moan struck her from inside and out as the fluted columns twisted and ground against each other. Arvada tried to clap her hands over her ears until the pain reminded her that one hand was no more than a burned stump.

The lights playing across the machine's face blurred into splotches, all fractal order disintegrating into spastic jerks. Pieces began to crack off the columns. Arvada, already huddled on the floor, watched the Grinders and Peregrines beyond the boundary of light hit the floor as the translucent shards shot whirling through what had a moment ago been an impermeable barrier.

Beams of light speared through the holes left by the broken sections. They lit up the room beyond in overlapping, glaringly bright colors. Arvada saw the separate holobrains in their rows of webbing glow to white heat as they began to vibrate ever more violently.

Time to get the hell out of here.

Arvada ran through the fast-fading wall of light into the welcoming arms of her troops. Normally they would not have dared touch their Captain, but the loss of her hand made them eager to support her.

And at first she needed it; the loss of blood and perhaps even more the shock of watching Sahan sink into the horrors of the Terror Barrier overwhelmed her. Had she known how to join him, in that moment she would have.

But if that option ever existed, it was clearly dying along with the wreck of the machine that, transmitting the Group Mind, also served as a bridge.

"Suits!" shouted, pushing away the supporting hands. "Everyone! Move, move, move, people!"

The Riggers and Marines ran to the front of the hall, a few lingering as they saw her stay right where she was. They could not leave her alone before the Grinders, all suited up with weapons in hand.

"I said *move*, dammit!"

They moved.

Arvada braced herself. She'd felt steadier in life, but she'd do. She had to take command.

She faced the Grinders. The lights emanating from the machine, more frantically now, still played across their faceplates. But she didn't need to read their expressions. Some connection to them, faint but perceptible, lingered through the holobrain, distressed and weakening as it was.

She sensed no fury, no aggression among them. Dread she felt, a profound confusion over what should happen next. Never in their existence had they known one wholly unguided moment. Now the holobrains had fallen silent.

She felt in them too a profound sense of loss. Had the ghosts instilled that in them through some sort of resonance? They were after all the Grinders' ancestors. The Grinders' brains might still retain something of a mirror-image reflection of the emptiness that was all their Christian forebearers had been left with.

Now the Grinders tried to fill that emptiness with an image of....

Sahan?

Sahan. His picture, his Grinder form, came clear to her through the holobrain.

Arvada suppressed a sudden impulse to cry. It just struck her as miraculous how Sahan, even as the anger-bound creature the Evolved had made of him, still managed to infuse these wild, half-human beings with something as close as their circumscribed brains could fathom to love. Even if such emotions far exceeded their ability to express or even accurately feel them.

Which left her where? The Grinders had watched her and Sahan pass together into the cave of light. They'd seen the two of them fight. They'd seen Sahan cut off her hand.

Yet now it was the Peregrine Captain, not Sahan, who stood here before them. The one against whom their leader had led them in vendetta.

Had he lost? Incredible. The idea presented a whole new world they were wholly unequipped to face.

And what of the Masters? Where had they gone? Had this Peregrine killed them too? Appearances suggested nothing else.

Should they avenge Sahan? Or bow down before this creature of clearly overwhelming power, who might yet offer them the only guidance the universe might hold out to them?

Arvada became aware of what felt like a weakening of gravity. At first she thought it another vaguery of the dampers.

Or a ship beginning the plunge down into the heart of the sun.

And without that far to go.

Get out. Fast.

And the Grinders? Leave them here? They didn't seem much of a threat. And they'd just hinder the evacuation of her own people.

Decide. *Now.*

For Sahan, then.

"The war is over," Arvada told Grinders. She doubted that under normal conditions they would understand her. But her recent emergence from the holobrain seemed to offer some degree of communication.

"The Evolved — the Masters? — are dying. Sahan, Sahan your leader, killed them. To free you from them. Because he loved you. He paid for your freedom with his life."

All she could sense was more uncertainty. Another sliver of glass whistled by to smash off the suit of a Grinder close to her. Her back felt dreadfully exposed.

"I will lead you now," she told them. "I, Arvada Sattar. I was never your enemy, only the enemy of the Masters. Now they are gone, and Sahan his given this task to me. I will protect you. I will ... I will love you, as Sahan did. But we must leave this ship right now. Grinders and Peregrines together. So put down your weapons, and follow me."

The uncertainty increased. In another moment she would have to walk away. Would they kill her as she turned her back?

Further up the corridor her people had suited up. The held their battle-saws in their hands. Several gestured frantically at her. The Grinders stared at their now suited and armed opponents, and their doubt increased.

"Put your weapons down!" she shouted toward the Peregrines.

They too hesitated, naturally enough. A whizzing piece broken off the great machine took a small but not wholly insignificant slice out of her right thigh. She buckled, but recovered. She didn't dare fall in front of the Grinders; she didn't know if their instincts could resist such weakness. She could barely stand as it was.

From the sound of it, the great machine was developing the mother of all bellyaches. The ship was definitely headed down.

"I said put the freaking saws *down!* One of you — just one — come forward to help me. Then begin evacuation. Make sure the other wings understand we haven't much time."

Slowly, with obvious reluctance, her people obeyed, trailing out the way they'd come. One brave soul walked unarmed up to her. Arvada thought she recognized her as Mevrian Tornoval.

Arvada turned back to the Grinders.

"I will lead you to a new life. For Sahan. If you stay aboard this ship, you will die. Now I am leaving. Those of you who would live, put your weapons down, and follow me."

It was a very long three minutes as with much help from Mevrian, she got back into her suit.

First one Grinder, then another, set their weapons on the floor and slowly straightened. They were creatures of habit, creatures of the herd, and within the next minute all weapons were down and they stood ready to receive her orders.

"Come with me."

She began her walk out of the Evolved ship. Past the body of Duncan Mallory, lying in a pool of blood with his body cut almost in half, not four meters away.

So many sacrifices, she thought. Later, maybe, I can put them all together, and understand.

But when I begged Sahan to take me with him, I meant it. And I never gave a thought to where.

Chapter 39

"TAKE A SEAT," SAID Solange O'Grady, ushering Arvada into the Captain's quarters aboard the *Dysis*. Arvada saw that a more bucolic air prevailed along the walls; slowly shifting scenes of forests, lakes, and the snow-sloped mountains found gracing the end cups of the grander cylinders. Not a gauge or meter in sight.

Solange wasn't planning to retire, was she? She looked ready for some time off. Her once fiery red hair had dulled around maverick streaks of gray, and wrinkles hid the freckles that once danced at the corners of her eyes and mouth. Arvada wondered guiltily just how much she herself had contributed to that stress.

For the occasion Solange wore her full-dress Admiral's blues, medals and all. Showing the flag. Arvada sat opposite the Fleet Commander, expecting a thorough and well-merited ass-chewing.

But Solange appeared quite mellow, at least on the surface.

"Someday," she said, taking in the room with a sweep of her hand, "all this will be yours. Sooner rather than later, actually."

"You're not thinking of leaving the service, are you, Solange? You can't. Not now. We need you. I need you."

"*You* need me? Well, better late than never." Solange reached across the table to pour coffee from a golden urn into Arvada's cup. "Drink up. There's plenty. I got my commando team into Raisa Catalan's little nest before anyone else and lifted her entire stash. I'm going to see her tomorrow. I must say I'm looking forward to asking how the coffee in the penal colony compares."

Arvada, lifting the cup with her right hand, found the taste, that had gone flat in their previous meeting, returned in full aromatic glory.

"But to answer your question," said Solange. "Retiring, no. They're kicking me upstairs. Head of Naval Command. Which means I'll have to chair regular meetings, then liaise with the Citizens' Council. That's a reward? Bet you can't guess who's taking my place as head of the fleet."

"Not me. Please say it's not me."

"Don't blame me," said Solange, not without a certain smug glow. "I pleaded. I cajoled. I mean Arvada, I all but fell down on my knees begging for them to give Naval Command to you instead. I was *so* looking forward to disobeying your orders for a change." She issued a deflationary sigh. "But with precious little else to recommend them, the Council is searching for some reflected glory to bask in. I think it's that silver hand finally decided them. Very dashing. Brings out the pirate in you. I'm thinking of getting one myself. Though I rather think I may settle for a silver glove."

Arvada turned her hand to demonstrate its glinting silver surfaces. "It's still a little clumsy yet."

The memory blew into her mind of Sahan taking her hand off as she lunged. The feel of it, anyway; she could not claim to have actually seen the blow.

What wires had gotten crossed in her head that she could find such a memory poignant?

"Actually," Solange continued, "Naval Command was my second choice for you. Before that I strongly urged that you be airlocked. For insubordination unique to the entire history of the Peregrine Navy. Maybe the history of any Navy."

She shrugged philosophically. "But civilians, they think insubordination is cute. Until they're the ones who have to deal with it. Who would have thought that the chief qualification for head of the fleet was to be" — she threw her up hands at the perversity of the world — "like you. Wish somebody had told me early in my career. I'd of had a lot more fun."

"Solange, I'm sorry."

"No you're not."

"No," Arvada conceded, "I guess I'm not. Sahan had unique knowledge of the enemy. Then I did, if on a lesser scale. Things that were hard to make those who hadn't lived through them understand."

"That's certainly true. I'm still trying to get it all figured out. Like for instance, we *did* win the war, didn't we? We aren't going to have to do it all again?"

"I tracked the two Evolved ships all the way down into the sun, where they dematerialized. The Master Holobrain was destroyed."

And Sahan along with it. A mercy, realistically. It still hurt.

Following the loss of the two Evolved ships, and the Master Holobrain along with them, Raisa Catalan's forces had crumbled. She tried to initiate negotiations, but rebellious officers shut down the planetary defenses, and when Solange swept in with the Alliance fleet, those few Collaborationist ships who came out to meet her soon surrendered.

"See," said Solange, settling back in her chair with an air of easy familiarity that belied the tension between them, "I've read your report. And like you say, it's all very strange. I'm still not sure I have even a half-assed idea of what actually happened. I mean, Mirai Allan and the Christian purge, as you call it? That's reaching back a ways. Hypatia Wren, the psychopath who murdered her own crewmates? You make her out to be the Savior of the Universe. Only I'm not clear just how. As for Sahan Kotori, well, let's just say Sahan's always been something of a gray area. Still, for a man who cut off your hand, then tried to drag you down into the Terror Barrier, you appear to have, ah, cut him a lot of slack, to say the least. Then these ghosts you mention. Christian ghosts, at that. Who ultimately crushed the Holobrain by what? Flying in and making spooky faces? Thumbing their noses, perhaps?"

"*Ghosts* was an approximation."

"Yes, but approximate for exactly what? What I come away with, after you nabbed half the fast cruiser force and most of the infantry available to the Resistance without so much as a by-your-leave — we'll let that pass for now — Sahan tried to kill you, and failed, barely. Some sort of weirdness then took place in the holobrains, which resulted in the two remaining Evolved heavies in Peregrine space opening fire on each other, then diving into the sun in what looks more than anything like a suicide pact. I mean, it's not exactly Actium or Trafalgar, is it?"

"Solange, I'm still trying to put it all together myself. The whole event involved forces with which we are not familiar. Then in the midst of it all I lost my hand, verged on losing my mind, and lost the man I loved."

"The man you loved, who just happened to be the one who cut off your hand in the first place. Courting rituals have changed since my time. Following which he tried to drag you down into this obscure but clearly nasty place you call the Terror Barrier. I admit I lack your poetic soul, but eternity in a horror show does not strike me as a romantic idyll."

"Yes, but...." Arvada could think of no way at all to explain.

"I know, it's complicated," Solange completed for her. She shook her head. "Very well, let us return to these ghosts of yours. Because while I know it does not seem of any great significance to you, I *am* head of Naval Command, in name anyway, and I should have at least some rough idea of just how we won the war. Or if we really did."

Arvada spread her hands, one flesh, one silver, in a placatory gesture. "It all started with Mirai Allan. While still a teenager, she fell in love with a member of the Christian community aboard the *Stephen Hawking*. Some conflict between the two groups occurred, and in response the Riggers of that time excised all thoughts of religion from the Christians' brains. Synapse by synapse. It was a brute-force solution, and I gather the Christians came out of it with something like the intellectual capacity of a young child. An a profound sense of inner emptiness. In truth they became slaves, robbed of both their freedom and their humanity."

"The Riggers," Solange mused, "were trying to keep a sinking ship afloat. I wonder if we'd do any different, in the circumstances."

"Before the war, I would have said yes. Now, maybe, maybe not. But Mirai Allan, at least, could not accept it. She went on to join the neuroscience program that would ultimately produce the holobrains and the Group Mind.

"Her true purpose, however, was different. She believed that all records of what amounted to psychological genocide would be destroyed as soon as they were no longer needed for research. So Mirai secreted away a number of transcripts that had been made during the purge. But how to safeguard them? First she found a way to preserve the transcripts by inscribing them into her own brain tissue."

"My God, she was as mad as you," exclaimed Solange. "That's brain roulette, even if you use what was once called the redundant areas."

"Dangerous, yes. I don't know just when she did it. I would imagine it must have been quite late in her life, when the Group Mind was beginning to function. The critical problem for those who would later call themselves the Evolved, was the translation from individual existence to the collective consciousness. There were failures. And these formed what I called—" she faltered, thinking of Sahan.

"The Terror Barrier," Solange completed. "Yes, I got that far. But this Terror Barrier, even while not part of the Group Mind itself, remained within the the holobrain?"

"Yes. And it appears to be, or to have been, somewhat, oh, shaded, around its borders. The Barrier itself was a realm of complete madness, where the primordial terror our conscious minds have suppressed runs free. I also believe that was where" — she gulped down the bile that rose at the thought — "where Mirai Allan was engulfed, after she deliberately took her own life in such a way as to fall into the pit."

Solange scrunched her face. "*Nobody's* that brave."

"Mirai Allan was," said Arvada. "Sahan was. Mirai knew the Barrier was the only place the Evolved would never find and destroy the records, because they did not dare look. She hoped that someday, when all memory of the Christian colony and the purge it suffered had been covered up and forgotten, a way would be found to extricate the lost souls from the Terror Barrier. And then the proof would emerge from the evidence in her head."

"My God. She was serious, your Mirai."

"Incredibly so. Only no such attempt was ever made. The Group Mind was too afraid to probe. So there she languished. You can't imagine what it was like."

"Can you?" Solange asked curiously.

"I had a glimpse. No more. And that was ... bad enough. But over all those years the transcripts, which had begun as no more than patterns of brain tissue, with no individual life of their own, began to absorb a form of sentience from the holobrain. Somehow they incorporated the quality of individual awareness from those trapped within the Barrier."

Solange grimaced. "Talk about a marriage made in hell."

"Exactly. But once the individual transcripts began to gain some element of self-awareness, they began to extend beyond Mirai Allan. To become what I called ghosts, and reach into those netherlands surrounding the deepest part of the Terror Barrier itself. That's where Sahan encountered them. And Mirai Allan, who apparently managed to follow them."

It all seemed so unreal, sitting here. Only the constant pain of Sahan kept her from doubting her own experience.

"When I fought Sahan in the holobrain, he could easily have killed me, or dragged me down into the Terror Barrier. But then he saw Mirai. Her pain, Solange! Her need! It truly was beyond our imagining. Sahan turned from me, and...." You can do this. "And he went to her. He knew exactly what he was doing. He touched her, and took her suffering into himself.

In that moment, the ghosts were freed. Sahan, who'd travelled wider through the holobrain than Mirai Allan, formed the bridge she could not."

Solange stared open-mouthed. "My God. Sahan Kotori...." Her hands waved helplessly.

"Yes." Tears started up, passed just as quickly. Grief came in waves these days. Now it subsided to a dull stone in Arvada's chest. "Hypatia Wren played some role in all this. I don't understand it, but I think as soon as Sahan first entered the holobrain, the first true human since her to do so, she began forming a plan. But in the end, it all came down to Sahan. Despite everything the Evolved could do to him, Sahan chose love over hate. And sacrifice over revenge."

Solange contemplated her cup, unable to meet Arvada's eyes. "We always knew that Sahan was a brave man, as well as a most capable one. But he had a sense of, of *honor* to him, that I'm afraid I never gave him proper credit for."

Nor did I, thought Arvada. Or rather, I always knew that about him, but I held him at arm's length anyway. So many wasted, painful years.

"Once Sahan freed the ghosts," she said, "they made straight for the Group Mind. They'd spent all those years searching for some God to fill the emptiness in their souls. It must have looked like the closest approximation."

"Only it wasn't."

Arvada shook her head. "No. But the Barrier had been breached. The Evolved seem to have believed that once an individual made it past the Terror Barrier, they jettisoned the primordial fear forever. That it could no more flow upward into the higher form of life they represented than a swamp could scale a mountain. But that was hubris. They'd found a way to tiptoe around it, but in the end they could not escape their human roots. It drove them mad, and to escape, they plunged themselves into the sun."

Solange ran one finger around the rim of her cup. "I hated them. I really, truly, hated them. But now they seem almost pathetic. More like, well, us. Which I guess they were, weren't they?"

"Much more than either they or we thought. But it gets worse. Beck thinks such a catastrophe to the Master Holobrain here at Harrar's Reach would have communicated itself back to the other holobrains in their homeworld. In which case their reaction would be much the same. We may have committed genocide."

Solange grimaced. Then sighed, heavily, and shrugged her shoulders. "We didn't start this war. When Sahan destroyed the first Master Holobrain, why didn't they just withdraw? It wasn't like we were going to go after them once they left us alone."

"Only their legends indicated that we would. That's why they fell upon us in the first place."

Solange sipped her coffee, made a face. Rising, she tossed the lukewarm brew into the sink. Coming back to the table, she refilled her cup.

"So many people dead," she said. "So many ships, so many habitats destroyed. The civilian government in shambles, a quarter of the population displaced from their homes, and now we may have gone and committed genocide ... I hate myself for saying it, but sometimes I could almost wish we were back at war. It all seemed much simpler then."

If I could have Sahan back, Arvada thought, I'd choose war too. No question. That's how civilized I am. "It's always easier to destroy than to build."

Solange considered her. "You can write your own ticket, you know. If you choose to go into politics like your mother, I'm thinking you could run the whole Peregrine Alliance within a year."

"Maybe. I had something else in mind. And since you're still my superior, I'm asking you for permission."

"What a refreshing change. Though I think I'll just save myself some aggravation by saying 'yes' right now. Instead of refusing permission, then have you go ahead and do whatever your mind's set on anyway. So what is this permission I'm technically granting?"

"To take a small expedition — three fast cruisers — to the Evolved Homeworld. My personal feeling is that the Master Holobrain there will have self-destructed. Or gone mad. But there's no sure way of knowing aside from going there. Or staying on a war footing while we wait for them to come back here."

"Can you find it?"

"Beck seems to think so."

"If the Evolved haven't been destroyed," Solange pointed out, "they may be less than overjoyed to see you."

"At least then we'll know. But I don't believe that even if the Master Holobrain there has survived, the Evolved will choose to go on with this war. They've lost everything they sent into our space. From their point of view, it's looking like we may possess a Doomsday weapon. No, if the Group Mind is still active, my bet is it will either be eager to establish peace, or be in full flight for decades to come. Of course the Living Evolved, those who have not made the transition to the Group Mind, should still survive. But what have they got to fight for now?"

"Maybe building a new Master Holobrain?"

"Maybe," Arvada acknowledged. "But it's not that easy, and certainly not quick. Especially if they want to eliminate the Terror Barrier this time. There is another consideration."

"Yes?"

"The Grinders. We have so much work to do with them. And little real idea how to do it. Are we going to try to reverse engineer them back into something that looks like us? Or without changing their bodies and brains, try to get them functioning on an equal footing, when they were deliberately tampered with to be unequal? I told them I would take care of them, and I mean to fulfill that vow. But first I want to visit the Evolved and let them know that a prerequisite for any sort of peace is to stop cloning new Grinders, and either find some means of rehabilitating the ones left to them, or turn them over to us."

"And if they say no?"

"Then my vote would be to go on with the war."

Solange shook her head. "You are a bloodthirsty little savage, aren't you?"

"The Grinders are an evil with a long history. One we Peregrines share in, at least in part. I for one am not going to declare peace until we find some way to deal with them in a humane and reasonable manner. Whatever that may turn out to be."

"And as to this 'permission' you're requesting, it won't really make any difference if I say yes or no, will it?"

"To whether I go or not, no. To you and me, yes. Please, Solange. Consider this a formal request to Naval Command, from the head of the fleet."

Solange threw her hands wide in exasperation. "Head of the fleet! Are you thirty yet?"

"Three months."

"Very well, I agree some attempt to reach whatever remains of the Evolved should be made." She seemed about to say something more, but held back.

"Yes?" Arvada prompted.

"And what of Sahan? I'm sorry, but is he really...."

"Dead?"

"Yes. It's just so involved."

Arvada kept her voice perfectly level, even as her silver fingers tightened on the edge of the table. "Sahan is dead. He died along with the holobrains, in the fires of Thais. And that was a mercy."

"I am sorry, Arvada. The two of you ... working so closely ... so many years...."

"He stood his watch."

"And there can be no finer epitaph for any soldier."

They raised and clinked their cups lightly together.

"I should get back to my ship," said Arvada, close to being overwhelmed by memories, and remorse. "There is much to prepare. Permission to leave?"

"Granted."

Arvada walked toward the hangar deck, hardly noticing her surroundings, or the briskness with which those she passed snapped fully erect, saluting with a vigor that threatened to bloody their eyebrows. Such display had gone out of fashion in the Peregrine navy of late. But for Arvada Sattar, the Eagle, winner of the war, those aboard the *Dysis*, every one of them veterans of combat, were proud to make such a show, feeling themselves included in a grand pageant that would forever be acclaimed in Peregrine history.

But though Arvada returned about half the salutes in an absent-minded fashion that would see her put on report at the Academy, her thoughts remained far away.

Sahan was dead. It was so hard to be certain about anything connected with the holobrains. But this she must accept. Sahan was dead, and she would be going forward without him.

The sensation of loneliness drained her of.... Well, of Arvada Sattar, was what it felt like. Like all these people were saluting someone else. Someone who had once lived, but died with Sahan.

You cannot accept that. Cannot believe that you have followed him into death. Hold firm instead to the faith that if Arvada Sattar was never wholly herself, then that part of her that was Sahan still walks with her. Make it life that will dominate. The life, and the love. Not the death.

Oh Sahan, I truly was willing to join you. At that moment when you pulled me toward the Terror Barrier, I was ready to go. With you. To share your fate. Our fate. Together.

Forever.

But you chose another sacrifice.

Forever.

I can only hope that in that moment, you finally knew I loved you.

And just how much.

Epilogue

He felt her need.

Mirai.

He touched her. Lightening-shock twisted through him.

A void opened, sucking out his very soul. Emptying him of all but horror.

Then from another realm came an exultant cry. Recognition briefly flared — the collective voice of the transcripts Mirai Allan nourished within her until the holobrain gave them sentience.

The Christian ghosts had just broken free from the Terror Barrier.

In that moment of release, their lost God beckoned to them. An entity beyond vastness; all-seeing, all-powerful, all-certain. Their souls' long starvation pulled them straight toward Him, crying out in joy.

Which abruptly broke into confusion, then fear and disbelief, as the Group Mind tried to pull itself in against the onslaught.

Too late. Not only the ghosts, but the traumatized spirits of all those Living Evolved who had fallen into the Terror Barrier came twisting through the holobrain's defenses like cracks spreading through ice.

And when that ice finally broke, beneath it lay only the primordial fear.

In an instant all identity, group and individual alike, vanished.

Swept up in the flood, terror spun Sahan loose of all associations. Screams sounded from within and without. Some from the ghosts, some from himself, some from a vast but disintegrating entity far beyond his comprehension, and now beyond its own.

Fragmented bits and pieces of lives streaked by. A scattered few struck chords of memory, but most were wholly alien, wholly incomprehensible. The emptiness in him grabbed at any flash of recognition, frantic to build some pattern that might hold his disintegrating will in place. More fragments hurtled past, shrieking in a multitude of voices as they dissipated into the void.

Then pain fixed a point amid the chaos.

His eyes!

Lacking any voice, he still screamed as the luminosity of the sun seared the eyes out of his head.

But with the pain, came a memory. A memory connecting these sparse fragments he clung to with a vision from ... another life, now coalescing more firmly than the disintegrating present.

The same blinding light, the same pain, uniting his broken soul in one final cry of love and joy:

ARVADA!

About the Author

Richard Quarry writes science fiction, fantasy, crime, and historical adventure. His short fiction has appeared in *Fiction River* and *Blaze Ward Presents*. He lives in Seattle, where he enjoys hiking the hills and beaches of the Northwest with his wife Claire. For more of his books and stories, go to richardquarrywriter.com.

The God Machine concludes *The Evolved* series. For a look at another science fiction adventure, *Absent From Felicity*, please keep reading. And if you enjoyed this book, please consider leaving a review. Thanks.

Absent From Felicity

I stooped to pick up the doll half buried in the dust. It looked like some 19th century period piece; calico dress around lumpy stuffing, frizzy red hair, lots of freckles in a round pink face, tiny button nose, and wide dead marble eyes.

Yet the doll was close to four feet long. Too big for a child's toy, surely. I squeezed experimentally.

"Ah-*OOH*-ga! Ah-*OOH*-ga! Dive! Dive!"

I hurled it from me. "What happened here?" I bawled at Lieutenant Bau.

Holding the sensor high, he made another sweep of the devastated landscape. Steady, deadpan Lieutenant Bau. An Ophelian, strong as an ox and about as sociable. Of the eight of us who had started down the spoke to the main torus, only the two of us remained. Him because of his Ophelian toughness, me because ... well, that was one more mystery, and I feared the question might soon prove moot.

I stared at the rows of orange lights flickering two thousand feet overhead. A lifeless, billowing gray ocean of debris swept gently up toward the down-curving horizons of the torus roof for a mile in front and a mile behind. Scarecrow frames of collapsed buildings reached up as if having died in vain supplication. Zephyrs of gray silicate rose and spun in the fickle drafts. The air smelled of scorched metal.

Sixteen thousand people had been living aboard the *Tycho Brahe* when the black hole lurking at the center of the galaxy spasmed outward and swallowed the habitat whole. Skeptics predicted we'd find no fragment big enough to clog a salt shaker. Well, we'd proved them wrong.

Alas, I feared few would ever know. Because along with the gruesome loss of our six comrades, we'd lost all radio contact with our ship. And we still had to get back *up* the spokes.

"They're all dead, aren't they?" I said.

Bau tucked the sensor away. Hoisting his rocket launcher, he peered through narrowed lids, searching for any threat the machine might have missed. "There are other sectors."

Even more than the silence of the ruins, the thing I found most deeply disturbing were the *toys* lying thick on the dust around what remained of the recyclers.

Toys, I say, and yet a parody of anything that might ever have been designed for play. As expedition historian I recognized the designs, mainly early to mid-twentieth century. The Golden Age of Christmas catalogues, before children's dreams went online.

But what were they doing here, lying atop the debris of whatever catastrophe had struck? What use could survivors have had for a model train set, or a rocking horse, or a pedal-driven model of one of the great Empire of Waste finned monster cars? What possible use for a complete life-size, solid model of a barn, surrounded by similarly scaled chickens, pigs and cows, cast from bonded silicates and weighing, at a guess, from one to four hundred pounds? Or a cowboy hat big enough to form a hot tub?

Mockery. Sheer mockery of the family life that had once flourished aboard the *Tycho Brahe*. As if some evil intelligence — but I could not submit to mere superstition.

"Tidal forces," I declared, trying to shut the freakish pseudo-toys from my mind. "From when the torus plunged through the event horizon. Nothing else could rip rents like that in the *Brahe's* hull." Or create the jumble in the spokes, that demented, ear-splitting battle of machinery our exploration team kept trying to dodge. And falling short by one disappearance and five mangled bodies. Or maybe two disappearances and four mangled bodies; hard to be sure. "The gravitational distortion must have killed everyone aboard."

"Men—" Bau hunched involuntarily as Thor's hammer, or something sounding painfully like it, came clanging around between the hull and the outer shield again. Obviously the gyros, designed to keep the spinning donut hull of the torus from smashing into the radiation shielding, were going their own way like all the rest of the systems. I wondered just how much more pounding the *Brahe* could take.

I lowered my hands from my ears as the metallic roar passed on.

"Men fought here," completed Bau.

"What? How can you tell?"

"Look around you." As I gazed clueless, he shrugged. "Let's get moving."

We tramped through the rubble, wheezing in the thin atmosphere. Twisted tie-bars, exposed ends of I-beams, and loops of reinforcement webbing clutched at our feet like the fingers of drowning men. My legs burned as I topped an ashen dune and followed Bau down into a bowl in the rubble desert.

He stood crouched, the rocket launcher suddenly pointed straight out from his shoulder.

"Lieutenant?"

"Shut up."

Something pinged off my backpac. Turning, I caught a hint of movement, then nothing. Bau grunted sharply.

"What is it?" I cried. Then I saw the vaned rod poking from his side.

I whirled and fell as a sudden piercing ache jerked my arm around. Bau fired his launcher. Fifty feet away the explosion kicked up a spray of dust and something that looked like a head. I saw a bloody red tear in the arm of my blue plasticene coverall. Bau fired again, and once more, then kept firing as dark, crouched figures scuttled across the depression.

"Stop! Stop!" I shouted, on my knees and waving my arms frantically. "We're friends!" I could do little else; Bau was the only member of our party to carry weapons.

A thin, ragged figure sprang up from the dust before me and pointed something in my direction.

"We come in peace!" I tried.

I thought I saw a grin on the filthy, cadaverous face. Then the figure exploded, the upper half disappearing in a crimson spray while the legs, unjoined, toppled apart.

Bau staggered sideways, missiles still streaking from his launcher. He looked like a murderous St. Sebastian, with short rods sticking out of his body while dust, blood, and body parts spurted in gouts all around.

I wanted everyone to stop shooting and establish a dialogue. "We've come to help you!"

A jet of flame belched forth from the rubble at Bau's feet. His dark form, engulfed, struggled in the center of the fireball.

Quick gray forms scrambled low to the ground, more like rats than humans. Bau collapsed. Slowly the flames flickered out.

They closed in on me then, cautiously; thin, crouching, outlandish figures, clad in rags and grime. Some brandished crossbows, others more strange-looking weapons. Most looked little more than children. Tall, creeping, spider-limbed, sinister children.

I got up off my knees. "We're from Earth! Don't you understand? You're rescued!"

One, a veritable patriarch from his soot-stained beard, stalked in close, holding an improvised mace and chain. His lips drew back over a gap-toothed mouth as he started twirling the head: a silver rocket ship, its exaggerated fins honed sharp. "*Maa*-ma, *Maa*-ma," it wailed. My attacker's expression wavered between temerity and mad glee.

Then he pitched forward, raising a fresh cloud of dust as blood welled from a huge hole in the back of his skull.

The ragamuffin band scattered like minnows as a giant came bellowing down the slope, pistol in hand. I say, and perceived, a giant, but I doubt he stood much over seven feet, and built like the Hulk. It was the sheer volume of his fury, as well as the bronze shade of his skin, that exaggerated his already considerable stature.

"I wanted them alive!" He kicked Bau's still smoking body for emphasis. Beneath layers of dust he wore a mélange of bright tatters and irregular sections of black body armor.

His minions, as I now took them to be, gibbered an unintelligible host of excuses as they cowered out of reach. A second bronze-skinned goliath topped the rise.

"Damn. Well, at least we got one of them."

Their size! That bronze skin. Ophelians for a certainty. What were *they* doing here? The logs of the *Brahe* listed none among the population.

The giant strode down and with one great hand hoisted me up off my feet so that we stared eye to eye.

"We come in peace," I burbled, without much faith.

"TOUGH SHIT!"

A sharp pain spiked upward from my neck and exploded through the top of my skull, taking consciousness with it.